Praise for Catherine Cavendish

'If there is a crown for queen of Gothic horror,
[Catherine Cavendish] should be wearing it.'
Modern Horrors

'Cavendish draws from the best conventions of the genre
in this eerie gothic novel about a woman's sanity slowly
unraveling within the hallways of a mysterious mansion.'
Publishers Weekly on *The Garden of Bewitchment*

'Well-rooted in classic gothic traditions, the novel doesn't
furiously spill the blood like most modern horror, but
it maximizes its unique advantages. [...] An atmospheric
and gently scary tale that will appeal to horror fans and
Brontë enthusiasts alike."
Booklist on *The Garden of Bewitchment*

'Cavendish sets the scene exceptionally well and the book
is atmospheric and spooky throughout.'
The British Fantasy Society
on *The Haunting of Henderson Close*

'Cavendish breathes new life into familiar horror tropes
in this spine-tingling tale of past and present colliding.
[...] The story of female resilience at the heart of this
well-constructed gothic tale is sure to please fans of
women-driven horror.'
Publishers Weekly on *In Darkness, Shadows Breathe*

T0273654

CATHERINE CAVENDISH

THE AFTER-DEATH OF CAROLINE RAND

This is a **FLAME TREE PRESS** book

Text copyright © 2023 Catherine Cavendish

FLAME TREE PRESS
6 Melbray Mews, London, SW6 3NS, UK
flametreepress.com

US sales, distribution and warehouse:
Simon & Schuster
simonandschuster.biz

UK distribution and warehouse:
Hachette UK Distribution
hukdcustomerservice@hachette.co.uk

Publisher's Note: This is a work of fiction. Names, characters, places, and
incidents are a product of the author's imagination. Locales and public names
are sometimes used for atmospheric purposes. Any resemblance to actual
people, living or dead, or to businesses, companies, events, institutions, or
locales is completely coincidental.

Thanks to the Flame Tree Press team.

The cover is created by Flame Tree Studio with
thanks to Shutterstock.com.
The font families used are Avenir and Bembo.

Flame Tree Press is an imprint of Flame Tree Publishing Ltd
flametreepublishing.com

A copy of the CIP data for this book is available from the British Library
and the Library of Congress.

1 3 5 7 9 8 6 4 2

HB ISBN: 978-1-78758-740-3
US PB ISBN: 978-1-78758-738-0
UK PB ISBN: 978-1-78758-739-7
ebook ISBN: 978-1-78758-741-0

Printed and bound in Great Britain by Clays Ltd, Elcograf S.p.A.

CATHERINE CAVENDISH

THE AFTER-DEATH OF CAROLINE RAND

FLAME TREE PRESS
London & New York

For Colin
Who saw more of the 1960s than I did
but still never made it to Laurel Canyon

CHAPTER ONE

"What the hell am I doing here?"

Alli Sinclair slammed the door of her red Micra. She stared around at the immaculately groomed lawns that seemed to stretch forever along both sides of the gravel drive. The weather was perfect. Almost too perfect. Five minutes ago, a hailstorm had battered her small car, threatening to smash the windows, then, as soon as she turned down the lane to reach the house, the storm stopped and the sun came out. Now not a cloud troubled the pristine azure sky. "Bloody typical British weather. Four seasons in one day." Had she really said that out loud?

Her mother's voice sounded in her head. "If you keep talking to yourself, the men in white coats will come to get you." How far away was Tuscany anyway? It didn't matter. Jessica Marconi Sinclair's words knew no border controls.

The sunshine should have cheered Alli up. Instead, it was having the opposite effect. She tried to shake off the bad mood that had hung around her for days, not even knowing why she felt like this. For some reason, that made it all much worse. Oh well, she was here now. Might as well make the best of it. Alli tossed back her long dark hair over her shoulders and started off toward the house.

Ahead, a recently built or – at the least – restored stone wall was fringed by box hedges trimmed within an inch of their existence. The house itself seemed to bask luxuriously in the warm June sunshine. As Alli's sandaled feet crunched gravel, she took in the light reflecting off the golden stone walls. The building had once been an abbey and monks had strolled around these grounds in centuries past. Closing her eyes for a second, Alli half-imagined she heard their voices, unified in plainsong as they chanted their psalms and proceeded to the various offices of the day.

So, this was Nancy Harper's place. Who would have guessed the girl Alli hadn't thought about in years would turn up with such a mansion? But then, who would have guessed she would even have remembered Alli's existence, much less invited her for a long weekend after all these years? The wonders of Facebook. Not just any weekend either. This one was to be Sixties themed. All guests were to channel their inner hippy and think Summer of Love. Well, 1968–69 anyway. Alli hummed a tune to herself. 'Mr. Tambourine Man'. That ought to get her in the mood.

On she trudged. *I should have parked closer to the house.*

Finally, she was within fifty yards or so of the front steps and could see an area clearly meant for parking. If only she had turned down that nondescript, overgrown track she had sailed past, she would have been sitting down with a glass of something chilled by now. That's what happened when you weren't concentrating properly. The rigors of her journey had been too fresh, and her hackles still raised at the sheer lunacy of the succession of trucks and cars packed to the rafters with so much holiday luggage the driver had no chance of seeing what was behind them. Judging by the appalling standard of driving, few of them knew how to use wing mirrors either. Alli had lost track of the times she had needed to slam on her brakes and swerve to avoid being hit by a car wandering over while she was overtaking it. Bloody weekend drivers.

I really don't need this. Not right now. She had lost count of the number of times *that* thought had flashed through her mind. More than once she had been tempted to turn off at a service station and go right back home.

Of course, she didn't *have* to accept Nancy Harper's friendship request, but the woman had caught her on a bad day. A day – and there were rather too many right now – when Alli was feeling alone and vulnerable. Losing a job you loved and which had been part of your life for a decade and more was never easy. It would have been so much less difficult if she had received any real warning. It seemed one minute everything was fine. The company she worked for was apparently on the up, with business booming. She was certainly making a great salary and, thank goodness, had saved much of it. She would need it all now, that was for sure. Four weeks ago, she was delivering a weeklong series of seminars on marketing for groups of executives in Dubai. Then, an email. *A stupid email, for Christ's sake!*

'Sorry, Alli, the company has gone into liquidation.'

It had been signed by her boss, Lincoln Wardrow. Alli's lip curled as she thought of when she had last seen him – sitting in his bespoke black leather chair, owning all the space it occupied. Practically owning *her* until they had decided to stop their personal relationship and keep things strictly business. That had been three years earlier. Now, all she merited was eight words. Eight lousy, stinking words. It took a day or two, but she finally made contact with Lincoln's secretary, whose wavering voice carried the weight of a thousand tears drowning a broken heart.

"He's gone," the distraught woman – Laurie – managed after a few false starts. "The tax men are chasing him, and he's skipped the country. You'd better come home. There's no money to pay you. Or any of us. I'm clearing out my stuff and then I'm off. I'm sorry, Alli. I know you were here much longer than me."

Only eleven years longer. "You'll be fine, Laurie. I'll write you a good reference. You'll soon get fixed up."

"Oh, it's not that. Well, it is, but…." Out it all came, in one almighty flood. "He told me he loved me, Alli. He told me he wanted to marry me."

Didn't he always? "Lincoln says a lot of things. Don't waste your tears on him. Take it from someone who knows. He's not worth it."

Maybe it was the bitterness Alli couldn't keep out of her voice. Or maybe Laurie simply didn't know about the two of them. Wardrow Associates was the kind of setup where physical interaction didn't take place most of the time. Alli could count the number of days she had spent in the office over the last six months on the fingers of two hands and still have two to spare. She and the other consultants were not paid to sit around socializing with work colleagues. They barely knew each other. Each had their own portfolio of business clients they worked with to help them improve their market share. Training and developing the key staff. That was her role, along with six others like her, working on contracts from China to the USA, Australia and South Africa, not to mention most of the countries in Europe. Except Liechtenstein. Alli had always wanted to win a client in Liechtenstein, for no other reason than no one else in the company ever had. It never happened and now it never would.

Coming home to an empty apartment in the heart of London – surely the loneliest city in the world when you had no one in your life – proved hard. She had never even considered that before. Home was always merely a place to sleep, catch up on washing, do a bit of shopping, before packing and jetting off to the next assignment.

Within two weeks, the walls seemed to have encroached at least two feet all round her, penning her in. Claustrophobia was setting in big time. She had to get away. It came as a shock to realize she had no friends in London. The only people she had known there had been attached to Wardrow Associates. With a sudden start, she realized she didn't have any home contact details for any of them. Not even Laurie.

And that was why, at around seven one evening, Alli booted up her laptop and logged in to her barely used Facebook account. She ignored most of the notifications and messages, which were mainly of the spam variety anyway, but one caught her eye. A message request from Nancy Harper.

The name rang a vague bell from the past. School days. But which school? Alli had led a peripatetic childhood and changing schools had been a regular event. She clicked on Nancy's profile, and the memories flooded back.

She looked a world away from the gawky schoolgirl with the mousy plaits Alli remembered from those far-off days. Staring back at her was a confident, striking woman with long, immaculately coiffed blonde hair, bright red lipstick, exquisitely styled eyebrows and long eyelashes.

Whatever she's done, it's worked out well for her. I'll bet that look cost her a small fortune.

Alli leaned back in her chair and let her recollections wash over her. St. Margaret's High School. First day of the new term and, for Alli, yet another first day at a new school.

Alli did as always on such occasions. She sat at the back of the class, kept her head down and got on with her work, trying to assimilate as soon as possible into the new regime's way of doing things. Friendships, she hoped would follow, but this school felt different from others she had attended. The pupils here seemed more sophisticated somehow. Older, even though they were all her age. And, of course, they already had their own groups of friends. Hard to break in when you were the new girl in class.

"Will you be my friend?"

Alli had been lost in her own thoughts when the girl with the mousy plaits and reedy voice approached her.

"I'm Nancy. Nancy Harper. I haven't been here all that long either. My father's in the Army and we only came back from Germany last year."

"I'm Alli Sinclair. Thank you. I'd like to be your friend very much."

So had begun a friendship that lasted the three years she spent there. When the inevitable happened and her parents took her on the move again, she had promised to keep in touch with Nancy and had done so. For a couple of months. Then it fizzled out. New friends came and went. Alli felt a pang of guilt as she remembered how, on her last day at St. Margaret's, there had been tears in Nancy's eyes as she said goodbye.

Alli had experienced bullying from some of the other girls who insisted on calling her by her full list of forenames – Allegra Carmen Isolde – knowing she hated it. Nancy always stood up for her, even though that frequently meant the bullies turned on her as well. As she recalled this, Alli felt more than a little ashamed of herself. When she left, did the bullies turn their full attention to Nancy? She hoped not.

Anyway, here she was, messaging her on Facebook and looking as if she had spent a fortune on hair, makeup and a gorgeous dress. Surely that was a Versace, wasn't it?

Alli opened Nancy's message. It was dated a week earlier.

'Hi, Alli. Long time, no see. Wondered if you fancy a get-together? I've recently bought an old abbey in Wiltshire – Canonbury Manor on the outskirts of the lovely little village of Canonbury Ducis. Not far from the M4. It's like stepping back in time. The house is mostly around five hundred years old and its last owner was Caroline Rand. Have you heard of her? She was a folk/rock star in the late Sixties. She had a massive hit with that psychedelic song, 'Lady Gossamer'. Then she went to the States and flopped, so she came back here and bought my house. I'm planning on having a hippy late-Sixties-themed weekend for a few friends – a sort of combined housewarming and tribute to her. I would love for you to come. Message me or ring me so we can sort out dates and so on. Longing to hear all your news. You've obviously done well for yourself. Nancy.'

Not half as well as you have, Nancy.

The name Caroline Rand stirred a distant memory. Not Alli's generation though. Her parents'. Alli's talented musician parents had been much in demand for their prowess with piano and keyboards (her mother) and guitar, or any other instrument possessed of strings (her father).

Alli hesitated, fingers hovering over the keyboard. *Oh, why the hell not?* After all, it wasn't as if she had anything else planned and everything about Nancy's message intrigued her. Where had she accumulated such wealth? Her family certainly wasn't wealthy. At least not when she and Nancy had been at school together. Curiosity, tinged with that remaining thread of guilt, won her over. Alli dashed off a quick acceptance and now she was here.

As she looked across at it now, Canonbury Manor was exactly the sort of house she had dreamed of living in one day. Set in acres of its own grounds and with a few ghosts for good measure, no doubt. Exquisite. Alli carried on strolling up the path.

To either side, clumps of vivid blue columbine rustled in the light breeze. Their bonnet-shaped flowers seemed to nod at her. Bidding her welcome perhaps? Alli smiled. What was it about columbines that always made her do that? They seemed a cheerful flower, although she couldn't explain why.

Alli ascended the handful of steps up to the stone entrance porch. It must have been part of the original building. The sandstone was weathered and pockmarked with age. Alli looked around for a bell and found an old-fashioned iron pull. She tugged it and was rewarded with a reassuring echoing ring coming from inside the building.

A smell of incense wafted toward her and she located the source. On both sides of the porch, small bushes of pinky-red roses gave off a heady aroma. What a fitting smell for a former abbey.

Footsteps approached, heels clattering on a stone floor. The scrape of a bolt being drawn back, a slight creak and the heavy wooden door opened. A smiling face greeted her.

"Allegra Sinclair, how lovely to see you."

"Hello, Nancy. And it's Alli. Please."

"Oh yes, sorry, I remember. Those nasty girls, what were their names?"

"Clarissa Davenport, Maryella Whittard and Natalie something-or-other."

"Ah yes, I remember now. They used to tease you a bit, didn't they?"

"Only every day. You stuck up for me and earned yourself a bellyful of sarcasm from Clarissa. She was a prize number one cow, wasn't she? I don't know if I ever thanked you, by the way, so I'm thanking you now."

Nancy made a dismissive gesture with her hand. "That's all forgotten now and consigned to ancient history. It's wonderful to see you. Do come in. You're the first here."

Alli felt underdressed in her jeans, sandals and white t-shirt. Nancy had already dressed the part in a long flowing gypsy skirt, with swirls of purple, red, orange and green. A chain belt glinted and tinkled at her waist and her black velvet top sparkled with tiny mirrors among the intricate beading and embroidery. Around her neck, a selection of chains of differing lengths added to the authentic hippy chic. She wore her hair long and straight, a beaded headband around her forehead. As she moved, waves of patchouli hung in the air. Alli felt as if she had just stepped into a different world.

She followed Nancy down the long, wide hallway, resplendent on either wall with oil paintings of serious-looking men in robes. They looked like senior members of the Catholic church of a bygone era.

Nancy caught her looking at them and smiled. "They came with the house. Previous abbots, I believe. I almost got rid of them, but they seem to suit it here, don't you think?"

Alli smiled and nodded, hoping this was an appropriate reaction. Personally, she wouldn't have given any of the grim-faced characters house room. *Especially* that one. She shivered and hurried past one especially piercing gaze preserved in oils.

Nancy started up the stairs. "Have you left your suitcase in your car?"

"Yes, I thought I'd announce myself first. Rather stupidly I missed the first entrance and left my car at the end of the drive beyond the lawn."

Nancy gave a light laugh. "Oh, everyone does that the first time. I'll get a proper sign put up one of these days. There's still a lot to do here. You wouldn't believe the state it was in when I arrived. I can't imagine how Caroline Rand managed to live here as long as she did. Nothing worked. Not the plumbing, heating, electrics.... And talk about overgrown.... It was like a forest out there. Anyway, I'll show you your room and get you a drink. I'll bet you could do with one after that drive. I heard on the radio that the roads are a nightmare today. All the holidaymakers going to the South West."

"It wasn't a barrel of laughs, and you're right. I could certainly do with a long cold drink. It's just what I need right now."

At the top of the carpeted stairs, Nancy turned to her right and opened a beautifully polished wooden door.

The distinctive scent of honeysuckle tickled Alli's nose, and the room, with its theme of lemon and white chintz, suited it.

"I hope you'll be comfortable in here."

"It's beautiful. Thank you." Alli took in the double bed, covered in a pretty, floral coverlet. It was a little too girly for her taste but suited the room. The curtains matched; the small bedside lamps, made of chrome and glass, sat neatly on top of white cabinets. A selection of novels lay ready for her to dive into, and the floor-to-ceiling windows were slightly open, allowing the gentlest of breezes to flutter the drapes.

Along one wall, a mirrored set of fitted wardrobes added extra depth to the already quite spacious room.

Nancy proceeded to open another door in an adjoining wall. "Your bathroom's in there. If you need any more towels, let me know. I've put out some toiletries, so I hope you have all you need."

"I'm sure I will. Thank you, Nancy."

"My pleasure. I'm so happy you could come."

"I'll bring my car out to the front here, get my case and unpack now, if that's okay."

"And I'll fix that drink. Iced tea okay for you?"

"Perfect, thanks."

Alli followed Nancy back downstairs and her host indicated where she would be when Alli was ready to join her.

So far, so good. Alli's earlier dark mood had evaporated, and she felt more lighthearted than she had for days as she hurried back to her car.

Alli swung the Micra back onto the road and took the turning she had missed previously. It was well concealed – even more so when approached from this direction – and hardly surprising she had gone past it before she spotted it. This was even more like a track than the turning she had taken previously. It appeared disused, with not much more than a hint that vehicles had ever come up and down here. Only the odd tire-shaped rut at the verges. The car bounced valiantly over potholes and small rocks, past overgrown hedges and brambles that scraped the bodywork of the Micra and made her wince. *My car's going to need a new paint job if this goes on much longer.* Finally, the lane opened up into the immaculately tended and empty parking area at the side of the house. Hers was the only car there.

Unpacking didn't take long. After all, Alli had only come for three nights and the theme was to be hippy-style dress throughout. She quickly changed into her own gypsy skirt. Hers wasn't the artist's palette of colors that Nancy was sporting. Alli had opted for more muted shades of mauve, blue and gray. Her loose white cotton top was embroidered in shades of blue. She braided her hair into two plaits that reached halfway down her back and added the obligatory headband before accentuating her eyes with black kohl. Large gold hoop earrings completed her look and, having satisfied herself that she had channeled her inner hippy-chick Cher-wannabe, she dabbed some Shalimar behind her ears and thrust the contents of her usual handbag into a dark brown suede tote she had found in a vintage clothes store. Its fringes were so long they threatened to trip her up on the stairs as she made her way down to join Nancy.

Having descended the final step, she glanced along the wall of portraits in the hall, unable to resist taking a closer look at *that* one.

Abbot Hippolytus Weaver, his name emblazoned on the gold plaque beneath his portrait, stared out at her and Alli shivered. That look…. No wonder it had disturbed her earlier. You would spend a long time searching that face for the pious grace of a man of God. In the flesh, this priest wouldn't have consoled, he would have intimidated. Maybe worse than that.

For heaven's sake, where was her imagination wandering off to now? She tore her gaze away and brushed aside the impression that, even though she had turned her back on them, the eyes in the picture were watching her every move. And disapproved of every inch of it.

The door to the living room was ajar, allowing the gentle sounds of a late-Sixties song to drift toward her. She listened for a moment before recognizing it. 'Summer in the City'. The group's name eluded her.

"The Lovin' Spoonful," Nancy said as Alli joined her. "To get us in the mood." She wafted a spliff around before offering it to her guest. Alli had never smoked and wasn't about to start now. She politely declined.

"Oh, that's a shame. It's great stuff. The best quality. All the more for me then. And Ric I expect. Ric Vargas, do you know him?"

Alli shook her head and accepted the highball glass filled with ice and tea, sprigs of fresh mint and a glass straw. "Thanks," she said.

"My pleasure. Listen, we're probably all going to be getting high this weekend. You'll be out of it if you don't try this stuff."

"I'll be fine. Don't worry. I just don't do drugs, unless my doctor prescribes them. It doesn't mean I don't know how to enjoy myself."

"I can respect that."

"Good." Alli wanted to withdraw that. It sounded judgmental. She hadn't intended it to be. Suddenly she didn't feel quite so happy anymore and, once again, the question flashed into her mind, more heartfelt this time. *What the fuck am I doing here?* And, she had to admit that if she didn't know this was Nancy from school, she would never have guessed. Apart from the cosmetic changes, this woman seemed to have undergone a total personality change. *We were only twelve years old at the time. People change. Life intervenes.* It certainly had in her case.

The doorbell rang and broke the awkward moment. Nancy rested her joint in a nearby porcelain ashtray where it sent a lazy, aromatic curl of smoke upward. Alli moved away from the sickly-sweet scent.

"I expect that's Ric. Actually, there won't be many of us. Only you, me, Ric and Mike. The others I invited couldn't make it." Nancy excused herself and Alli decided to inspect the room while her host settled her next guest in. From the hall, she heard a pleasant male voice and Nancy's girlish laughter, retreating as she took the man upstairs to show him his room.

The music changed to The Beach Boys. 'Do It Again'. An old favorite of her mother's and Alli remembered dancing around the living room to it when she couldn't have been more than six or seven. In a rash moment, her mother had confessed to having a schoolgirl crush on the drummer, Dennis Wilson. She said that Alli's father reminded her of him and that was what had first attracted her to him. That and Christian Sinclair's bad-boy reputation.

With Nancy gone, Alli took the opportunity to survey the large rectangular room. It was traditionally furnished with comfortable-looking sofas, small tables, and an original-looking stone fireplace along one wall. Above it, a painting, of a very different kind to those in the hall, drew Alli in.

The subject was a young woman, her long blonde hair draped over one shoulder, a wistful expression in her vivid blue eyes, which were fringed with long dark lashes. The artist had chosen to paint her languishing in a chair, the detail of which was largely lost under her voluminous silk shawls in rich purple and scarlet. These fell away to reveal a slender arm culminating in a hand with long sensitive fingers and perfectly manicured, shell-like nails.

The subject in the portrait dominated that part of the room and, as a sound behind her announced the arrival of her hostess, Alli found it hard to drag her eyes away.

"She's almost real, isn't she?" Nancy said, at her elbow.

"Who is she?"

"The lady herself. Caroline Rand. Back in her day everyone wanted to photograph her. Most of the greats did. David Bailey, Lord Lichfield,

Lord Snowdon. She sat for all of them. Cecil Beaton even. Then came the portrait artists but, one by one, she turned them down. All except Lucius."

"Lucius?"

"Lucius Hartmann. He's largely forgotten now. His heyday came in the late Sixties and early Seventies when he was the darling of the King's Road. All the Chelsea set loved him and none more than Caroline Rand. She adored him. They had this wild affair, or so the story goes. She's supposed to have been pregnant by him when he painted that portrait, hence the shawls. They could cover up a multitude of sins, couldn't they? I mean, look at that arm and those cheekbones. She wasn't a chubby girl. In fact, if you look at the photographs, she was as thin as Twiggy."

"Do you have any? Photographs of her, I mean?"

"Loads. Albums full of them. When I bought the house, I went into the attic and there were boxes and boxes of her stuff. I'm wearing her clothes." She performed a perfect pirouette. "I love the way this skirt flows. It's like gossamer. Pure silk, you see."

"It's lovely. May I borrow the albums to look at? Just while I'm here, of course."

"Sure. Help yourself. I brought them downstairs and put them over there." Nancy indicated a bookcase built into a wall near the window. "I left everything else up in the attic. It's a bit creepy up there, especially…. Well, you know what attics are like. Attics and cellars." She gave a mock shiver. "Be back in a minute. Need the loo."

Alli wandered over to the bookcase and selected an album at random. It weighed heavy. *There must be well over a hundred photographs in there.*

She took it over to a central circular table and laid it down, opened it and let the pages fall where they settled.

The photograph was in black and white. It was autographed – 'Lichfield' – and dated 6th September 1967. Caroline Rand wore a simple white trouser suit and matching patent leather boots with a low, chunky heel. Mary Quant probably. A white slouch hat partially obscured one eye and her stark makeup, with heavily kohl-rimmed eyes and frosted lips, contrasted sharply with the ivory paleness of her skin. Her cheekbones had been contoured with blusher to give her an almost gaunt appearance.

She posed with one knee bent, her foot resting on a wooden chair, and a hand draped over it. Her lips were slightly parted and she looked as if she were about to speak.

"Stunning, isn't she?"

Alli jumped. She turned to see a man with a bushy chestnut beard and matching long curly hair.

"Sorry, I didn't mean to startle you." He touched her arm lightly, then withdrew his hand. "I'm Ric Vargas. You must be Allegra Sinclair."

Alli cringed inwardly at the sound of the hated name. "Alli," she said. "Please, do me a favor. Never use the other name."

"I hear you. I'm Ricardo Pasqual Montoya Vargas by birth and the only person in the entire universe who is allowed to call me Ricardo is my mother."

He smiled, and Alli warmed to him. She felt her muscles relax and her nerves untangle for the first time since the awkward moment with Nancy. "Good to meet you, Ric. That look suits you by the way."

It was no lie. Ric looked at home in his bell-bottomed denims, tie-dye t-shirt and denim sleeveless jacket festooned with sewn-on badges celebrating the Grateful Dead, The Doors and Jimi Hendrix. "I bought it like this. Local street market. It's the real deal apparently and it certainly smelt like it. Took two runs of the washing machine to get the whiff of grass and sweat out." He sniffed the lapel. "Smells all right now though. Lenor. Can't beat it."

Alli laughed.

Nancy joined them. "I see you two are getting along. That's great. Love your jacket by the way, Ric. Reminds me of one I saw in a photo of Caroline. She was standing next to her then manager, Arthur something."

"That would be Arthur Sedgemoor," Ric said. "He managed all sorts of bands and artists at that time. I don't think Caroline was with him very long. Now *that* was a strange business. Do you remember, Nan? He was killed by a train, wasn't he?"

"Yes. The London express. Not far from here actually. The poor driver never stood a chance. He had a nervous breakdown afterward. He said Arthur dashed out from the bushes at the side of the track, straight in front of him. He spread his arms out as if he was nailed to a cross. They gave a verdict of suicide owing to Arthur's state of mind at the time."

"He must have been under a terrible amount of strain to do that," Alli said. "I mean, if you're going to be so desperate as to commit suicide there are a lot less painful ways to do it."

Ric sighed. "The speed that train was going I would say death was pretty much instantaneous, but I get what you're saying. There was one other factor that made it really odd though."

"Oh?" Alli asked.

"I saw Arthur literally hours before he did it. He was over the moon. He'd proposed to his girlfriend and she'd said yes, he'd just landed a massive contract for a top band he was managing and, to cap it all, he'd been paid a healthy advance for his autobiography. Life had never been sweeter. He told me so himself. Twelve hours later, I heard the news. The thing was, there never was anything wrong with his state of mind. Not that I knew of anyway. He didn't do drugs either. Not even weed. He rarely even took an aspirin."

Nancy coughed. "Can we change the subject? I'm sure Alli doesn't want to hear all the sordid details about the suicide of someone she never even met."

"Oh, not at all," Alli said. "This is fascinating. Carry on, Ric."

Ric clearly didn't need much encouragement. "I always wondered if someone didn't want him to reveal some deep dark secret in his tell-all autobiography. Mind you, if he did, we shall never know because it never saw the light of day. He knew Caroline of course, although there was no record of him coming here that day, nothing in his diary, and his girlfriend had no knowledge of it. It was rather odd he should die so close when he had no other business being within miles of here. I do wonder if he had threatened to expose some murky details from her past and...."

"You mean he was murdered?" Alli asked.

Ric took a swig of the Scotch Nancy handed him. "Maybe," he said. "But he literally ran out onto the track. The driver was adamant he didn't see anyone push him."

"Could he have got it wrong?" Alli asked. "I mean he must have been in shock."

"It's possible, I suppose," Ric said. "Anything's possible when you come down to it."

A cold breeze made Alli jump. Iced tea slopped over the side of her glass.

"You okay?" Ric asked.

"Yes. Yes, I'm fine." Alli forced a smile. She couldn't shift the sensation that someone was standing right behind her, watching her every move. She jerked her head around. Nothing. This was different than her experience in the hall. This felt more…tangible.

"Are you sure you're all right?" Ric's concern, directed at Alli, was unexpected and welcome. It had been a long time since a man had paid her that sort of attention. It was usually business, business and business again.

"I felt a bit of a chill suddenly. Didn't you feel it?"

He shook his head. "Can't say I did." He glanced up at Caroline's portrait. "Maybe *she* doesn't approve of all this. What we're doing here."

Alli wondered why she felt so reluctant to follow Ric's gaze when, only a few minutes ago, she had barely been able to tear herself away from those clear blue eyes. Now she had to force herself. But she didn't expect the sight that met her. "She's not the same. Her expression. It's changed."

Nancy gave a light laugh. "What are you talking about, Allegra? It's a *painting.*"

"It's Alli, Nancy. My name is Alli. Please try to remember that. You always used to…. And I know it's a painting. I'm not entirely stupid. I'm telling you, her expression has changed. She looked calm and serene before. Now…." She stared in disbelief at the beautiful face whose expression showed fear in those amazing eyes. Fear and something Alli couldn't define. Some sort of…emptiness. "It's as if someone has switched portraits."

"That's crazy. It looks exactly the same to me. Oh, come on, let's stop this nonsense and have another drink. I have champagne chilling in the kitchen." Nancy swept out of the room, her skirt billowing behind her.

Ric stared out of the window. Alli continued to gaze at the portrait. She felt at any moment the figure would move, blink its eyes....

Nancy returned, bearing a Georgian silver champagne bucket containing a bottle of Bollinger in one hand and three champagne flutes, which she held by their stems, in the other.

"Now we can really get started." She set the bucket and glasses down on a table and proceeded to pour. When they all had a glass, she sat on another chair.

"Mike's been held up in London, so he'll be joining us tomorrow if he can get away. For tonight, at least, we're all met. Let's raise our glasses to our real hostess. Caroline Rand."

They faced the portrait and Alli was relieved to see the original expression she had first seen on the face of the beautiful dead singer.

"Caroline Rand," they echoed as they raised their glasses.

A familiar intro started up and Alli realized Nancy had pressed a button on a remote control she had fished out of her pocket. The acoustic guitars and gentle rhythm accompanied Caroline Rand on her most famous song, 'Lady Gossamer'.

Nancy sighed. "She had a voice that could span three octaves – some said four on a good day."

Alli settled herself on a nearby sofa and drained her glass, letting the music wash over her.

> She flies through the heavens on gossamer wings,
> Flies free and open and lets her heart sing,
> The earth is her canvas and on it she'll paint
> Her portraits of pleasure – of sinner and saint....

No one spoke a word through the entire three minutes plus. As the song faded, Nancy picked up the remote and pressed the stop button. "I always think there's a touch of Joni Mitchell in her voice," she said. "The same kind of wistful innocence."

Alli nodded. "It's a pure voice. Judy Collins had that too. And Joan Baez."

"More champagne." Nancy was issuing an order, not a suggestion.

Alli wasn't about to argue. She handed over her glass.

"So, what's the plan this weekend then?" Ric asked.

Nancy paused in the act of pouring. "Tonight, we'll have a typically Sixties-style buffet. The caterers will come at around six and set it up in the dining room across the hall. After that, we can just chill, drink, get high, while we listen to Caroline and other music from the era."

"And as I'm the only guy, we're channeling the era of free love and I believe you two are straight, there will be sex," Ric said, rubbing his hands together and smiling. "Looks like I'm in for one hell of a night. I hope I can keep up with you. No, strike that. I hope *you* can keep up with *me*."

Alli stared at him. Could he really be so crass? In this day and age?

Nancy laughed. That sound was beginning to grate on Alli. She was a thirty-five-year-old woman for heaven's sake, not some giggling schoolgirl. Hell, Alli couldn't remember her giggling like that when she *was* a schoolgirl.

"Oh, Ric," Nancy said between bouts of the girlish laughter. "You never change, do you?"

"I sincerely hope not."

Ric sat next to Alli. "I hope you didn't think I was serious," he said.

"About the sex? Well, this *is* meant to be 1969 so I suppose…. Yes, I did, actually. Until you did that thing of rubbing your hands together." Alli felt herself relax once more. She hadn't realized how her muscles had tensed in the past few minutes.

"Oh, don't get me wrong," Ric said, "I wouldn't say 'no', but I'm not going to leap on you either. I hope we're a bit more enlightened these days."

"I'm sure *I* am," Nancy said.

Alli sipped her champagne. It had been so long since she had even been on a date. Were men more enlightened these days? All the ones she had known had seemed preoccupied in parting her from her clothing in the shortest possible time, resulting in awkward maneuvers and some swift exits.

Alli's eyes drifted upward to the painting. She was aware of Ric's gaze following her.

"What is it about that picture?" he asked.

"Yes, I was wondering that too," Nancy said.

Alli set her glass down. "What do you mean?"

"You said it wasn't the same," Ric said. "That it had changed somehow, even though we know that's impossible. I mean, you know it's impossible, right?"

Alli nodded. "It's hard to explain. It was her expression. Everything else was the same, her dress, the pose. It was her eyes. How the portrait is now, she's looking out at us, her gaze is wistful and a bit faraway, but she's at peace and seems happy."

"She was probably high when it was painted," Nancy said.

"Maybe so, but you can see what I mean when you look at it now. What I saw was a different expression. As if her eyes had come alive and she was terrified. It was so real I could actually *feel* her fear. Only for a few seconds…. It felt as if she was reaching out to me." Alli shivered at the memory. It seemed strange putting into words what she had previously only felt. "What I don't understand is why I was the only one who could see it."

Nancy stood, wielding the empty champagne bottle. "I'll go and get another." She swept out of the room.

Ric was silent. He seemed to be processing what she had said. Or maybe he was wondering how he could excuse himself from the company of a madwoman without appearing rude. Either way, Alli wished he would speak because, for the life of her, she hadn't a clue what else to say.

When he finally did, it wasn't what she had expected.

"Have you ever been to Laurel Canyon?"

"What? Where? Laurel Canyon? No." She nodded up at the picture. "That was the place to be in *her* day, wasn't it? I don't think it's like that now though, is it? I mean, these days, it's full of expensive houses and that whole music scene is long gone."

"I take it you're a fan of late-Sixties music then?"

"I grew up listening to my parents' record collection, and that was pretty extensive, I can tell you. They're both professional musicians and that was their favorite time, when they were just starting out. I didn't spend much time with them when I was growing up because they were away on tour so much, or else recording, but I did spend a lot of time with their music collection. So, yes, I suppose I am quite a fan. It was music of its time, wasn't it? I used to listen and let my mind drift away, imagining what it must have been like living there in Laurel Canyon in its heyday. Everyone who was anyone in music lived there or visited there. The Mamas and the Papas, The Doors, The Beach Boys, Hendrix, Joni Mitchell...."

"And that's why you came here this weekend. Hoping to soak up a bit of Sixties nostalgia."

"Oh no, this is the result of a rash moment. Nancy friended me on Facebook and invited me to come down for this long weekend. I was at a loose end, you see. I'd lost my job, totally out of the blue, and I accepted her invitation. The only thing of Caroline Rand's I really know is 'Lady Gossamer' – the track Nancy just played. And I think the last time I heard that I was probably around thirteen. You never hear her stuff these days, do you? I struggled to even remember her when Nancy said she'd bought her house. Then it started to come back to me. My parents used to talk about her, years ago."

"Would I have heard of them? Your parents, I mean."

"Probably not. My father was – still is – Christian Sinclair, and my mother's professional name is Jessica Marconi, her maiden name."

Ric looked thoughtful. "The names are familiar. Christian Sinclair.... Got it! Guitarist, right?"

"Yes. Mum plays keyboards."

"That's right. I remember. When I was first starting out, she played on that hit by The Village Queens. I used to manage them. I was ridiculously young and inexperienced and they were my first major band."

"Mum talked about those sessions, and she didn't do that often, so they must have been memorable. The lead singer was a bit of a diva, I seem to remember."

Ric raised his eyes and took a deep breath. He exhaled slowly. "Tell me about it. Angel Dovronevsky. She went as Angel Dove. More like a bloody vulture. Prone to hissy fits if she thought her voice was mixed wrong." He struck a diva-esque pose. "'No one can hear *me*, Ric. No one can hear *me*.' God, she went on. Happiest day of my life when I waved goodbye to Angel Dovronevsky. Last I heard she was driving an HGV."

Alli laughed. "She's probably causing havoc at every truck stop along the motorways and main roads of Britain."

"Oh, nothing so mundane. Angel moved to the States. She's a long-distance truck driver there these days. Probably goes down a storm in Texas and Oklahoma."

"So, what do you do now, Ric?"

"Public relations at Largos Creative. You won't have heard of them. Small, boutique company with an exclusive roster of clients. Business by personal recommendation only. That's how I came across Nancy. We both worked for the same company for a while."

Nancy swept back into the room, bottle in hand. "Fresh supplies," she announced, brandishing it and topping up glasses.

Alli pulled out her phone from her bag to check any messages. Not that she expected any. Since her job had finished, the calls had all dried up.

"I wouldn't bother. It won't work," Nancy said. "No signal. We're in a dip...a bad reception area. They're supposed to be installing a new mast somewhere. It's so annoying because if you go into my bedroom, and it's a clear day like today, you can look across and just about see the existing mast, but you have to walk around a hundred yards down toward the village before you get any bars on your phone."

Alli put her phone away. "That must be awkward."

"Oh, I have a landline and broadband, so I'm still connected. To be honest, I haven't missed not being disturbed at all hours by junk text messages and calls, but if you need to call anyone, feel free to use my phone." She grimaced. "You'll have to excuse me. What goes in, must come out. I need the loo." She left them.

Ric nudged Alli's arm. "I'll bet Nancy didn't tell you she had bought Caroline Rand's house with Caroline Rand still in it, did she?"

Alli stared at him. He tapped the side of his nose with his right forefinger. "Come with me, before Nancy gets back. She'll assume I've whisked you off to have my wicked way with you. After all, it *is* 1969."

Ric led her up the staircase. "Not a word now," he said as they reached the top landing. "I'm not sure exactly where it is. Like you, this is my first time here, but Nancy can be very loose-lipped when she's either drunk or high." He stopped in front of a door at the far end of the hallway. "I believe this is Nancy's room. It used to be Caroline's. If I'm right, there's another door in here, and it leads to a rather interesting little attic room." He turned the handle and the door opened smoothly.

Once inside, Alli admired the peaceful coloring of soft gray walls.

Ric beckoned to her. "Over here." Two doors stood side by side. One would lead to the bathroom, no doubt, the other....

He opened it and Alli joined him. A slight fusty smell greeted them as of an unaired space. They had entered a small anteroom, clearly part of the original abbey. An ancient, narrow and steep spiral stone staircase wound its way upward to the left of them.

"It's up here."

With a knot of fear clenching her insides, Alli followed Ric up the stairs.

CHAPTER TWO

The door at the top of the stairs creaked and seemed reluctant to open. Ric put his shoulder to it and it shuddered ajar. A rush of cold air hit Alli, taking her by surprise.

"Must be a window open," Ric said, crossing the threshold.

The room was pitch black. There didn't appear to *be* any windows. Alli followed Ric and waited as he felt around the wall for a light switch. A sudden burst of light illuminated the room from a central fitment; a striking black cast-iron candelabra with a dozen flickering bulbs cast shadows into corners yet burned bright enough to reveal walls painted in swirls of psychedelic color, now faded, either through the passage of time or, as no natural light penetrated here, the poor quality of the paint.

"This is the place all right." Ric spoke in an almost reverential whisper.

Alli hugged herself. The sudden rush of cold air had come as an unwelcome surprise, especially as, looking around the room, she could see no sign of a window or orifice capable of allowing any kind of atmosphere in. The place smelled musty, damp, unused and unloved. An overwhelming feeling of sadness and loss enveloped her, and she wanted to get out of there. "What are you looking for?"

Ric moved around the room, examining a few cheap paperbacks that seemed to have no real place here. He waved one at her. "*Valley of the Dolls*. The ultimate sex, drugs and Hollywood novel. We used to have it at home. Mum caught me reading it when I was about eight. It disappeared after that." He grinned.

Alli smiled. "I always meant to read that. Maybe I'll have time now…. You know, this place looks like a shrine of some sort."

Ric paused in rummaging under some cushions on a dilapidated sofa that seemed to be missing a leg. "If it's the place Nancy told me about, it *is* a shrine."

Despite her initial reaction, Alli's heartbeat was settling down a little and she took in her surroundings. She picked up old teen and fan magazines that lay scattered on the floor. They were all dated 1968 and 1969. The paper, aged brown at the edges, felt as if it might disintegrate under her touch. As she was always a lover of nostalgia, this was a fascinating collection for Alli. She flicked through each one, noting titles such as *16, Tiger Beat, Jackie, Fabulous 208*. Photographs of long-dead rock stars smiled from their pinup pages. She could have spent hours going through those, immersing herself in a bygone and more innocent age, but there was no time now. Alli sighed and stacked them carefully in a pile on the floor away from the door.

There was little furniture in the room and nothing to indicate what it had been used for. It was part of the original fabric of the building, that much she could tell from the stone walls. They felt cold and clammy to her touch. Here and there, traces of greenish-black mold infested the faded orange, green, purple, yellow and red swirls.

She gave in to an urge to lay her hand flat against the wall and closed her eyes. Strange swirls of light penetrated her eyelids. She tried to open them, but they resisted, staying stubbornly shut while unfamiliar voices wafted toward her…came nearer…surrounded her.

Grace Slick's powerful voice…a song about Alice…and chasing white rabbits.

"Hey, Caroline…."

Alli's eyes snapped open. She let her hand fall and turned to see Ric staring at her from across the room. He held a purple velvet cloth of some kind.

"Alli? Are you okay? What was that about?"

"You called me Caroline."

He laughed. "Me? When?"

"Just now." Alli rubbed her forehead. Someone *had* called her Caroline, but the voice hadn't been Ric's. Her earlier apprehension flooded back. "I think I'd like to get out of here. I don't like this place."

"Agreed. It *is* a bit creepy. That was a pretty good rendition of 'White Rabbit', by the way."

"What?"

"That song by Jefferson Airplane. Grace Slick has a fantastic voice, don't you think? I mean, that song must be fifty years old by now – no, more – but her voice makes it so fresh, and you sounded just like her. I thought someone had switched an iPod on. Oh, of course, it would have been vinyl back then."

Alli pointed to the velvet cloth. "What's that?"

"I found it. It was covering this. The reason we're here, actually."

Reluctantly, Alli crossed the floor and looked down.

"What do you make of that?" Ric stepped back and Alli found herself face to face with an elaborate-looking metal urn. Grecian in design, glinting a dull silver in the artificial light. She stared at it.

"Look at the base plate," Ric said.

Alli peered at it and read the inscription. "Caroline Rand. Born 10th April 1942." She touched the metal. It felt oddly warm. Carefully, she turned the urn around, searching for a date of death. It wasn't there. She met Ric's gaze.

He nodded. "Strange that, isn't it? If you're going to put a birth date, you would at least think they would have completed the story. There's plenty of room for it."

Alli felt a tingling sensation in her fingertips where they touched the metal, which suddenly felt oddly fluid under her touch. She withdrew her fingers and wiped them on her skirt.

"Maybe she commissioned it before she died but her relatives never put the date on. I presume this really is what we think it is. Her burial urn?"

Ric grinned. "I sneaked a peek. The top screws off and there you are. Straight into the business. Loads of ash. Have a look if you don't believe me. Go on, open it."

"I'll take your word for it. So, this is what you meant when you said Nancy had bought this house with Caroline still in it?"

Ric nodded. "She and I went out for a drink one night and she had a couple too many. We were celebrating the completion of the renovations on this place. That's when she told me about this room and its contents. Well, its main content. The builders found it. Downstairs, the entrance to the staircase we came up was blocked off, so no one knew about this room. The builders discovered the door when they tore down some horrible old plywood. As the urn was exactly where it is now, Nancy decided to leave it there, and to keep the room as they had found it."

"There's something that's been bothering me since I first opened that message from Nancy on Facebook inviting me here." Alli spread her arms wide. "It's this. The mansion. The money. She must be worth a fortune. Do you know how she came by it?"

Ric looked away. "Perhaps you should ask her. I heard stuff, but—"

A sudden blast of air distracted Alli. She shivered. "Did you feel that?"

Ric nodded. "Come on, let's go back down." He strode out of the room.

At the entrance, Alli paused. She stared over at the wall where she had experienced that strange sensation and heard the Jefferson Airplane song. For a second it had almost been as if she had slipped back in time. Back to a time when someone could have called Caroline's name…and received an answer.

★   ★   ★

Nancy looked up as Ric and Alli rejoined her. Her eyes held a question. Alli ignored it and resumed her seat. Ric winked at Nancy, picked up the Bollinger and refilled his glass, before taking it over to Alli and topping hers up.

"So, Nancy," Ric said, breaking the silence. "What's been going on in your life apart from acquiring a mansion? You left Largos Creative suddenly. There were lots of rumors."

Nancy laughed. "Oh, don't tell me. Apparently, I married some wealthy hermit and was living a Howard Hughes-like existence in a luxury Mayfair penthouse. Or maybe I inherited a shedload of cash from a wealthy uncle I never even knew I had."

"Yeah, I heard both of those. I prefer the one you told me yourself."

Nancy's smile died on her lips. "*I* told you? Really? I don't remember discussing that part of my life with you."

"In fairness, you were drunk at the time. Or high. Maybe both." Ric took a swig of his drink and set his glass down.

An awkwardness had descended on the room.

"Drink?" Nancy circulated the room with the bottle, topping up glasses, until she drained the last drop. "Oh dear, time for another, I think." She left them, a little unsteady on her feet. At least half that bottle had gone down her own throat.

"What's this version of hers?" Alli asked.

"It wouldn't be fair. It really ought to come from the horse's mouth."

Within seconds, Nancy was back, bottle in hand. "Who's for more?"

Ric nodded while Alli felt her head beginning to swim from the effects of alcohol on an empty stomach. "I'll pass this time, thanks," she said and pushed her half-empty glass away.

Nancy set the bottle down in the cooler and rearranged herself on the sofa. She looked from one to another and Alli felt her penetrating glance uncomfortable.

"My, don't you both look serious?" Nancy said, draining her champagne glass. "This is supposed to be a fun weekend." She reached in her pocket and brought out the remote. She pointed it in the direction of the iPod.

Alli caught her breath.

The distinctive opening chords of 'White Rabbit' filled the room.

"Remember this one, Alli?"

Did she know Ric and Alli had recently been exploring a room they had no business being in?

Nancy wasn't finished. "You only have to hear the first verse and it takes you back to the time when it was played everywhere. I don't think there's another song that so perfectly encapsulates the mood of the late Sixties, with one exception. Caroline Rand's 'Lady Gossamer'." Nancy flipped the switch again and the strident Grace Slick was replaced by the sound of the former owner of the house they were now sitting in.

Next to Alli, Ric coughed. "You may as well tell her, Nan. Alli's curiosity won't go away. She was asking me earlier, and we have the whole weekend to get through. Tell her the secret of your vast wealth."

Alli wanted to smack him. But, he was right. The longer she stayed here, the more curious she was becoming.

Nancy glared at Ric for a moment before her features softened. "Secret? Oh, there's no secret. In fact, the answer couldn't be more straightforward and simple. I signed a pact with the devil."

CHAPTER THREE

The words hung heavy, as if echoing throughout the room. Surely Nancy hadn't just said that. A pact. With the devil. She would burst out laughing in a moment. She would laugh and say it was all a big joke.

The laugh didn't come.

Next to her, Ric shuffled his feet. Alli looked back at Nancy, who stared at her. Her eyes held a penetrating gaze. Alli did her best to stare her out. She had done it plenty of times with a succession of cats when she was growing up, and she usually won. Or the cat simply grew bored with the whole exercise and sauntered off. This time it wouldn't work. Nancy was keeping up the stare. Didn't the woman even need to blink?

Alli couldn't stand the silence any longer. "For heaven's sake, Nancy, what are you talking about? Pacts with the devil only happen in horror stories."

Nancy reached for the Bollinger, topped up her glass and drank deeply. Still, she said nothing. The silence grew more awkward by the second.

Ric coughed. "Come on, Nancy, enough's enough. We've come down here for an entertaining hippy weekend to toast your new house and its former inhabitant—"

"Not sure 'entertaining' is the word I'd be looking for right now," Alli said. "This house is beginning to give me the creeps. What happened in the attic...." The words were out, and she couldn't retract them. Ric glared at her.

"Oh, don't worry," Nancy said. "I might have guessed it wouldn't take long for someone to find that door. And I was very drunk that night, wasn't I, Ric?"

"You remember then?" Ric said. "I thought you might have forgotten."

"What did you see up there, Alli?" Nancy asked.

"I'm not sure. I.... There was a voice. It called Caroline's name. And for a second, I saw the walls as they must have looked when they were first painted. Psychedelic swirls of red, orange, purple. All the colors of the rainbow. It was over as soon as it began. I thought I must have imagined it."

"Now you're not so sure, are you?" Nancy asked, her voice softer.

"No. I'm not."

"You want to know where all the money came from? Well, I didn't win the lottery for a start. I know the stories about the rich uncle, and they're partially true. Only it wasn't a rich man. It was a rich woman and she was my grandmother. I'm Caroline Rand's illegitimate daughter's equally bastard child. In other words—" she raised her glass to the portrait "—that lady's granddaughter."

"*What?*" Alli cried.

Ric started to laugh and began a slow handclap. "Oh, you're good, Nancy. You're very good."

"It's true, Ric."

"This can't be right. You introduced me to your parents. I remember it distinctly. It was at that 'do', when you won that award for best creative. A couple of years ago."

"You're right. Those people. That lovely couple who brought me up.... For thirty-four years, I believed they were my parents, and, to all intents and purposes, they were. Needless to say, when the truth finally came out, it took some adjusting. I didn't believe it at first. A solicitor contacted me out of the blue and told me I needed to make an appointment to see him. When I got there, he read me the contents of Caroline Rand's will and told me I was her sole heir. She had a daughter she gave up for adoption on the day she was born. That child grew up and got pregnant when she was just a teenager. The baby was me and, like her mother before her, my birth mother gave me up for adoption immediately. A few years later, she died of a heroin overdose. So that left me as Caroline's sole direct descendant. I didn't buy this house. She left it to me. Along with £13 million."

Ric whistled through his teeth.

"How did she make so much money?" Alli asked. "I thought 'Lady Gossamer' was her one massive hit and everything after that was…well…. I mean she never really charted again in the States, did she? Over there, she was pretty much a one-hit wonder and that's where the big money was. Still is, come to that."

Nancy's face clouded over. "Don't ever say things like that. Not in this house. Never." Her gaze darted about, as if she was suddenly scared.

Alli felt the woman's fear transmit itself across the room. "What's the matter?"

Nancy seemed to compose herself. "Caroline wasn't a one-hit wonder. 'Lady Gossamer' may have been her only big hit in the States but, over here, and in Europe, Japan and elsewhere, she had a string of hits – both singles and albums. She was careful with her money as well. And there were…investments."

Alli prickled at this. She remembered the clutch of Caroline Rand albums gathering dust in her parents' collection. They hadn't aged well and her songs were never played these days, nor had they been for years before Alli was even born – apart from 'Lady Gossamer' of course. Granted she may have made good money at the time but how long would it have lasted? And what about those investments Nancy mentioned? Something she couldn't yet explain niggled at Alli. Nancy's 'pact with the devil'. What kind of shady business had Caroline been into? Or was she simply being paranoid? This house had that effect. It made you jump at nothing and be suspicious of everything.

Ric cleared his throat. "I heard, or read somewhere, that she upped sticks, moved to Laurel Canyon and bought a bungalow a few doors down from Joni Mitchell. She arrived there in 1968 or '69 and left a year or so later. By then things were changing in the Canyon and she wasn't the only one moving on."

Nancy nodded. "That's mostly right. 'Lady Gossamer' was a global number one in 1968 and Caroline had always wanted to live in the States. She had read about Laurel Canyon and how the West Coast sound was developing there. She found this perfect little world. Only a short drive up from Sunset Strip but it could have been miles away, in its own countryside microclimate."

"With a perfect view over the smog of LA," Ric added.

Alli closed her eyes. "It must have been magical there then. There was still so much innocence." She felt herself beginning to drift pleasantly. Ric brought her up sharp.

"Then along came Charlie Manson and blew it all away."

"Harsh, Ric," Nancy said.

"Harsh maybe. True though. Those so-called 'flower children' were living in a bubble. They were young, rich, pampered, drugged up…. The perfect target for a madman."

"So," Alli said, anxious to return to Nancy's story, "that's how you acquired your money – and it must have been a hell of a lot to take in at the time. This was, eighteen months ago?"

"About that. It's taken this long to get probate through and renovate. There's still more to do. You should have seen it when I first laid eyes on it. The grounds were in a terrible state. Nature had taken over and it doesn't take long. Apparently, ten years earlier, the formal gardens were as you see them now. Thank goodness for landscape gardeners."

"You said you made a pact with the devil," Alli said. "That's the bit that's bugging me."

"Yes, I did, didn't I?" Nancy looked upward. Alli got the distinct impression she was searching for the right words, maybe wishing she hadn't said what she had earlier. Finally, she spoke.

"Caroline Rand was a complicated person. I'm still trying to fathom her out. My biological grandfather was the artist who painted that portrait." She nodded over at the painting above the fireplace. "Lucius Hartmann. He was a lot older than Caroline."

Ric smacked his hand against his thigh. "Lucius Hartmann, of course. From what I've heard over the years, he was bad news for anyone he came into contact with. Come to think of it, he had some dealings with poor Arthur at one point. He, Hartmann that is, also preyed on young women. He had a reputation for being ruthless and almost uncannily successful. Just when you thought he would be bound to wind up in jail, off he went on some other scheme. Same old story – one rule for the rich and well connected and another for the rest of us. Rumor has it he used Caroline's bank account like his own, with full power of attorney. She'd made a bit of a mess of things early on and lost a small fortune. In rides Hartmann to the rescue like some kind of knight in shining armor and, hey presto, she's solvent again. Not only that but she can somehow afford a mansion in leafy Wiltshire."

A thought struck Alli. "Could that be why Arthur committed suicide? He found out about Hartmann's business dealings and was going to expose him in that autobiography of his?"

"Nice try," Ric said. "Unlikely though. Arthur died…oh, about ten years ago now. Hartmann's been dead around thirty. So, unless his ghost pushed him in front of that train…."

Nancy laughed. A hollow sound.

A shudder passed through Alli's body. *Maybe…just maybe that's not so far from the truth….* She dismissed the thought. Too ridiculous.

Nancy lit a cigarette. "Lucius Hartmann certainly did pull all Caroline's strings."

"You mean like…Svengali?" Alli said, her lip curling.

"There were resemblances. Lucius operated in a different way. He was like a Svengali figure when it suited him. Highly charismatic and able to convince someone as young and naïve as Caroline that he had all the answers and knew what was best for her. She, in turn, was flattered by the attentions of a famous artist who seemed so much more confident and worldly-wise than she was.

"So, she had to do what he said even when she became pregnant with his child. 'Lady Gossamer' had shot up the charts, and she went into seclusion to have her baby. My mother. Within minutes of her birth, her new parents were holding her in their arms. Hartmann had set all that up without Caroline even knowing about it. It's possible he even forged her signature on the adoption papers. Either that, or money changed hands somewhere. The solicitor had a letter with the name of a Catholic adoption agency. When he checked it out, no official record exists of any such organization. As soon as Caroline had recovered from the birth, off she went to the States and bought that little house in Laurel Canyon just as you said, Ric.

"She was still in love with Lucius and heavily influenced by him, despite what he had done. But she had been through a lot, emotionally. Laurel Canyon was to be her little world away from the real world. I suppose it suited Hartmann for her to live there, away from too many prying eyes, apart from those of the sympathetic, many of whom were also damaged in their own ways. And there were some great neighbors around. Mama Cass, by all accounts, befriended her. All these musicians, singers and bands may have been deluded and drugged up half the time, but they were real people living real lives. Here were people who would inspire her and, in doing so, make more money for Hartmann, who was already written into all her contracts. Not her manager officially, more as some kind of personal adviser, as well as being her lover. At first it suited her to let him take care of all her financial affairs, especially after her manager had swindled her out of everything she had."

"How do you know all this?" Alli asked. "She was dead before you even knew she was your grandmother. Lucius Hartmann is dead too. Did you get it from your adoptive parents?"

Nancy shook her head slowly. "No, not from them. But you make a lot of assumptions."

"I do? You said Caroline's dead and Lucius is dead. Caroline's ashes are in an urn upstairs, unless I'm very much mistaken, and Lucius…I don't know where he is. He died back in the Nineties, didn't he?"

"That rather depends on your definition of dead, I suppose."

"Well, that's enigmatic, I'll give you that," Alli said. "I still don't understand what a pact with a devil has to do with this. Or what you're implying about the fate of the late – or maybe you think, not-so-late – Lucius Hartmann."

"Oh, he's dead. In the way you mean. His body no longer walks this earth. He's buried in Highgate Cemetery in London. The problem is his spirit. His spirit is still very much alive."

A cold shiver shot up Alli's spine. "Are you saying he's here. In this house?"

"That's exactly what I'm saying."

"So," Ric said, speaking slowly and deliberately, "you believe this house is haunted by the spirit of a dead puppet master?"

"I'm saying there is *something* in this house and I know that because one night I did an extremely foolish thing and now I'm paying for it. I'm hoping you two – and Mike when he eventually gets here – can help me."

"What happened, Nancy?" Alli asked.

"On the night I moved in the atmosphere felt strange. I looked up at that portrait and, like you, Alli, I could have sworn her expression changed. I told myself I was being stupid. It's an old house; the creaks and noises I heard were all easily explained by that. The change in her expression? The sun was going down. Different shadows formed. I poured myself a Scotch and water, slammed in a few ice cubes, sat down and read for a while. But I kept looking up at that picture, and I swear she stared right back at me. That her eyes could see me. These weren't the cold, dead eyes of a mixture of oils, however skilled the painter and, whatever you say about Hartmann, he *was* a gifted artist—"

A crash cut off her words.

The three shot out of their seats.

"What the hell?" Ric reached the door first. He threw it open. Out in the hall, under the picture of the priest with the disturbing eyes, a crystal vase lay smashed on the stone flags.

Alli and Ric looked at Nancy.

"That's the third one so far," she said, her voice too calm. "I'll get a brush."

She moved, almost robotically, toward the kitchen. Alli and Ric stared at the shattered shards of glass.

"Did you see where that was before this happened?" Ric asked.

Alli searched her brain, trying to remember. "I think it was on that table." She pointed at the long, narrow, polished wood table set against the wall. The vase lay a couple of feet away from it.

Ric tested the table. It held firm. No wobbles. "Was it perched on the edge?" he asked. "It could have slipped off."

"I don't think so. I think I would have noticed that. Unless someone dislodged it after I came in."

"I don't remember it at all, so you have one up on me there."

Nancy came back. "Oh, it was perfectly safe. It wouldn't have slipped off. It was thrown."

"But there's no one to throw it," Alli said.

Nancy shrugged, crouched down and swept up the glass onto the small hand shovel, taking care to catch every splinter. She stood. "He didn't like me referring to him in the past tense. He never likes that."

Alli and Ric watched Nancy return to the kitchen. They went back into the room. "I don't know about you," Ric said. "I could do with a drink." He reached for the champagne bottle.

"Seriously?" Alli indicated the bottle. "After what she said about making a pact with the devil?"

"Do you honestly think she wants to poison us? She's just asked us for our help."

"True. Help to do what, though?" Alli held out her glass. "What the hell, eh?"

"My sentiments exactly." Ric topped up her glass, before emptying the rest of the bottle into his own.

Nancy was back within a couple of minutes. She seemed to have pulled herself together remarkably quickly. Gone was the scared, blanched face and distant, vague sense of doom.

Alli decided to plunge in. "You honestly believe this house is haunted, don't you?"

Nancy turned her eyes to Alli. "Of course it is." She might have been discussing the weather. "The question is not whether the house is haunted, but by whom and how many."

Alli exchanged glances with Ric, who raised his eyebrows.

"Oh, I know you think I'm mad, but you can't deny you felt something up in the attic, didn't you, Alli? And I'm betting you're not immune either, Ric."

Ric coughed. "I wouldn't go that far. It's an old house. Old houses are, by definition, spooky. And having an urn full of the ashes of your late grandmother in that room doesn't really help dispel the atmosphere."

"If they are indeed her ashes," Nancy said quietly.

Alli stared. "You're not seriously suggesting they belong to someone else?"

Nancy shrugged. "Right now, I don't know. Did you read the inscription?"

"You mean the name and date of birth?" Ric asked.

"Yes. You see what I'm getting at."

"Not really."

The memory of the engraving flashed into Alli's mind. "You mean the fact there's no date of death?"

"Precisely," Nancy said. "What if she's not dead?"

"Woah." Ric exhaled heavily. "She's dead all right. The solicitor contacted you after she died and read you the will. Clearly, she couldn't have been alive then, any more than she is now."

Meanwhile, Alli was racking her brains. "Nancy, do you mind me asking…. How did Caroline die?"

Nancy sighed. "She committed suicide. In this house. Hanged herself. At least that's what they told me. That's what the coroner's verdict said. No one else involved. No one else here. She was found by her cleaner the following day. The poor woman had to be sedated for shock. I phoned and asked her if she would come back and clean for me, but she refused point blank. Can't say I blame her. Can you imagine? Walking into your place of work on a normal day like any other, and you find your employer hanging by the neck from the top banister?"

A chill settled itself in Alli's bones. How could Nancy say all this in such a matter-of-fact tone? This was her birth grandmother for heaven's sake. Alli shook her head and lowered her eyes.

The shadows were lengthening in the room and Nancy got up to switch on a selection of lights and lamps. She closed the window.

"The caterers will be here shortly. I'll get the room ready for them." She shut the door behind her.

Ric stood and looked up at the portrait. "What secrets lie behind those enigmatic eyes, Caroline Rand?" He turned back to Alli. "How old would she be if she were alive today, do you reckon?"

"She was born in 1942 according to the urn."

"Ah yes. So, what made her decide to end her life at such an advanced age, and in such a manner?"

"Loneliness?"

"She could have made contact with Nancy. I mean, she knew where to find her, didn't she?"

"Not necessarily. The solicitor may have had to conduct a search."

"Okay but if *he* did, then *she* could have. In fact, surely that must have happened or else how would she know that the daughter she gave up for adoption and never saw again had herself produced an illegitimate child? She obviously had some feelings for her, else why bother tracing her and leaving everything she possessed to her? She could have saved herself the effort and left it to a cats' home."

"Maybe she didn't like cats."

Ric gave her a look.

"All right. I get your point. She could have left it to a charity, or any one of a number of great causes but she decided to leave it to the child of the child she gave up for adoption all those years earlier. My guess is guilt. After all, it doesn't sound as if she was a wholly willing partner to her daughter's adoption in the first place. Lucius Hartmann pulled the strings there."

"I was right. He really was a puppet master," Ric said. "He seems to have had a genuine talent for manipulating pretty much anyone he came into contact with."

"And may still be doing so." Alli wondered why she had said that before the words were even fully formed. But Nancy's fear seemed real enough. "I don't believe she got us here for a hippy party at all. I think that was simply a ruse to make sure she wasn't on her own this weekend."

"Oh? Why this weekend particularly?"

"I've no idea. And maybe it doesn't matter which weekend. She wanted witnesses to corroborate her suspicions. She wants other people to experience what she has, so she'll know she really isn't going mad. That it's all real."

Ric remained silent for a minute. "So, she wants us to believe that Lucius and/or Caroline are still alive in some way, and in this house."

Alli nodded. "I know it sounds crazy, but that's the whole point, isn't it?"

The door opened and Alli jumped as Nancy bustled in.

"And I thought I was the jittery one. The caterers have arrived. Dinner will be served in a few minutes. Do either of you want anything to drink?"

"No thanks," Alli said. Ric shook his head.

"I'll get myself one then." Nancy picked up the remote, aimed it at the iPod and left them once more, leaving the door partially open. In the distance, the sound of plates, glasses and cutlery echoed across the hall.

The Mamas and the Papas started up. 'Monday, Monday'. Images of Laurel Canyon sprang into Alli's mind, although from where she had no idea. Maybe she had watched a program about it or read a book. "Nancy's going to an awful lot of trouble considering there are only three of us," Alli said. "Even if her friend Mike had arrived in time, there would still only have been four."

Ric nodded. "All the more for us then."

They lapsed into their own thoughts. Alli's grew more and more troubled. This was not the weekend she had thought it would be. She wanted to leave, but it would be so rude and insensitive to go now. Maybe when Mike arrived tomorrow, she could make some excuse, say she had to get back to London immediately. It wasn't as if she and Nancy were particular friends. Ric knew her most recently and so, presumably, did Mike, whoever he was.

Why did her conscience insist on pricking her? The fact remained that she had never been one to turn away from someone when they were in trouble. Even people she barely knew. Perhaps a result of her relatively lonely childhood. Apart from all the changes of school, she was virtually ignored at home, where the sole topic of conversation revolved around music whether classical or modern. She learned a lot from listening to her parents. After all, she had little to contribute to their chats, but occasionally little snippets of gossip would drop into the conversation and she found she could make herself popular with girls at school by imparting stories of their favorite singers or bands they would never have heard otherwise.

Not that Alli saw all that much of her parents anyway as they rehearsed for the next tour or recording session. Mealtimes were the only real times they spent together and then only when one or both of them happened to be at home. Then, straight after dinner, she was packed off to her room to do homework, watch her own small television on her own, read or play with her toys. Until she was old enough to fend for herself, one or other of her mother's friends would be drafted in for babysitting duties. The unmarried ones would stay with her. Those with their own families would add her to their number. All the moving around taught her self-sufficiency, but it stinted her ability to form meaningful relationships. She always kept a part of herself back. It wouldn't do to be too open. That would expose her and make her vulnerable and this belief never changed. Sometimes she felt lonely, but she learned early in life not to complain to her parents.

"What have you got to complain about, Allegra?" her mother would say. "Do you realize how lucky you are? You have the best toys, your own television, a beautiful room. What a selfish, ungrateful child." Alli would feel guilty, mumble her apologies, and retreat back upstairs. She may not have spent too much of her life with her, but her mother's words never failed to have a profound effect on her.

No, it was never a good idea to complain. So Alli kept her loneliness to herself. She kept everything to herself. As she grew older that became easier. She simply kept people at a distance, but she was always there to help anyone in trouble or needing a shoulder to cry on until their own crisis passed. Sometimes someone would try to cross the boundary into her inner sanctum. At that point, she gently backed away, avoiding them until they drifted off themselves. It was better this way. Less chance of getting hurt the way she had been by her parents' constant pushing away and rejection once they discovered that, while she enjoyed music, she had no talent whatsoever for playing an instrument of any kind. They had been unstinting in their efforts to develop any latent talent. Early violin lessons were abandoned quickly to preserve sensitive eardrums. Piano tuition ceased after one too many discordant chords. Finally, guitar. She could never seem to progress beyond the basics. One, then both her parents, admitted defeat until one day Alli came home from school to find not only her parents away on a tour (which she knew about) but also her guitar missing. She never saw it again and there were no more music lessons.

Alli's need to be needed persisted, and people turned to her. So, given Nancy was in such dire straits how could she walk away from her? The answer was simple. She couldn't. She would stay. At least for now. At least until she found out what the hell was going on in Canonbury Manor.

The door opened wider and Alli became aware the music had changed. Now John Denver. 'Leaving on a Jet Plane'. Such a lonely song in so many ways. She had always identified with it and had often chosen to play it out of her parents' collection.

Nancy entered and broke her reverie. "If you come with me, we can get started. I hope you're both hungry. I'll be eating this all week if you're not."

The spread was a banquet of a cold buffet. A whole poached salmon, vol-au-vents with a variety of delicious-looking fillings, quiches, tartlets, open sandwiches, a selection of cheeses, fruit, artisan bread that smelled as if it had come straight from the oven, salads and dips. Sixties style it may be, but gourmet style.

"You've got enough here to feed an army," Ric said, already piling his plate.

"It's beautiful, Nancy. Thank you," Alli said. She took a mouthful of smoked salmon and cream cheese vol-au-vent. The pastry almost melted in her mouth.

"I'm glad you're enjoying it," Nancy said. For the next ten minutes or so, very little conversation punctuated the consumption of the delicious food. Eventually Alli set her plate down, followed by Ric. Nancy set hers down too and Alli noted that she had barely touched a morsel. The table looked as if maybe a couple of mice had taken the odd nibble. There was so much left.

"I hope you have plenty of fridge space," Alli said. "Let me help you."

Nancy was already beginning to collect up plates. "Thanks, Alli."

"I'll pitch in too," Ric said. "We'll soon get this lot put away."

It took the three of them half an hour before they were able to wrap up the uneaten food that would keep another day, dispose of what couldn't be saved and, finally, pile dishes and plates into the dishwasher.

Fortunately, Nancy's well-equipped, spacious kitchen had a massive American-style larder fridge, which was practically empty when they started to fill it. By the time they had piled in all the remaining food, little space remained. Nancy shut the heavy door.

"Cognac?" she suggested and, with the agreement of her guests obvious by their enthusiastic nods, she reached up to a glass wall cupboard and took down three crystal brandy goblets.

Strains of The Monkees' 'Your Auntie Grizelda' wafted across the hallway. One of their lesser-known tracks. Alli remembered her father saying it was a shame Peter Tork didn't sing lead on more of their songs as his voice had such personality.

The sound of the grandfather clock chiming the hour interrupted Alli's thoughts and prompted her to count. At nine, Nancy's hands visibly shook. The bottle of Courvoisier clanked against one of the glasses as she sloshed a generous measure in. Without thinking, Alli put her hand out to steady her.

"My God, Nancy, your hand. It's ice cold."

Not only that, she could see through Nancy's translucent skin. Dark blue veins were clearly visible in her fingers and the back of her hand. Blood pulsed through them as each heartbeat sounded in Alli's ear.

Nancy pulled away. Cognac splashed on the floor.

"Hey, steady." Ric put his arm out to catch Nancy, who looked as if she might faint at any second.

She thrust the bottle at him. "Here. Take this. I'm...I'm sorry. I...

don't feel very well. I'm going to bed. You can look after yourselves, can't you?"

Nancy didn't wait for an answer, shot out of the kitchen and raced up the stairs. A few seconds later, the noise of an upstairs door banging shut echoed around the house.

Ric set the bottle down on the sink. "What the hell do you suppose that was about?"

"I haven't a clue. It seemed to get much worse when the clock started to chime."

Ric looked thoughtful. "Yes, it's strange about that clock."

"What is?"

"Do you remember it chiming before? We've been here a few hours now. We would have heard it. I don't remember, do you?"

Alli thought back. "You're right. Surely if a clock is going to chime, it does so every hour. Not just one of them."

"You can get the sort that run silently during night hours but that's not the same as only chiming at nine o'clock. Come on."

Alli followed Ric into the hall. The clock stood against a wall equally distant from the open doorways of the kitchen and the living room and diagonally opposite the dining room.

Ric moved closer to it. "This is the real deal, I reckon. I'm no expert but it looks pretty old to me."

Alli peered up at the clock face. "There's the maker's name. Johnson of Fleet, London 1876."

She looked down the casement. Through the glass, the pendulum swung rhythmically and steadily from left to right. The tick was deep, but not noisy. "I can see why we wouldn't hear anything but the chime. We had a grandfather clock at home, and it made quite a noticeable 'tock' noise. This one seems well insulated."

"Except at nine o'clock."

"Let's test it then," Alli said. "We'll stay in the kitchen until ten and see what happens."

"Agreed. Don't these clocks sound the quarter hour as well?"

"Some do. Maybe not this one. That, at least, isn't terribly unusual."

Back in the kitchen, they sipped their brandy.

Alli sat on one of the stools set around the central island. Ric joined her, taking one opposite. "What do you make of all this?" he asked. "This is not the Nancy I used to work with. That Nancy was confident, self-assured.... She would have laughed in your face if you'd mentioned the term 'haunted house'."

"We were in the same class at school together for a while," Alli said. "I was the new girl, joining the school in the second year. She was a bit of a misfit as well, having only started at the school six months ahead of me. She became my only proper friend for the time I was there, and she would defend me when a group of girls decided I was fair game. They used to tease me unmercifully about my name. I was a bit chubby as well then, so when they weren't chanting my full name, they would call me 'Fatty Alli'. It's okay. You can laugh now. It bothered me back then, but I lost the puppy fat when I was eighteen. I lost touch with Nancy long before that, when I moved on to another school."

"I wasn't going to laugh," Ric said. "They called me beanpole at my school. I was the tallest in class and thin as a rake. I've been this height since I was around fourteen. Kids can be fucking cruel, right? I didn't know Nancy all that well either, but I did work on some projects with her. She has a quick brain. Highly creative. And nothing like the scared, quivering wreck that shot out of here like the devil was after her."

Alli shivered at his words.

"What's wrong?"

"What you just said. It almost seems to sum her up. 'Like the devil was after her', you said...."

Ric shifted on his stool. "If this house was left to her by her grandmother, then surely she'd want the best for her grandchild. You don't leave someone a vast house and a fortune only to turn on them and drive them insane."

"You're talking about Caroline Rand. What about Nancy's grandfather? He's the one who, allegedly at least, wanted her mother adopted and out of the way, and we know that, by reputation at least, he's a master manipulator."

"Was."

"Sorry?"

"You said, 'is'. You said he *is* a master manipulator. The man is dead, Alli."

"And what if he isn't? What if Nancy's right and somehow he's found a way to come back?"

"Are you serious?"

Alli leaned back. Was she? She had heard her words, but she couldn't believe that she had said them. "I haven't the faintest idea." The music wafted through from the living room. The Doors' charismatic lead singer, Jim Morrison, singing 'Riders on the Storm'. Such an atmospheric song, complete with sound effects that seemed especially real this evening. Alli hugged herself against the sudden chill that seemed to have descended on the room. Her skin felt cold. *Like this damned house.* "Look, I only know that when I looked at Nancy's hand a few minutes ago, I could see the veins through her skin. I could see the blood pumping through them. Did you see that?"

"To be honest, I wasn't looking. I was more concerned that she was going to smash that expensive bottle of cognac. And, while we're on the subject, have you noticed how well stocked her drinks collection is and how little food she had before we filled her fridge earlier? I reckon she's living on alcohol. That's hardly likely to help her sense of perspective."

A groaning creak interrupted them. Like someone opening a door close by. A door that had been closed for too long. Alli froze.

"It's probably Nancy come down for a glass of water or to apologize," Ric said.

They both stared at the kitchen door. No one appeared.

Ric stood. "I'll go and check."

Alli jumped to her feet. "I'm coming with you." No way was she going to be left in that kitchen alone.

CHAPTER FOUR

The only light came from the open doors of the living room and the kitchen. Alli kept close behind Ric. So close she could smell his aftershave. "I don't remember the hall this dark," she said.

"It wasn't," Ric said.

A shadow flew across the wall opposite them.

Alli cried out. "What the hell was that?"

Ric's voice trembled slightly. "I've no idea. I don't even think I *want* to know."

Another shadow shot across the wall, then another and another. Silent, swirling. Gone in an instant.

A blaze of light cast out the shadows as the wall lights came on.

"Oh my God, Ric. What the hell's going on?"

"We need to go to Nancy."

They tore up the stairs. Ric hammered at her door.

"Nancy. It's Ric and Alli. Can you open up? We're worried."

Alli turned the handle. Locked. "Nancy, it's Alli. Please open the door."

Ric put his shoulder to the door. It wouldn't budge. "Here goes." He stood back and kicked it open.

The dying rays of a burning sunset cast fiery shadows across the bed where Nancy lay, fully clothed.

She opened her eyes and struggled to sit up. "What's the matter? What's happening?" Nancy put her hand to her head, her hair disheveled.

"Thank God you're all right." Alli sat on the bed. "Didn't you hear us banging on the door?"

Nancy shook her head. She seemed to be having difficulty focusing.

Alli took her hand, grateful to see her skin looked normal again. Nancy withdrew from her light grasp. Maybe she didn't like being touched.

"I need to tell you," Alli said, "after you dashed out of the kitchen, we heard a noise downstairs. The lights in the hall were off and we saw shadows we can't explain shooting across the walls. Then the lights came on again, all by themselves. Does that sound familiar?"

Nancy blinked. "It happens every night," she said. "Always at the same time. Nine o'clock. It's the only time that clock ever strikes. The only thing I can guess at is that I was told the time of Caroline's death was estimated between around eight p.m. and midnight. Maybe nine is the actual time she took her last breath. All I know for sure is that it's happened every night since I moved in here. I hoped with you being here it might not. I hoped it would give me a rest. I'm so tired." Nancy slumped back onto her pillow, tears streaming down her cheeks.

Alli put her hand on Nancy's shoulder. This time she didn't recoil. Through the thin fabric of her top, Nancy's skin felt ice cold – like before, only now it felt clammy, as if she had broken out into a cold sweat.

The sunset faded, and a gloom settled on the room.

"It's too bloody dark in here." Ric flicked a switch. The central light came on.

Nancy averted her eyes from the strong light. "Please turn it off. It hurts my eyes. Put a lamp on if you must."

Alli reached over and turned on a bedside lamp, which gave off a muted soft glow. Ric switched off the main light. A wave of sympathy swept over Alli. The cheerful, happy woman who had greeted her mere hours earlier had evaporated, to be replaced by this quivering wreck who, even now, was drawing her legs up in an apparent effort to curl into a fetal position. Anything, it seemed, to gain some modicum of comfort.

Ric touched Alli's shoulder to get her attention. She switched her gaze from Nancy. He touched a finger to his mouth. Alli took the hint to keep quiet and followed him into the hall. Nancy's eyes were closed. If she could sleep, she might feel better, more able to fight whatever was in this house.

Alli pulled the door closed behind her.

A loud creak made them both jump.

Alli hugged herself. *It's listening to us. It can hear what we say.*

In an instant, the air around them grew thick. Fog misted Alli's eyes. Ric's eyes became black hollows in a face that was rapidly disintegrating.

Alli cried out. "Ric! What the hell's happening? I can't see you."

His mouth opened. It kept on opening. It opened into a tunnel, a black, never-ending tunnel.

It wasn't in a face anymore.

It wasn't a mouth anymore.

Alli wasn't there anymore.

She was falling, rolling over and over, trying not to breathe in the noxious smells of smoke, ether, sulfur, rotting vegetation. All assaulted her. All tried to smother her. Alli coughed, heedless of phlegm spewing vileness out of her body. Her head spun with the constant rolling motion and bile shot up into her throat.

A cacophony of noise, music played far too loud, so loud it was distorted. A jangling mass of guitars and keyboards, backed by throbbing drums echoed the banging in her head.

Through the blackness, a dim light gleamed in the distance. A blueish white light that flickered and beckoned to her. She still had no control over her movements, turning wherever the momentum took her. Willing herself to move closer to the light. But it seemed to grow no closer. Now it seemed she was rolling over and over in the same spot. She swallowed hard, dreading the moment she wouldn't be able to hold back. Bile, burning with acid that didn't belong outside her stomach, welled up inside her.

Then it stopped. No more sickening rolling motion. She was sitting on a floor.

"Hi." The voice was male, unfamiliar.

Alli tried to open her eyes, but the muscles wouldn't work.

"Hey, man, are you all right?"

All around Alli were voices, happy, laughing. Music played in the background. Music she hadn't heard since childhood. She struggled to remember it. A famous song.

"Hey, hey, little girl, open your eyes, let me see you're okay."

Alli concentrated all her effort on forcing her eyelids to work. When they did, the light nearly blinded her, and she couldn't focus.

"Woah, steady, steady. It's okay. Everything's groovy."

Groovy? Who says groovy anymore?

"Try again." The owner of the voice had shuffled down on the floor next to her. She was on the floor, sitting on top of something soft. Cushions probably. And leaning against more of them. The smell was of incense burning. Sandalwood, or similar, by the aroma. Had she fallen asleep? Had she dreamed all the crazy stuff she thought she had experienced with Ric? That's what must have happened. Maybe Nancy had recovered and spiked the champagne for some sort of twisted lark. And that's why the light hurt her eyes. At least her head had stopped throbbing.

Next to her, the man was stroking her hands as if trying to massage some feeling back into them. Who was he anyway? Not Ric. This guy had an American accent.

"Hey, John?"

Another male voice she didn't recognize. And another American. Where had they all come from? Now she could make out more of what was going on around her, even though her eyes still wouldn't work properly, Alli could hear individual voices. All with American accents.

"Who's your friend? I don't remember her arriving."

"I think she just got here. Seems out of it. Maybe a bad trip."

"Need some help?"

Alli pushed forward and opened her eyes. Everything seemed fuzzy and blurred for a second or two before coming together, as if someone had adjusted the lens on her own personal camera.

Standing above her, looking down, was a smiling man with collar-length sandy-colored hair. Next to her, the man who had appointed himself her savior responded. His voice was light, cheerful and he wore round wire-framed glasses. His blond hair was shoulder length, and he sported a wide grin and even teeth.

He smiled at Alli and looked up at the other man. "No thanks, Pete. I think she's coming round now. You had us worried there...what's your name?"

"Alli." Her voice was cracked and dry. She badly needed a drink. "May I have some water, please?"

The man called Pete let out a guffaw. "Water? Seriously? At one of Cass's parties?"

"Excuse me?" Alli stared at him.

"I think she's serious," the man she now knew as John said. "Probably the best thing for her if she's coming down."

"Well, okay, I'll get it, but that's a first."

He moved away, bypassing young women with long, natural hair, floor-length dresses or hot pants, men in jeans, their hair as long as the women's. All smoking…tobacco or some such.

Alli shook her head, trying to clear it.

"You're British then?" John said.

"Well, yes." It seemed a strange question to ask someone in their own country.

"Far-out," John said, laughing. His eyes twinkled. Alli warmed to him. She couldn't get the thought out of her mind that she had seen him somewhere before and pictured him wearing a Stetson while strumming an acoustic guitar.

"I'm Alli," she said.

"Yep, you already said that. I'm John. At your service, ma'am."

Alli stared. Then she remembered. "Cass?"

John spread his hands expansively. "This is her house. But you must know that. You were invited, right? Or did you just drop in? It's open house at Cass's and there's always plenty of food. Good, wholesome, delicious food. Reminds me of home in Colorado. It's the Jewish mama in her, I guess."

'Pete' returned with a glass of water, two giant ice cubes floating in it. He knelt a little unsteadily and handed Alli the glass. She noted he had kind, warm eyes. She took the glass from him, thanking him.

"Pete, meet Alli," John said. "Alli, this is Peter Tork. Late of The Monkees. But you knew that anyway. I'll bet you saw all their TV shows."

Alli stared blankly. She hadn't, not that it mattered. Her parents, in their lighter moments, had reminisced about watching a zany show about four guys who wanted to be as famous as The Beatles. But this was the twenty-first century. In rural England. Nancy's weird, increasingly scary house, except.... 'Your Auntie Grizelda'. That had been playing on Nancy's iPod. That must be it. She had heard it, fallen asleep and this was a dream. Even if it didn't feel like one.

Everything made too much sense. She could smell the incense, taste the water. You weren't supposed to be able to do either in dreams, were you? Okay, so it must be real then. Except...

...it was all wrong. Nothing fit. This *couldn't* be Nancy's Canonbury Manor. Right now, if someone said she was somewhere in America in 1968, she would, in all probability, believe them.

That wasn't possible. Right? So, she must be dreaming. If so, it was the most realistic dream she had ever experienced. Alli shook her head. She hadn't a clue what was going on here. The safest bet seemed to be to go along with it. At least for now.

Alli swallowed hard. "Hello, Pete. I'm Alli Sinclair and I wish I'd come up with a better persona for this party."

Pete gave her a quizzical look.

John let out a belly laugh. "Far-out, man. This girl's far-out."

A large female figure loomed toward them, dressed in a voluminous, tent-like dress of pink, lilac and yellow swirls, her long, thick brown hair draped over her shoulders. John stood and helped Alli to her feet. She staggered.

"Man, that's some heavy stuff you've been on," he said.

In a minute he's going to ask me for the name of my supplier.

He didn't. The woman who had joined them commanded their attention. She stood in front of Alli, appraising her, but not unkindly. A smile twitched the corners of her lips.

"I don't believe I've had the pleasure," she said.

Alli stared. She knew she must look stupid, but the resemblance was uncanny. The Mamas and the Papas had been one of her parents' favorite groups of that era, along with The Beach Boys. They had loved their close harmonies.

"Cass," John said, "this is Alli Sinclair. British and, I'm guessing, new around here."

A beaming smile transformed Cass's heavy features. "Well, let me welcome you to the Canyon and to my home. I'm Cass Elliot and my door is always open. I also happen to have the best grass in town, with the possible exception of Dave Crosby, and it's a real pleasure to meet you."

"Thank you."

Without warning, Cass wrapped her in a massive bear hug before releasing her and moving on.

When she was out of earshot, Alli asked, "Is she related to the real Mama Cass? I think she had a daughter, didn't she?"

John stared at her, and Alli wondered if she had grown another head.

"You really don't know where you are, do you?" he asked.

"I thought I did. Although these past few minutes have been probably the weirdest of my life. I think Nancy must have spiked my drink earlier. I'm in Nancy Harper's house on the outskirts of Canonbury Ducis in Wiltshire, England."

Again, the laugh. "*Far-out.*"

That expression was becoming just a little irritating.

Alli waited for John to regain control of himself. He did. Wiping his eyes, he said, "You're in Mama Cass Elliot's house in the heart of Laurel Canyon in the hills above Los Angeles, California in the good old U.S. of A. I sure as hell know where England is even if I haven't a clue about this Canon…wherever. You're at least five thousand miles from there."

Alli looked from John, around the room, surveying it, seeing faces that belonged in history books. In a corner, she saw a young woman, not pretty, swathed in a massive feather boa, feathers stuck in her long, unruly brown hair. Her skin seemed pasty, and she swayed as she swigged from a bottle of Southern Comfort. Next to her, a strikingly handsome man in tight black leather trousers laughed and took deep drags on a large, untidily rolled spliff.

A man with a beard in urgent need of a trim swayed past her, also smoking. He eyed her up, grinned, winked at John and moved on. Familiar faces everywhere. But they all belonged in the past. The same era. Late Sixties. Her parents would have been in their element. Throughout the room, guitars were strewn everywhere, some plastered with labels, others gleaming new and expensive looking. The man she had been introduced to as Peter Tork took up a banjo and played a song Alli didn't recognize. Plenty of the partygoers did though, and soon joined in. Cass's voice soared above them, drowning out the quieter ones. She had some magnificent lungs on her.

In the surreal atmosphere, the man who had winked at John wandered back.

"Hey, man," he addressed John and his voice was gruff, gravelly. "Is she yours?"

Shocked, Alli realized he meant her.

John answered, "No, man, she just got here. I never met her before."

The man made a grab for her arm. Alli drew back. He looked startled.

"Hey, come here, let's party. You and me and one of Cass's deep soft beds."

Again, he grabbed for her.

"*No.*" A couple of heads turned. Alli didn't care. How dare this man, this *stranger*, treat her like a piece of meat.

He looked startled, as if no woman had ever said 'no' to him before. Maybe they hadn't.

"Hey, girl, what's the matter with you? This is a party. We're all here to get high or get laid. Preferably both. Aren't we?" He nodded at John, who laughed, a little nervously this time.

"I have no idea how I got here, or why," Alli said. "But I can assure you, I am not here to get high or *laid* as you put it."

"Ah, that explains it. British. They're all frigid. Come on, let's see if this California beach boy can warm you up a little." Once again, he made a grab.

He had well and truly crossed the line. Alli was putting a stop to it. The sound of her hand slapping his face was sufficient to pause Cass in mid-flow. Conversation stopped and all eyes focused on how their hostess would react.

The man put his hand to his cheek and glared at Alli. Beside her, John shuffled his feet.

Then, from across the room, a guffaw, followed by a huge belly laugh, broke the tension. Soon one, then another, joined in.

"Looks like you met your match there, Dennis," Cass called over to him, as she wiped tears of laughter from her eyes.

The injured man whirled round, then spun back again to face Alli. He lowered his hand and a grin stretched across his whiskered face. "Feisty lady," he said, wagging his finger at her. "Feisty." He moved away, to be swallowed up by a gaggle of girls who didn't look as if they really belonged there. Too thin, raggedy, undernourished and looking as if a good bath wouldn't go amiss.

The room returned to its version of normal.

John let out a deep breath. "You're too much, lady. Far-out."

Alli stared at her hand. Dennis Wilson. She had just slapped the face of The Beach Boys' drummer. The sexy one of the group. The one all the girls screamed for. The one her mum had confessed to dreaming of all those nights as she gazed up at his poster on her bedroom wall.

Dennis Wilson. The *late* Dennis Wilson.

Alli looked over at Peter Tork. She had read about his death far more recently. Cass Elliot had passed away years before. And so had...Janis Joplin. She was the woman with the Southern Comfort, and she was standing next to...Jim Morrison. He really was as good looking as his photographs suggested.

I'm believing all this. It can't be true, but I believe it.

Alli scanned the room once more. Still so many faces she knew she had seen somewhere....

Is everyone in this room dead?

They didn't look dead. They didn't seem like ghosts. Her brief contact with Dennis Wilson's cheek had been with warm flesh, not the cold of some graveyard specter. She had a sudden urge to touch John. Would she feel warm flesh there too? Who was he? He looked so familiar, but she still couldn't place him.

Alli tried to think logically. The problem was this wasn't a logical situation. Her mind ticked off the possibilities. They came down to two. Either she was dreaming, or she had somehow slipped back into the very world Nancy had been seeking to recreate with her weekend party. And, given what had already happened in Canonbury Manor.... She turned back to John, who was eyeing her with some concern. "What date is it?"

"June 3rd."

"And the year?"

"The year? It's June 3rd 1968."

It came as a shock. It hit her brain like a speeding train. Even though what he said fit perfectly with everything around her. "You wouldn't lie to me? It really is the third of June, 1968?"

He touched her hand, and she felt the warmth of living, breathing skin. Blood flowed through those veins.

"Hey, man, what is this? Do we need to get you to a hospital? Did you hit your head? It might be a concussion."

Alli shook her head. "No, please. I'm as sure as I can be that I didn't hit my head." Alli felt around her scalp anyway. No bumps, bruises or tenderness anywhere, and now that she had become accustomed to the light, her vision was normal, and her balance restored. Only the circumstances were off. Way off. "We are definitely in Laurel Canyon?"

"Sure are. And everyone who is everyone is here. Oh look, here's a new arrival. She's British too. She's Number One on both sides of the Pond right now."

John moved forward to greet the newcomer. So did a number of others. Greetings were shouted, a few cheers. Alli couldn't see over the mass of heads or between the press of bodies until they parted momentarily to let the young blonde woman through.

She smiled and made straight for Alli, who stood rooted to the spot. And then she was right in front of her.

CHAPTER FIVE

Caroline Rand looked exactly like her portrait. Long, slender arms and impossibly long fingers, which would have been the envy of any piano player or guitarist. Her lithe body was encased in an ankle-length floral dress that moved with her. Her straight hair draped her shoulders, like a gleaming gold shawl. Her eyelashes seemed real, although surely too long to be natural, framing luminous blue eyes. Her understated makeup enhanced her high cheekbones and fine skin. She was, to quote a term Alli had heard her father use, classically beautiful.

"Do I know you?" she asked Alli.

"No. I'm Alli Sinclair."

Caroline Rand was clearly waiting for some explanation, a description of her reason for being there, what she did for a living perhaps, or which group she was in, even who she was dating. Anything. All Alli could think of was that they had someone in common – Nancy, this young woman's *granddaughter*.

An awkward silence fell between them. Until Caroline spoke.

"I'm Caroline Rand and I've only just moved over here. I've bought a bungalow a little further down on Lookout Mountain Avenue. We could be neighbors. That's if you're going to be living here? Or have you moved in already?"

"No, no," Alli said. The awkwardness was getting worse. This woman had died. She had committed suicide in her own home – the same home where only minutes earlier, Alli had been. Oh, why not go for it? "I live in England. Canonbury Ducis. Maybe you've heard of it?"

The answer came back immediately: "Canonbury Ducis. What a lovely name. I'm sure I would have remembered it if I had. Where is it?"

"Wiltshire. Really handy for the M4."

"They're still building that one, aren't they? There are so many new roads opening everywhere these days in Britain, there'll be no countryside left soon."

Alli smiled and nodded.

"Caroline!" Cass grabbed the startled woman by the arm. "You must come and meet someone you're going to love. He writes great songs and I know you'll want to work with him."

Caroline shrugged apologetically at Alli, who watched her propelled by the irresistible force that was Cass Elliot. A light breeze fluttered through the open picture window and blew Caroline's hair over one shoulder.

Alli gasped. Livid purple against fair skin, rope marks, etched deep enough to reveal bruises. Right around her neck, disappearing under the curtain of hair.

At that moment, Caroline turned toward her.

And her misted eyes poured blood, like tears raining down her cheeks.

Alli turned to John. He was no longer there.

The music drifted away. No smells of summer, incense, pot and sandalwood. Only the burnt stench of ashes, catching in the back of her throat. Rotting vegetation leached the miasma of compost. The walls ran with rainwater, saturating the black and green mold and quenching the thirst of ferns, lichen and moss that covered the wooden floors and timber-framed walls.

Alli's legs gave way under her and she slid to the slimy floor. The cold and wet penetrated her skirt, chilling her. Everywhere, black beetles crawled, large spiders spun gossamer webs. She looked up and nearly passed out.

A figure – apparently human – swayed back and forth, like a grotesque pendulum. Its face was turned away from her, too far gone to be recognizable as either male or female. A long, thick rope held it suspended from a crossbeam. Alli closed her eyes and prayed it all away. She could hear the sounds of a forest. Birds singing, the distant bark of a fox, but the evil stench remained ingrained in her nostrils.

She opened her eyes and dared to look upward.

With relief, she took in the ceiling. No crossbeam. No rope. No figure dangling dead above and in front of her. Alli struggled to stand. Her feet slithered across the floor, and her legs would not support her. She fell back down again.

She must think. Somehow, she had ended up here, either in her mind or in fact, so, surely, she could extricate herself.

A sudden cracking noise, like bones breaking, sounded to the left of her. She looked. Nothing there.

To the right.

Again nothing.

In front of her. She turned her head and screamed.

Caroline Rand was dead. Her body stood, gown filthy and in rags, hair in clumps, skin gray and sloughing off white bone. Skeletal fingers reached out to Alli. Skinless jaws clacked together like the carapaces of a hundred beetles. Wide, staring eyes. No pupils, just ugly yellow irises crisscrossed with ruptured veins of long-congealed black blood.

Alli screamed. "You cannot be there. This isn't happening. *I am not here.*"

The creature's head lolled to one side as if struggling to hear and make sense of what she was saying. Its jaws clacked again.

The sound sent cold fear coursing through Alli's body. "Go away! Go back to wherever you came from. You don't belong here." As if *she* did.

The jaws made another sound. Almost a whisper. Indistinct, it resonated in Alli's brain.

Help me.

Alli clapped her hands over her eyes. She drew her knees up to her chin and let her hands fall to clutch them tighter, the need to make herself as small as possible overwhelming.

She dared open her eyes.

The creature had gone.

Everything had gone. Alli looked down at a polished wooden floor, at the male hand extended to her. She inhaled the scent of Nancy's patchouli, which seemed to hang everywhere, as gradually her senses returned.

Ric helped her to her feet. "You had me worried there for a few minutes. Has this happened before?"

Alli's head felt muzzy. "No. Never. Did I pass out?"

"You went out cold. One minute you were saying that someone was listening and the next I was breaking your fall."

"I need to sit down."

"I'll help you to your room."

"What about...?" Alli nodded toward Nancy's room.

"Not a peep. I reckon she probably fell asleep again. Exhaustion I shouldn't wonder."

"You wouldn't believe what I've just experienced."

In the peace and quiet of her room, Alli recounted everything she could remember. Ric said nothing. He listened, appeared to be taking everything in and only when she had finished, did he inhale deeply.

"That's some story, Alli."

"Clearly I never left here so it must have been in my mind. How it got there, whether it was some kind of hallucination brought on by this house or something Nancy put in the champagne, I haven't a clue. I swear to you that everything I've told you is as real to me as you standing there now."

"And you've never been to L.A.?"

Alli shook her head. "My parents went when I was a child. They were on tour with a band, and they played the Hollywood Bowl. I was too young, and it was school time, so I stayed at home. I remember bawling my eyes out for days because I wanted to go so much."

"I went a few years back. I have a friend in San Diego and I stayed with him and his then wife. It was a great experience. We drove up into the Hollywood Hills though and I remember we went to Laurel Canyon. Stan – my friend – pointed out all the famous landmarks. Joni Mitchell's bungalow, where she lived with Graham Nash and he wrote 'Our House'."

"The one with two cats in the yard?"

"White Persians apparently. We drove past Frank Zappa's place. They called it the Log Cabin, I think. He was sort of the godfather to everyone as the Canyon gradually filled with rock, pop and folk musicians. The Doors had houses there. Alice Cooper, can you imagine? Dusty Springfield. Cass Elliot—"

"You actually saw her house?"

"Yes. I would guess it's been renovated since the Sixties. Since...."

"You don't have to say it. Since I was supposedly there. Imagined myself there.... God, if I could only accept it was a dream. You don't smell anything in dreams, do you? It's one of the ways you know you're dreaming. But I could smell all those aromas, feel the slimy coldness and the sudden change in atmosphere. And I knew that whatever happened, I was truly there. When it turned bad, I knew I was trapped and couldn't do a thing about it. To me, it was all real. No dream."

Ric exhaled in a whistle. "All I can tell you is that you were there, lying on the floor, all crumpled up, for a few minutes and then you began to come to. It did seem more of a passing out than a falling asleep. Maybe that's the difference."

"Maybe." Alli knew it wasn't, even if she had no alternative explanation to offer.

The unexpected scrape of a door handle startled them both. Alli scrambled off the bed and joined Ric, who was peering down the hall. Nancy's door slowly opened.

Alli held her breath, moistened dry lips and felt her heartbeat quicken. She exhaled as Nancy's tousled head appeared round her door.

"Hey?" Nancy sounded heavy with sleep. "What's happening?"

"Oh, not much," Alli said lightly. Too lightly. "How are you feeling?"

Nancy emerged fully, her skirt rumpled, her movements unsteady, as if she were hungover. "I had a strange dream. I wasn't here. I'm not sure where. Somewhere.... There was a party, full of dead people."

"Sounds like the same party you went to, Alli," Ric said.

Alli wished he hadn't mentioned that.

"What do you mean?" Nancy's eyes were glazed. She was clearly having trouble focusing. "You had the same dream?"

Alli thought quickly. "He's joking, Nancy. I fell asleep as well and had a weird dream. Obviously not the same as yours."

"I need some water," Nancy said. "My throat's on fire." She turned and swayed.

Ric raced forward to catch her before she fell. "I think you should go back to bed and stay there until morning. I'll fetch you that water. Alli, you might consider going to bed as well. You're looking pale and it's been a weird day. In fact, let's all get some sleep. Tomorrow we can start trying to work out what's going on here. What time is Mike arriving?"

Leaning heavily against his shoulder, Nancy stirred. "Somewhere around eleven I think."

"Okay. Let's get you back to your room, Nancy. Alli, I've got this. You get yourself off to bed."

"Thanks," Alli said. She retreated back into her room, changed into a nightdress and wrapped a thin cotton robe around her. She was tying the waistband when a soft knock sounded at her door. A smiling Ric brandished a tall glass full of water.

"Thought you might like this. I was getting one for Nancy anyway."

"Thanks." Alli took it from him. She had to tear her eyes away from his face. The face she had seen so horribly disfigured before she found herself five thousand miles and more than fifty years away.

"If you need anything, I'm right next door. Good night and sleep well."

"I hope so. Night, Ric, and thanks for looking after us."

Ric smiled and moved away. Alli closed her door and, as she made for her bathroom to clean her teeth, she heard Ric's door shut softly.

★　★　★

She woke to moonlight pouring into her room, casting a silvery light that only served to enhance the depth of the shadows in every corner. There were no trees at her level, which was on the first floor, but a partially open window let some night sounds in. An owl hooted in the distance, an eerie sound, swiftly followed by the barking of a fox. A smell of night-scented jasmine floated on a breath of breeze, growing stronger as she recognized it. It floated all around her, a fragrant cloud of heady sweetness.

Her eyes tightly shut, as she willed sleep to return, Alli shifted position slightly. The breeze caressed her cheek. It seemed warmer now. And that jasmine.

What jasmine?

There was nothing outside her window. She had seen the house when she arrived. The stone walls were devoid of any growth. There was no jasmine clinging to the walls, trellis-work or anywhere near, only those incense roses by the main door. If the smell was this strong, its source couldn't be that far away.

Alli's eyes shot open. She wasn't in her bed. She wasn't even in Nancy's guest room. Or Nancy's house.

The small bedroom had plain timber walls. Moonlight filtered through fluttering lace curtains that framed floor-to-ceiling windows.

Alli pushed back the sheet and her feet found a soft cotton rug covering the polished wood floor. She looked around at the bed she had risen from. A simple double bedstead, once again made of wood. Pine probably, like everything else here. The pillows were soft white cotton, as were the sheets. Over the top of it, lay a quilt that looked hand-stitched in some Native American pattern. Even from a cursory glance, Alli could tell it was finely and expertly crafted.

She wondered why she felt so calm. She also wondered why everything seemed so familiar and comfortable even though she had never been here before in her life.

At the window she peered out. She was on the ground floor. The smell of jasmine was almost overpowering, and she saw the reason. It trailed up both sides of the window, laden with pale white and yellow trumpet-shaped flowers.

She inhaled deeply and listened to the unfamiliar sounds of a night she knew to be thousands of miles away from Canonbury Ducis.

Sounds echoed from the surrounding hills. Animals called to each other. Wolves? Coyotes? She had never heard either before so she could only guess. Somewhere closer, someone was playing a haunting tune on an acoustic guitar.

Alli stepped out onto wooden decking. Somehow, she knew that if she followed the walkway round, she would come to the front door. She took her first step, then another. The wood felt cool, not cold, under her bare feet. The jasmine extended a couple of feet and then petered out. She turned a corner and faced a short driveway, framed with bushes and trees left to grow naturally. No landscape gardener here. Ahead of her a streetlight's neon blaze seemed out of place. Without it, this place would have been like a Swiss chalet in the forest. She continued past the closed door, round the next corner, along the side. To the right of her, a garden overflowing with wildflowers played host to a stream. She could hear a frog or a toad making its guttural call and the sound of tinkling water.

The house was quite small so she reached the far end within a few seconds. She followed the decking around to the back, where steps led down to a path. In the moonlight, she could see that this wound its way past untidy flower beds on either side, before disappearing into a mass of bushes at the end, maybe half a football pitch away. She would need daylight to tell precisely.

Everything about this place felt right. More than that. It felt like home. More like home than she could ever remember feeling. She didn't know this place. But she knew where she was. Laurel Canyon.

And she knew she never wanted to leave.

CHAPTER SIX

"Alli. Alli."

She woke with a start. Someone was shaking her shoulder. She opened her eyes to see Ric looking down at her. "What.... What are you doing in here?"

"I tried knocking but I couldn't get a reply. I was worried, so I thought I'd better check. I was really concerned there. You were so soundly asleep."

Alli sat up, trying to gather her thoughts. She blinked in the bright sunlight that Ric let in as he drew back the curtains. "I had the most amazing dream."

"Good." He wasn't listening. "It's just after ten-thirty. Nancy's up and making breakfast. She doesn't seem to remember anything at all about last night. She reckons she drank too much."

"That's a possibility. She *was* hitting the champagne."

"Anyway, she's back to her old self. Mike's phoned to say he'll be here before noon, so get yourself up, showered and dressed and come down to the kitchen. Bacon and egg good for you?"

Alli grimaced. "I'm not that much of a breakfast person. Toast and coffee will be fine with me. Orange juice if she has any."

"Oh, she's got it. I remember seeing a couple of bottles of the stuff last night. And there's all that food left, remember. Whatever happens, we certainly won't go hungry this weekend and that's for sure."

Ric left Alli to it and, feeling more like herself, she quickly showered and got herself ready. Today's outfit would maintain the Sixties theme. Ric had donned bell-bottom denim jeans, adorned with a long paisley-patterned silk scarf threaded through the waistband. Alli selected a gypsy skirt in black with scarlet and green roses, a white off-the-shoulder embroidered blouse and a long silk scarf to tie around her head. A quick slash of black eyeliner, mascara and dark blue eyeshadow completed the look, topped off with a frosted pink lipstick. She slipped her feet into gold strappy sandals and made her way downstairs.

The sound of Nancy's laughter reached her at the bottom of the stairs. In the kitchen, Ric sat at the central island, sipping fragrant coffee, while Nancy, in an ankle-length, flowing multi-colored dress, fried bacon on the hob.

"Sleep well, Alli?" she asked.

"Fine, thanks. And you?"

"Perfect. I dreamed of jasmine. The most perfect, sweet-smelling jasmine."

Alli sloshed the coffee she was pouring from the cafetiere onto the worktop.

"That's a coincidence," Ric said.

Nancy looked from one to the other. "Is someone going to explain?"

Alli picked up a dishcloth and made herself calmly mop up the spill. "It's nothing really. I was telling Ric that I dreamed of smelling jasmine."

The doorbell rang. "That'll be Mike," Nancy said and hurried out of the kitchen.

"Saved by the bell," Ric said.

"It's not funny, Ric. Don't you think it's weird? I mean what are the odds that Nancy and I would dream about jasmine when there isn't even any around here?"

"The incense sticks?"

"They smell of patchouli. It's really distinctive. Jasmine is a whole different scent. Besides, look at what else has been going on here. It's as if this house is playing with us."

"Like we're puppets."

"Exactly like that."

Footsteps and animated voices interrupted them. A smiling Nancy led a slim man with dark blond dreadlocks that trailed down to his waist. Out of the corner of her eye, Alli saw Ric tense. The newcomer blinked behind heavy dark-rimmed spectacles.

"Alli, Ric, this is Mike Hathaway. Musician, poet, actor, writer. You name it, Mike's pretty much had a go at it."

Mike shook hands with Alli, and she noted the confident, firm handshake. She also noted the tattoos on his left arm. You couldn't really miss the vivid red and orange flames shooting out from his elbow. Around his wrist he sported a number of beaded bracelets.

"Pleased to meet you, Alli."

"And you, Mike. You look familiar."

Nancy laughed. "Not surprising. Mike was lead guitarist with Taranis. Massive a few years ago."

Alli remembered. Heavy metal, all male band in the Black Sabbath tradition. "'Thunder the Waves' was brilliant," she said, and meant it. Alli had never been a great metal fan but she made exceptions for some of the classics and 'Thunder the Waves' was way up there with 'Paranoid', 'Welcome to the Jungle' and a cluster of others. "I always wondered. Where does the name Taranis come from?"

He must have been asked this question a thousand times. How could she be so crass? Nevertheless, he smiled good-naturedly and answered her as if she'd asked something interesting. "Taranis was the god of the Celts, known as the Thunderer. Rather like Thor was to the Vikings. He was the god of storms and weather, could travel the world at great speed and was also associated with sacred wheels, which is why our set always featured a massive, stylized wheel. Apart from that, no one knows anything else about him. He made a lot of noise. It seemed appropriate for a heavy metal band."

"So, 'Thunder the Waves' is really about him then?"

"It seemed like a good idea at the time and a lot of people bought the record. I can live with that."

Ric had been standing silently. To Alli he seemed conflicted, anger mixed with...could it be fear?

Mike flicked a stray dreadlock over his shoulder and nodded at Ric. "Long time," he said.

"And a change of identity...Marcus."

"I didn't know you two knew each other," Nancy said.

"We don't. Not really." Ric turned away.

"That all happened ten years ago, Ric," Mike said. "She's not in my life anymore. She went off with some Canadian folk singer and last I heard they were living in a log cabin somewhere in the wilds of Saskatchewan. Look, we were all very young, high most of the time and crazy all of the time."

Ric's lips were set in a firm line. His anger wasn't going anywhere. Whatever – whoever – had caused this bad blood between them had cut deep.

"So, when did you stop being Marcus Aurelius then?" Ric's tongue slithered over the name.

"Around the time I grew up and realized naming myself after a Roman Emperor wasn't the coolest thing to do. It made no sense. I know nothing about Roman history apart from the blindingly bloody obvious and what I do know has nothing to do with heavy metal. Evidently Adrienne thought otherwise. Plain Mike Hathaway was less appealing than the more exotic Marcus Aurelius. When a Canadian called Finneas Androcles came along, she was off like a shot. You've got a fancy name too, haven't you, Ric?"

Nancy clapped her hands together. "Right, boys, time out please. Let's play nicely or not at all. I'll show you your room, Mike. Alli and Ric, will you make some more coffee and take it into the living room? Get some incense burning, smoke some pot, and put some music on. Preferably Caroline's. Let's get channeling our inner hippy. Peace and love, everyone. Peace and love."

Nancy made the peace sign with her fingers and linked arms with Mike.

Alli made a pot of fresh coffee and strolled into the living room with Ric, who brought in a tray laden with mugs, milk, spoons and sugar. She saw for the first time that the iPod stood in its deck on top of an old hi-fi, complete with turntable. Below this, a collection of old vinyl albums reminded her of when she was growing up.

Alli flicked through them and found Caroline Rand's *Madrigal for the Lost Temptress*. 'Lady Gossamer' was on side one, track one. Alli removed the fragile disc carefully. She slipped off the dust cover and placed the album on the turntable. As she lowered the stylus, it made a crackling contact with the beginning of the record.

"I thought I'd see what the original sounded like. Frying bacon hisses and all," she said.

Ric didn't reply. He was lighting incense sticks at various locations in the room and the warm scent began to drift toward them. There was no point in avoiding the subject. After all, the four of them were spending a weekend together and, if anything else went awry, they needed to be able to depend on each other. Alli cleared her throat.

"Ric, is Mike right? Did that girl and you split up ten years ago?"

Ric blinked at her. He was frowning and seemed to be battling to contain his temper. "Around that, yes. Look, some things are too important to sweep away just because a few years have elapsed. Adrienne was the love of my life. I haven't met anyone since who even comes close."

"Have you ever thought you would get her back?"

"Maybe. Possibly.... One day. I don't know. Can we change the subject, please? I'm not comfortable talking about this with you and, right now, I think I'm going to leave. I don't want to spend any time under the same roof as that bastard."

"No, Ric. Please don't." Alli bit her lip. She sounded as if she was begging a lover not to go. "I'm sorry, that came out wrong. It's just that...I haven't known Nancy for years, I don't know Mike at all, and you and I have been getting along quite well. I don't mean like.... You know what I mean. You were there when I needed help and I'm scared that if anything else happens and you're not here.... I know I could leave as well but...Nancy needs our help. I can't simply turn my back on her. Not like...all those years ago."

"No one else needs to go anywhere." Mike stood at the doorway, arms folded. "I'm the last one here so I can be the first to go."

Nancy squeezed past him into the room. "No one's leaving. I mean, please guys, please don't go. I really need your help. I have to know what's going on in this house and I can't do it by myself. I never told you what I did – the thing I should never have done. I called out to her one evening. Oh, I know nothing about séances and all that paranormal stuff, but I called her name. And she replied."

Alli stared at her. "She replied? Caroline Rand replied?"

Nancy nodded. Ric and Mike said nothing.

"She whispered my name," Nancy said, staring down at her hands. "Then the room went dark, and I heard this…chanting. Next thing I knew…. Shadows. Everywhere. They were moving and…I think I must have passed out because the next thing I remember it was really early in the morning. It scared the life out of me and that's when I decided I needed help." She looked at each of them in turn.

Ric turned on her. "There's a perfectly rational explanation for what you experienced. You fell asleep and had a particularly vivid dream. Look, Nancy, I'm sorry this hasn't worked out for you, but you're not exactly skint. You could simply walk away from this place. Sell it. Rent it out. Whatever you want. Hell, burn the fucking place down to the ground if you must. You could walk away and take the financial hit without batting a false eyelash. Why put yourself through this shit in the first place?"

Nancy looked as if he had just struck her. "Look, I know it doesn't make sense, and you're right. I should just pack my cases and go. The thing is, I have to know what happened – what *really* happened – to Caroline. To my grandmother. She didn't commit suicide. She was murdered. I know it and *he* knows it. Lucius fucking Hartmann." She jabbed a finger at Caroline's portrait. "Alli, you understand, don't you? You won't leave me."

"It's all right, Nancy. I'm not going anywhere." Alli's voice echoed around the room as if the place had suddenly emptied of all furniture. And that bloody incense kept getting stronger, heavy and cloying. She put a hand over her mouth and coughed, then swallowed hard and repeatedly. The other three stood like statues, staring at the portrait. Their stance seemed odd and unnatural, as if they were willing the picture to move.

The record stopped partway through the first track. No one moved to investigate. Not even Alli. She wasn't even sure she could if she tried.

The music started again.

At full blast. As if someone had pressed a 'start' button.

Nancy dashed over and lifted the stylus off the disc. Alli watched her set it down on its rest, switch the record player off, and unplug the machine at the mains.

Yet Caroline's voice continued to fill the room with her most famous song, soaring up to hit the high notes in perfect pitch and with exquisite timing.

Nancy stared down at the music center. No lights flickered. No power surged through it. The record lay still and unmoving. Slowly, she turned to face the others. "She's here. I can feel her."

Someone touched Alli's arm. The lightest and briefest of contacts, a mere fingertip brushing her skin like a feather, and it was gone. A waft of perfume. Not the patchouli incense. This was softer. A fresh, clean, dewy scent. Someone moved behind her. She heard the rustle of silk and glanced over her shoulder. There was no one there. Ric and Mike stood a few feet away. The four of them formed an almost perfect circle.

The men broke their gaze from Caroline's portrait, and, to Alli, their eyes appeared glazed, as if hypnotized.

"Ric?" Alli called. "Are you all right?"

He made no sign of having heard her. "Mike?" He also didn't acknowledge her.

"Alli, look." Nancy pointed up at the portrait, her finger shaking.

Alli followed her gaze and gasped.

The figure in the painting had shifted position. Her hands were now folded in her lap. The flowing scarves had been replaced by a lilac sweater and black skirt. Her eyes stared out, paler than before, crows' feet heavily etched at the corners, jowls heavier, bone structure less contoured.

Most startling of all, the seated figure's hair was silvery white.

"How can a figure in a portrait age?" Alli asked.

"Only the artist can do that," Nancy replied. "By painting another portrait. *He's* done that. Lucius Hartmann. He's painted another picture and substituted it somehow."

"He's *dead*, Nancy. He died before Caroline, and she must be…I don't know, eighty here?" Even as she said it, Alli remembered the inscription on the urn. Caroline Rand had been born in 1942 if that was to be believed. She had died the previous year, so she quite possibly did look like this toward the end of her life – her skin crisscrossed with deeply etched wrinkles, her eyes dull and hollow, filled with impenetrable, unutterable sadness.

"Maybe he was simply being cruel," Nancy said. "Guessing how she would age and leaving nothing to the imagination." She paused. "How did that picture get up there anyway? None of us have left this room. There's no one else in the house…no one we know of anyway. No one who should be here. No one living—"

A sudden movement attracted Alli's attention away from the picture. Ric and Mike seemed to have emerged from their stupor.

"What's happening?" Ric asked. "I seemed to lose track for a second."

Mike tossed his head back. "Same here. The weirdest feeling. As if I was floating, but I could still hear and see everything."

"The portrait," Alli said. "It's changed. Look at it."

"But it hasn't," Nancy said. "It's back as it was."

"Huh?" Ric looked at the picture and then back at Alli. "What's different about it?"

. Alli stared in disbelief. "Nothing. Absolutely nothing's different. Could we have imagined it?"

Nancy shook her head. "We both saw the same thing, Alli. Caroline as an old woman. It was there. It was definitely there."

"And now it's not."

Mike poured himself a coffee. "Would someone like to fill me in on what's been going on here? Because right now I feel as if I've walked onto the set of a horror film."

Alli sank down on a nearby chair, her head in her hands. An intense buzzing blurred her hearing. The animated voices around her receded into the distance, becoming less distinct with every second. The light faded; everything swam out of focus. Her head felt heavy and awkward as she tried to raise it. As if someone – or something – was pressing down on it. She tried to speak, but no words would form. Her neck would no longer support her head and it lolled to one side as her hands fell away to her sides and she slumped over the chair arm. Someone called her name. From far away.

The buzzing grew to a crescendo. Lights flashed, then went out.

Total blackness. Silence.

*   *   *

"Hey, hey." Someone was stroking her cheek. The aroma of sandalwood filled her nose. 'Lady Gossamer' played in the background. No. Someone was singing it. Someone not far away.

Alli struggled to open her eyes. She felt as if she had slept for hours. Maybe she had. One thing she was sure of. She was no longer in Nancy's house. No longer in England. When she opened her eyes, everything was as it had been a few seconds before she had zoned out here the last time. It was John trying to rouse her. Seeing her awake, or some approximation of it, he breathed an audible sigh of relief. "You have to stop doing that, Alli. You scared the shit out of me. What did you take?"

"Nothing. I swear. At least nothing I know of. I don't do that stuff. Who's that singing?"

"Caroline Rand, of course. I love that song. That's one I wished I'd written but, hey, I can't complain. I've got others, and," he tapped his head, "plenty more where they came from."

Alli pulled herself up into a sitting position on the floor cushions. She reached for the glass of water Peter had brought her earlier and took a deep gulp. It tasted refreshingly cold and pure.

Caroline finished her song and the audience, mostly of her peers, gave a resounding ovation. Loudest among them was their host, Cass. She hugged Caroline, who smiled broadly, caught Alli's eye and acknowledged her with a nod. Someone brandished a guitar and handed it to a long-haired man with a beard who bore more than a passing resemblance to George Harrison, the late Beatle. The man played a familiar intro and launched into the hauntingly beautiful 'While My Guitar Gently Weeps'. The distinctive nasal tones and trace of Liverpool accent transported Alli back to her childhood. Her mother loved this song and played it frequently.

What would she say if she knew her daughter was here, listening to the original? Only she couldn't be, could she?

Next to her, John seemed transfixed by the melody and the gentle lyrics. As the last note faded away, the applause almost deafened her.

"Far-out," John said and, for once, Alli agreed with him.

"May I have a word?"

Alli had been concentrating so hard on the beautiful song she hadn't noticed Caroline approaching. "Of course." Alli couldn't think of anything else to say.

"Do you mind if I speak to Alli in private, John?" Caroline accompanied her request with the sweetest smile. No way could he refuse.

He jumped to his feet and retrieved a Stetson and a guitar that were propped next to him. "I'll see you shortly, ladies. Time to go and sing for my supper."

Alli watched him go. He made straight for Cass. Alli tore her eyes away to concentrate on Caroline.

"You know, don't you?" Caroline said, her clear blue eyes friendly yet serious.

"I'm not sure what you mean. About what?"

Caroline positioned herself slightly to the side and in front of Alli and sat down, tucking her legs under her. "Let's put it this way. Neither one of us is where we should be right now, am I right? Isn't that how you feel?"

"Yes, but I...I don't know anything much about you. I know I shouldn't be here. I've never been here. And the time is all wrong. It's 1968 and you must be around twenty-six? But I've just seen a portrait of you when you looked eighty and that's not possible either because...." Alli's voice trailed off. Caroline's expression had turned from friendly to concerned, to mystified. "I'm sorry, Caroline. I know I sound crazy. I don't know what's happening. None of us do. Right now, I'm supposed to be in your house in Wiltshire, enjoying a nostalgic Sixties-themed weekend in your honor, and look at me." Alli made a sweeping gesture with her hands.

Caroline scrambled to her feet, all her poise set aside by her apparent sudden need to escape from the madwoman she had unwittingly cultivated. "I'm sorry too, Alli. I have to go. I…I'm sorry. So sorry…."

Caroline pushed her way past the nearest small cluster to the consternation of the drunk, or high, people concerned. One of the girls she knocked off balance blew a furious stream of bubbles at her from her party bubble bottle. "Who does she think she is, anyway?" she called, her words slurring. "Just another goddamn invading Brit. Haven't we got enough of them already?" At this, the girl glared at Alli, who looked away, still reeling from Caroline's odd reaction.

Across the room, John tuned his guitar, preparing to sing. Soon, his soaring voice reverberated around the room and conversation died down. 'Leaving on a Jet Plane'. Alli recognized the song immediately and couldn't stop herself from mouthing the words. John Denver. That's who he was. John Denver, who had perished when the light aircraft he was piloting crashed years ago.

Alli caught John giving her a surprised look. Cass joined in the song and the harmony was sublime. When it ended, to more rapturous applause, John thanked Cass and the crowd and made his way swiftly back to Alli.

"You like that song then?" he asked, a smile creasing his face as he sat down next to her.

"I've always loved it. I was brought up…." She stopped herself in time. John looked at her quizzically. "I mean, my mother played it – plays it – a lot."

"Your *mother* likes that song? Far-out!"

"It's a very pretty, very sad song."

"You really think so? Far-out. Thank you." He looked at her closely and Alli squirmed. His expression had darkened, and he looked at her in a strange way, almost scared. "I can't make my mind up about you. One minute you seem like the grooviest chick in here and the next…. Where did you come from, Alli…? What's your second name again?"

"Sinclair."

"Where did you come from, Alli Sinclair? Cass never invited you, did she? You don't know anyone here. Did you just walk in off the street?

You wouldn't be the first, and Cass would welcome you anyway. She has, hasn't she?"

"The truth is, I haven't a clue how I got here."

"There's something more. In your eyes...." His suntanned face blanched and he shook his head. "Motherf.... I don't believe what I just saw." He shot to his feet.

Alli stood, wavering slightly as her head swam. She leaned against the wall for support. "What's the matter? What did you see?"

His hands trembled. His expression one of terror. "In your eyes. I saw...I saw...." He shook his head.

Alli grabbed his arm. He shook it off as if she had burned him.

"Please, John, tell me. It's important. I have to know."

He stared straight at her, moistening dry lips. When he spoke, she had to struggle to hear him.

"I saw...death. I saw *my* death."

The words were barely out of his mouth and he was out of there, guitar in hand, hat crammed on his head.

Alli stared after him. She was certain now. However little sense it made, she was here. Back in time to 1968. And she was older than her own parents would have been. Hell, they could have been here as teenagers, mixing with musicians and singers who were among the finest of their generation while they themselves were starting out in the business. She looked around. No one paid her much attention. The occasional returned glance, a couple of lascivious looks from young men used to charming any girl they desired into bed. *Not this one, sunshine.*

Everywhere she looked, she saw even more familiar faces. All from the past. All dead.

She wasn't dead though. Alli was as sure as she could be that she was very much alive. Maybe she had been sent here for a reason.

So, what the hell is it?

She caught Caroline Rand studying her but, when she realized Alli had seen her, she averted her gaze. Yet Caroline had to be the link. Alli began her unsteady move across the room. She stumbled. The man who had so recently performed his eternal 'While My Guitar Gently Weeps' put out a hand to steady her.

"Thank you," she said.

He grinned, flashing a mouthful of gleaming white teeth at her.

Alli pressed on. She was just a couple of feet away from Caroline, who was deep in conversation with someone Alli didn't know. All she could see was the back of his balding head.

Then Caroline glanced her way. "No, Alli, don't come any closer." The man she was with turned to face Alli. He didn't look happy.

"Don't let her near me, Paul."

"I only want to talk to you, Caroline," Alli said. "I don't understand any of this either. I need your help. We all do."

"We?" Caroline said. "I don't see any 'we' here. Just you. I don't know who you really are. I don't know where you really came from, but I do know you're leaving."

"Please, Caroline—"

"Paul, make her go. Now, please. She *must* leave."

"All right." The older man clamped his hand around Alli's forearm in an attempt to drag her away.

"Get your hands off me!" Alli yelled. Heads turned their way. Through clouds of aromatic smoke and acid trips, people were stopping mid-flow, and taking an interest in the unexpected fracas.

The man called Paul wasn't over-tall, but he was stocky and strong. He also had the advantage over many of them there. He appeared to be sober.

"Time to go, young lady. You're upsetting Caroline and I'm her producer. You don't get to have an opinion on this."

He pushed her roughly toward the door.

Cass appeared from the kitchen. "Hey, Paul, what are you doing?"

"This young lady has upset Caroline, so she has to leave."

The smile died on Cass's face. "I think *I* get to say who stays and who goes, Paul Rothchild. This is *my* house, remember?"

"They can't both stay."

Cass made a sweeping gesture. "There's the door if you want to use it."

"You haven't seen how upset Caroline is."

Cass peered across the room. Alli followed her gaze. A smiling Caroline was engaged in conversation with another small group.

"She looks unharmed by her experience. I suggest you go back to her and leave Alli with me. She's new in town and not used to our Canyon ways yet."

The man hesitated, then moved away, after first giving a perfunctory nod to Cass.

"Thank you," Alli said, resisting the urge to kiss her.

"Save that for a while. You may not want to thank me later. The vibe in my house has changed and I couldn't get what caused it. Now I know. It's *you*. We need to talk, Alli. I need to know what you're doing here. And don't even *think* of lying to me."

Alli had no intention of lying, but whether Cass would believe the truth was an entirely different matter.

She followed her hostess up a flight of stairs. It was quieter up here. Cass led her into a bright, sunny and fresh room, full of the scent of early summer wildflowers.

"It can get a bit full-on down there. My own fault of course. I *will* keep an open house. My problem is, I *like* having people around me. People making music, being friendly, enjoying themselves." Cass settled herself on a wide double bed and indicated a chair next to it for Alli to sit on.

She took a step forward.

And found herself face down on Nancy's living room floor.

CHAPTER SEVEN

"Give her some air. Please stand back."

Alli recognized the voice as Mike's. He had an air of authority and right now, she could do with someone taking charge. She felt hopelessly out of control. "What's happening to me?"

Strong hands grasped hers and hoisted her to her feet. She swayed, dizziness threatening to overwhelm her again. Alli opened her eyes and let Mike steer her to a settee where she sank down. He lifted her legs onto it and Nancy handed Alli a couple of extra cushions so that she could prop up her head.

"I'll fetch her some water," Nancy said.

Ric moved into Alli's eyeline. "You gave us a scare for a moment. You were really out of it."

"I seem to be doing that a lot lately."

Ric knelt beside her. "You were talking to someone. Not one of us. You seemed to be somewhere else, and someone was asking you questions. We only heard your responses."

"I could see your eyes moving rapidly under your eyelids," Mike said. "It's typical of the stage we go through when we're sleeping and start to dream."

Ric's expression darkened. "Amateur psychologist now, are you, Marcus? Oh, I forgot. *Michael*."

"Please don't," Alli said. "I don't need you two fighting on top of everything else. What was I saying, Mike?"

"It was difficult to make out. You were saying stuff about being from England, not knowing why you were there or how you had got there and being confused about everything. You mentioned Caroline's name a couple of times. The thing was, you paused to allow the other person to speak and then carried on, literally, as if you were having a conversation."

"I was back there. In Laurel Canyon. In 1968."

"*What?*" Mike looked as if she had just struck him. "Are you serious?"

"It's not the first time it's happened since she's been here," Ric said. "You were late. You have a lot of catching up to do. That's if you stay of course. That's if any of us stay."

Nancy moved forward. "You must stay." It sounded like an order.

"Must, Nancy?" Mike's tone was reproachful.

Nancy shot him a glance and Alli felt a tension between them.

"I mean…" Nancy began. "I need you all here."

She handed Alli a glass of water, which she accepted gratefully, immediately draining half.

Nancy turned away, avoiding eye contact with everyone. "I have to know what this is all about. I have to understand what's going on here. This is my house. It was Caroline's and now it's mine. She left it to me for a purpose, and now I feel threatened. I was also attacked. I have no idea what happened…. Look." She thrust out her right arm.

An angry red welt extended from wrist to inner elbow. Alli touched it lightly and Nancy flinched.

"Did you burn yourself?" Ric asked.

Nancy shook her head. "I was in the kitchen getting the water for Alli. I turned on the tap and felt someone behind me. There was no one there. Then I felt a sharp pain as if a cat scratched me. I don't know. There was *nothing there.* I looked down at my arm and…. This had appeared. It stings like hell."

Mike looked at it. "You need to get some antiseptic on that. Have you washed it?"

Nancy shook her head. "I came straight in here and heard you say you were thinking of leaving. Please. Please don't leave me alone here."

Alli swung her legs to the floor and sat up. She didn't yet trust herself to stand. "Look, it's pretty obvious there's a lot going on here and none of it makes any rational sense. Maybe it's Lucius Hartmann and maybe it's…I don't know what…related to this house. From way back in its history."

As she spoke the words, the image of that picture in the hall flashed through her mind. "We need to get to the bottom of this. Running away is always an option but then we would never know, would we? Nancy would never know, except that she had been driven from her home by…an entity perhaps that she neither knew nor understood, any more than the rest of us. This is a beautiful house. It deserves to be loved and lived in. If we can…I don't know…cleanse it, maybe she won't have to leave at all."

"I agree," Mike said. "We need to search this house for a clue that might give us some insight into Caroline's life here and anything else that might help us understand what we're dealing with."

"I know you must think my experiences are all in my head," Alli said. "What if they aren't? It certainly doesn't feel like that and, as long as I have your word – all of you – that no one slipped anything into my drink or food since I've been here, then I have to assume that in some way I don't understand, I actually was there. In Laurel Canyon. Or at least some part of me was."

"I wasn't here when it started," Mike said. "And I will certainly swear I never slipped anything into your food or drink."

"Me neither," Nancy said.

Alli caught sight of a movement at the edge of her vision. She focused on it for a second. "Look," she said, then louder. "*Look* at the picture."

All eyes turned to the portrait.

Alli stood and moved slowly closer until she was directly in front of it. "She's crying." The beautiful face gazed out at them. In the corner of each eye, a tear had formed, and, on her right cheek, one was frozen in the act of tracking its way down her face. The tear glistened and shimmered. "It's so realistic."

Ric stood beside her; Nancy and Mike joined him. All four stared upward, mesmerized. Alli half expected the tear to continue to fall until it splashed out of the portrait.

Beside her, Nancy spoke, her voice cracking with emotion. "You see why I can't leave here. She needs help. For whatever reason, she couldn't acknowledge my existence in life, but she can now – in death – and she's trapped somewhere. I don't know how I know that, only that I do. Don't you feel it, Alli?"

Into Alli's mind flashed the memory of Caroline's expression when she had suddenly backed away from her. The woman had looked scared out of her wits. And Caroline wasn't the only one either. Both Cass and John had seen it in her eyes too. John said he had seen his death there. Could she be some kind of conduit between the living and the dead in whatever was playing out here? A shiver ran through her body.

"Ric," she said. "We need to go to that room. The one that leads off Nancy's bedroom."

"That place gives me the creeps," Nancy said. "When the builders first showed it to me, they left me alone in there. I felt a...presence. It came over me so fast. I had gathered up the photograph albums and...that's when it hit me. I couldn't get out of there fast enough."

Alli nodded. "I felt it too. But you've been back there, haven't you?"

Nancy nodded. "I had to. I don't know why. It's where Caroline's casket is."

"Her what?" Mike asked.

"Her ashes," Nancy said.

"They're in an urn," Alli said. "Her birth date is engraved on it, but there's no date of death."

"Well, *that's* different," Mike said.

"I heard someone call her name," Alli said. "When Ric and I were up there."

"That was around the time Alli gave a note-perfect rendition of 'White Rabbit', the old Jefferson Airplane song," Ric said.

Alli said, "I still don't remember doing that. I didn't know I had at the time. If you asked me to do it now, I couldn't. I hardly know any of the lyrics."

"Appropriate though, isn't it?" Mike pushed his dreadlocks back over his shoulder. "In a way, *we're* chasing rabbits down a hole."

"It's a song about getting high," Ric said. "The white rabbits are a metaphor."

"Obviously." Mike's voice had an edge to it again.

Alli put her hand up. "Stop it, you two. We've more important things to deal with now than your decade-long feud."

The two men looked as if they wanted to punch each other but at least they didn't act on the impulse. Alli hoped her warning glare to each of them in turn would help to keep them in check. At least for now.

Nancy led them up the stairs to her room and opened the door leading to the narrow staircase. "I'm glad I have you with me," she said. "Thank you for staying."

Alli exchanged glances with Ric. Did he also feel the change in Nancy? She was barely recognizable from the woman who had greeted her when she arrived. All the spark had been extinguished.

They trooped up the narrow steps. The closer they approached the top, the more the fusty smell increased.

Once there, it was as Ric and Alli had left it.

"Wow. This is some place," Mike said, touching the walls. "*Far-out.*"

Alli's blood iced. "What did you say?"

Mike looked at her. "Nothing. It's quite some place here. Like a time capsule. Someone has bottled 1969 and stored it here."

"No, I mean…. Didn't you just say, 'Far-out'?"

"Did I?"

"Yes, you did," Nancy said.

"Yep," Ric agreed.

"Then I must have. Not an expression I usually use. It's a Sixties/Seventies thing, isn't it? Must be the influence of this place."

"It's just that I heard that recently. When I was…*there*. Someone used it a lot."

"Well, there you are then. I'm being authentic."

He smiled at Alli, but the expression didn't reach his eyes. It was as if he had pasted it on.

"Here's the urn." Ric brandished it.

An icy chill descended around Alli. "Please be careful," she said.

Nancy whimpered. She pointed behind Ric. "Can you see that?" she said, her voice trembling.

On the wall, shapes swirled. Undulating shadows danced, mingled, arms waving, hair flowing. In Alli's head, distant music played. Some psychedelic track. Early Pink Floyd…'See Emily Play'.

"Put the urn down, Ric," Alli said.

He hesitated. Then did as she had instructed.

The shadows stopped moving, the music in Alli's head faded, and the atmosphere cleared. The temperature plummeted.

Alli's breath misted. Nancy moaned as her whole body swayed. Chanting filled the room. Like a song learned by children and sung by rote. Alli stared around her. Ric stood, white-faced, apparently rooted to the spot. Nancy was keening, her arms spread out as her body moved from side to side, occasionally dipping. Only Mike seemed apart from them. He looked angry.

"This will stop. It will stop *now*." His voice bellowed around the room, echoing off the stone walls. The chanting ceased. Nancy paused in her swaying and looked around her, as if she had no idea where she was. Ric broke out of his trance-like state.

"What the hell happened?" he demanded.

"Whatever it was, Mike stopped it," Alli said. "How did you do that?"

Mike shrugged. "Anger. I felt this wave of fury well up inside me and there was no way I could stop it. No way I wanted to stop it."

"It obeyed you," Alli said. "You must have some connection with it."

"I can't see how. I've never been here before. I only know Caroline Rand by reputation and hearing her music when I was a kid. My parents were proud, aging hippies."

"Did you feel as if you were no longer alone in your body?" Nancy asked. "As if you were possessed?"

"No. That's a pretty strange question."

"Everything's strange here," Ric said.

"Enough is enough," Alli said. "We have to find out what it wants. And once and for all, who it is we're dealing with."

Mike's face clouded over. "You'd better not be suggesting what I think you are."

"A séance. It's not an easy option, but how else are we going to find out what's going on?"

"I'm not getting involved in any bloody séances and that's final." Mike made for the door. Nancy stopped him. She darted forward and formed a human barrier between him and the stairs.

"Please, Mike. Alli's right. It's the only way."

"Out of my way, Nancy. I don't want to have to get physical here, but I will if you carry on."

"I'm not moving."

"Have it your own way." He made to shove Nancy aside.

Alli yelled at him. "Stop it!"

Mike spun round to face her. Alli flinched at the fear and fury in his eyes.

"You lot don't know what you're getting yourselves into," he said. "A séance is *never* the only answer. It should never even be an option. I know. I've been there and I saw my best friend die as a result. I've never been able to explain it. One minute he was sitting there, calm as anything and the next…. An invisible force threw him against a far wall, smashing four vertebrae and severing his spinal cord. Not content with that, it then set about tossing him backward and forward like some sort of lifeless ragdoll. The probable cause of death was a subdural hematoma, but he had multiple fractures and an array of internal injuries, any one of which could have rendered the final blow. If you think I'm going to put myself in that situation again, you must be mad. All of you. Now, get out of my way, Nancy. I'm out of here."

She hesitated, then stepped aside. Alli watched in stunned silence as Mike left them, his footsteps beating a hasty retreat downstairs.

Nancy was the first to break the silence. "I must go to him. He can't leave. None of you can leave. Not *now*. You can't leave *now*."

She dashed down the stairs, leaving Ric and Alli staring helplessly at each other. The atmosphere in the room was becoming increasingly claustrophobic.

Ric made for the door. "Come on. I don't want to stay in this room any longer anyhow. It's getting to me."

"I think that's the general idea," Alli agreed. She gave the room one more sweep with her eyes. The colors on the wall looked brighter. Fresher.

As if they had only been painted recently. Probably her imagination. Maybe some trick of the diffused light that seeped up the stairs, mingling with the flickering light from the candelabra. The feeling of being watched was ever-present, disconcerting and only partly to do with the room's strange appearance. And the urn. That thing overpowered the place. It wasn't even large, but its presence was overwhelming.

Downstairs, an argument raged. Mike insisted he was going. Nancy was equally insistent that he couldn't.

"Look, Nancy, if I'd known what you were getting me into, I wouldn't have come in the first place."

Nancy's attention was diverted by the sight of Ric and Alli descending the main staircase into the hall where she stood, blocking the main entrance. The door was firmly shut. She looked from one to the other, then slowly nodded. "Okay then, Mike. Fine. Okay, all of you. Off you go. I won't stop you." She stepped aside from the door.

"Fine," Mike said and grabbed the door handle. It turned smoothly and he opened it.

And Alli found herself back in 1968.

CHAPTER EIGHT

Alli stood on an unfamiliar street. It had a steep incline and twisted away from her. Gas-guzzling cars she recognized from Sixties films and TV shows flashed by, all gleaming chrome, with fumes belching from their exhausts. Lush trees and bushes framed both sides of the street and the sun warmed her back. She looked down at herself, relieved to see she was in the same clothes she had put on that morning. Typical Sixties gear. She fit right in, all the way to her ethnic headband and gypsy skirt.

Having no precise idea of her whereabouts, she gazed around. A few yards farther down, she spotted a street sign. Approaching it, she read 'Lookout Mountain Ave'.

"Hey, wanna ride?"

A red Porsche convertible had pulled up. Driving it was someone she recognized. Cass Elliot smiled, her hair wrapped in a silk scarf. Alli could have kissed her. "I'd love one," she said. "The problem is, I don't know where to."

"That's easy. Come to my place."

Cass opened the passenger door for her and Alli slid in. "I'm surprised you're stopping for me after what happened."

Cass looked bemused. "Sorry, you'll have to explain that one. What happened when?"

"The last time we met. At your house. You thought I was creating a bad vibe...."

It was clear Cass hadn't a clue what she was talking about. With all the tricks time seemed to be playing on her, it was probable that nothing Alli remembered about their last encounter had happened yet. They had clearly met, but as for the rest of it....

"Sorry, my mistake. I...I think I took something that didn't really agree with me."

Cass laughed. A great big belly laugh. "Honey, we've all been there. Don't worry. Come on. Let's get you back for a long, cold, refreshing drink. Cuba libre sound good to you?"

Alli nodded. Right now, it couldn't have sounded better.

Cass drove them around the twisting roads through the canyon, until they arrived at her home, where, in contrast to the last time she had been there, all was quiet. Alli was amazed to see Cass simply open her front door without using a key.

"Oh, no one bothers to break in here," she said. "We're just a bunch of hippies to them. Far richer pickings down below in the city."

Alli followed her in, welcoming the peace and tranquility. In spite of the impossibility of her situation, she felt safe here. Cass had such a commanding presence. Her huge, warm personality made the impossible seem almost possible.

"Come in, sit out back on the porch and I'll fix the drinks. Hungry?"

Alli shook her head. "The drink will be perfect. Thank you."

"You're so welcome."

Alli knew she meant it.

Out on Cass's porch, the cicadas were in full voice; their constant buzzing and clicking melded into a loud, insistent hum. The scent of wildflowers and eucalyptus provided a heady aroma.

Cass appeared, ice clinking in the drinks. She set them down on a table next to Alli and settled herself down, before taking a long slow drink. "So, wanna tell me what you're really doing here? In the Canyon in 1968? I mean, you just suddenly appeared. From nowhere. No one I've spoken to knows anything about you and there's something about you. Something I can't quite fathom. But whatever it is, you seem kinda out of place. I could almost believe you'd come from another time." She grinned. "I know, crazy or what?"

Alli took a moment to collect her thoughts. "The truth is I haven't the faintest idea what's happening. And despite the weirdness, whenever I'm here, I only know I don't want to leave. Ever."

Cass gave her a long look, then slowly nodded her head. "You may not have to."

"How is that possible? And how do you know I'm not supposed to be here?"

"Lucky guess, I suppose. As to your first question, I reckon you just need to figure out why you were sent here in the first place."

"I don't know. The only thing that makes any sense is that it's connected with Caroline Rand."

"Well, you're both British. I guess that's a start." Again, the booming laugh.

"I know her granddaughter. Nancy."

The laugh froze on Cass's lips. "Her *granddaughter*? I didn't even know she had kids. And when did she have one old enough to produce one of her own? Hell, you must start them young in England." She laughed.

Alli smiled but was fighting to find an explanation that would make any kind of sense. There was nothing for it, she would simply have to go with what she had. "It's complicated. I'm talking about the twenty-first century. Many years from now. She had one child and that child had a daughter – Caroline's granddaughter."

The laughter was history. Cass stared at her, a curious expression on her face. Not incredulity exactly....

Alli took a deep breath. "I know this is impossible to believe...." She couldn't think of one more thing to say. She waited for Cass to speak.

Cass studied her face, maybe searching for any sign that Alli was deliberately playing her for a fool. Finally, she spoke. "Who was it who used to talk about believing so many impossible things before lunchtime?"

"Lewis Carroll. In *Alice Through the Looking Glass*, the Queen said that when she was young, she used to believe as many as six impossible things before breakfast."

Cass nodded. "I'll have to read that to Owen one day. My daughter. She's too young now but give it a year or so.... Listen, I ate breakfast already, so I'll settle for believing one impossible thing before lunch. How's that?"

Alli laughed, her tension easing by the second. Cass was so easy to be with.

"I'll bet this granddaughter of Caroline's is a good-looking kid."

Alli nodded. "She is. And I'm supposed to be staying with her, at her house in England. The house used to belong to Caroline. She left it to her."

"Left it to her? So, in your time, she's dead then?"

Alli nodded. "I'm afraid so."

"And when is your time exactly?"

"It's 2023." *Please don't ask me.*

"Am I still alive then?"

Too late. Alli said nothing.

Cass sighed. "It's okay. You don't need to say anything."

Silence.

Birds sang overhead and in the trees all around. The day was perfect. Insects buzzed lazily. Bees went about their business, along with butterflies in colors Alli had never seen before. They fluttered and danced from flower to flower. It was perfect. And it was all wrong.

Cass broke the silence. "Just as long as I live long enough to raise my daughter right. That's all I ask."

Alli said nothing. How could she tell her the sad truth? No, she didn't need to know.

They sipped their drinks, and Alli let herself sink into the comfort of Mama Cass's back porch, listening to the sounds of Laurel Canyon, the sprawling smog-infested city of Los Angeles mere minutes away, yet it could have been on a different planet. Alli struggled to remind herself that this wasn't real. It couldn't be real. It had been created, or she had been sent back in time, or her mind had rigged it. Maybe she was going mad. Or maybe everything else was the sham. Perhaps she really did belong here in 1968 and she had imagined that other world. All of a sudden, her mind was reeling, and she was sure her blood pressure had shot through the roof.

She stole a glance at Cass, who was staring out toward the trees and hills beyond. This woman who had been dead for years, sitting here, so utterly real.

Cass caught her looking at her and their eyes met. "I wish I could figure you out, Alli," she said. "And I wish I could fix whatever's going on in your head."

"So do I," Alli said, and meant it.

"Then—"

Cass didn't finish her sentence. They were interrupted.

Alli stared in horror as the trees withered. Leaves showered down, turned yellow, brown, and crackled like the sound of a hundred log fires.

The beauty all around her vanished in a few seconds, leaving only decay and despair in its wake. Cass's warm eyes turned black. Her mouth moved as if someone was pulling strings to work her jaws. Words should have been issuing from her. None came. Only a meaningless, discordant chant, an assault on Alli's ears. One which filled her with despair, opening up a void of hopelessness of Hieronymus Bosch-like proportions. An infinity of pain and torment until she couldn't stand it any longer.

"Who are you? What do you want from me?" Alli's voice was lost in a maelstrom of wind and rain that beat down. It flattened the bushes and drenched her in an instant.

A furious rending tear ripped the timber of the porch roof from its nails, flinging it into the sky where it pitched and tossed before crashing to earth. The full force of the unnatural storm beat down on Alli. The rain scythed down her cheeks as it turned to hail, scratching her skin with the force of a handful of raking nails.

Alli dragged herself out of her chair and sank to her knees. Both chair and table toppled and fell. Shards of glittering glass swirled in the air, sharp and deadly. Alli put her hands up to shield her face.

In the chair where Cass had sat only moments earlier, nothing remained of her. Not a trace.

Alli pushed on. She grabbed hold of the doorframe, dragging herself around it. Her nails scraped claw marks on the wood. Trickles of blood flowed down her hands. Ignoring the pain, she thrust first one foot and then the other over the threshold, back into the room, but found no sanctuary there.

The ceiling had gone; the upstairs rooms and roof were gone. Only the ground floor walls remained. Everywhere, broken and ruined furniture tossed around in the impossible wind.

With her remaining strength, Alli clung to the one support she had, the doorframe. She closed her eyes and prayed.

The wind stopped. The storm stopped.

She opened her eyes.

All around her, blackness and no sense of anything there. No smells, no sounds. Alli touched her face with one hand, taking care to hang on with the other, until she realized she was hanging on to nothing. Her cheeks felt damp to her touch.

In front of her, a glow began. Like a flickering candle. Dim at first, then growing brighter as it seemed to take hold. She felt an irresistible urge to move toward it. She had no idea what she was standing on, only that it seemed like firm ground, even though she could see nothing. She took baby steps. One foot carefully in front of the other. The flame grew ever stronger. It changed form, swirling, swaying…undulating. An indistinct figure became clearer.

In front of her, a glowing face, that of a man she didn't recognize. It was distinctly human except for an elongated jaw and piercing black eyes, slanted diagonally down toward its nose. Its high cheekbones looked chiseled. Behind it, men dressed in monks' attire, hoods thrown back to reveal fat, bloated faces, reddened with the effects of too much drink imbibed over too many years. They were quaffing from mugs filled with a liquid that sloshed red onto their chins and over their habits. Wine perhaps, or…? Alli dismissed her second thought.

As the central figure emerged fully, the monks' ribaldry quieted. They stood as one, bowed their heads and lowered their hoods, concealing their faces. The sound of chanting began. It should have been holy. But this was a parody. A tuneless cacophony.

The demoniacal face opened its mouth to speak, revealing glittering teeth. "And so it begins," it said, its voice filling the space all around her, seeming to emanate from all directions simultaneously. "My world. My rules."

Heavy metal music Alli didn't recognize blared. So loud, it was distorted, hammering at her ears.

"Stop. Please *stop!*"

"What's the matter, Alli?"

The voice was Ric's. Alli opened her eyes.

She was standing in the hall. Mike still had his hand on the doorknob although the door was closed again. Nancy had tears in her eyes.

All of them were staring at her.

"What happened?" Ric asked.

Alli shook her head. "I...don't know. One minute I was here and the next...back *there* again. Only this time was different. I was there and then I wasn't *anywhere*. It's so hard to explain. It was like a black hole, nothing of any substance, until a face appeared. No, not *appeared*, it...it kind of formed in front of me. It looked human but at the same time...I don't know...alien. Like some sort of devil, and there were these monks, or they looked like monks, and they were in awe of it.... Oh God, none of this is making any sense at all. I must be having some sort of breakdown. Or it's this house. I don't know. I don't even know what reality is anymore." She caught sight of her hands. No trace of the ruined nails and blood streaks. No pain. Insanity. It had to be. She had tipped over an edge...or been pushed.

Alli shrank back into the living room. Ric followed her. He put his arm around her and steered her to a chair. Nancy and Mike drifted in. Their expressions were of concern, fear in Nancy's case. And almost... recognition. Suddenly Alli knew she wasn't the only one who had had a similar experience.

"How was *your* trip, Nancy? Who did you meet?"

Nancy blanched. "I'm not sure. I...I had a dream, that's all."

"A dream where you smelled jasmine, or maybe eucalyptus?"

Nancy hesitated, then nodded.

Alli took the plunge. "Were they all there? Caroline? Cass? If I said the names 'John' and 'Peter' to you, would you know who I meant?"

Nancy lowered her eyes.

"Well, Nancy," Ric said. "Aren't you going to answer her?"

"Perhaps she doesn't know what Alli's talking about," Mike said.

"Oh, I think she does." Ric glared at Mike. "Come on, Nancy. Alli's told us what she saw and experienced. It's your turn now. After all, none of us would be here if it wasn't for you. You want us to go through a séance which none of us are keen on. You owe it to us to at least tell us everything. Even if you don't think it's relevant, or you think you may have imagined it. Let's face it, Alli's told us some pretty far-out stuff."

"Please don't use that term," Alli said.

Ric looked at her questioningly. "What term?"

"Far-out. Mike used it earlier and now you…I hear it a lot when I go…there."

Ric shrugged. "Never used it before. I didn't know I had then. This stuff is catching. Like a virus."

"Don't make light of it, please, Ric." Alli shivered.

"Nancy," Mike said, "they won't let you go until you tell them whatever it is you've experienced. And this time, no belittling her, Ric."

Ric opened his mouth as if to protest, shook his head and closed it again.

Nancy looked up. She blinked rapidly. "Very well." She sat down hard on the nearest settee. Mike and Ric sat on chairs opposite her. "It started a few nights after I called out to Caroline. I was sitting outside enjoying the early evening sun. The first really warm day of the year and my chance to enjoy my garden for the first time. I was sipping a glass of chilled white wine and…. The next thing I remember is being in a room. There was no one else. Just me. The room was unfamiliar, but I *knew* it somehow. I knew if I went out of the door of the living room I was in, I would step right into the kitchen and there would be an old-fashioned set of fitted pine units which I would think were really modern.

"I followed my instinct and sure enough, there was the kitchen exactly as I knew it would be. I started calling out to see if anyone was in the house. No one replied. The back door was slightly open and the scent of jasmine wafted in. I opened it further and stepped outside onto a wooden stoop. I could see right across a valley to the hills beyond and all I could hear were tinkling sounds I soon traced to a set of wind chimes I knew would be round the corner of the building. Somewhere in the distance, someone was strumming a guitar. They stopped and I heard laughter...a light, girlish laugh. Then the guitar playing started again. Acoustic, folky. It was the strangest feeling because right at that moment, I felt at home. I knew this house was mine, even though it couldn't have been.

"I don't know how much time elapsed as I stood there, drinking in the relaxed atmosphere, hearing the birds sing, inhaling the scents.... Jasmine wasn't the only one; there were wildflowers everywhere. A real riot of perfume. I closed my eyes to better absorb it. When I opened them. I was back here. Exactly where I had been, my glass still in my hand. It seemed no time had passed."

"Was that the only time?" Alli asked.

Nancy shook her head. "A few days later, maybe a week, maybe a little more, I'm not sure now, I started noticing the clock striking only at nine in the evening, and I realized I had no idea if it had always done that. Then, there were the voices. Whispering. Making no sense. I thought it was air in the pipes and I called the local plumber. He checked everything. Of course, the house behaved perfectly while he was here. Not a whisper. He charged me some extortionate amount and left saying he could find nothing wrong. He even praised the work of the builders who had carried out the renovation. They'd put in miles of new piping and it was all functioning perfectly, he said. He'd only been gone half an hour when it all started up again. In my bedroom of all places. I had gone up there to change. I remember, I was pulling my top on when I heard someone call out Caroline's name. The next second I was back in that lovely little house. But this time, it was different. This time I wasn't alone."

Nancy stopped. She was wringing her hands in her lap and her lip was trembling.

"Go on, Nancy," Alli said. "You can't stop now. Just tell us what happened. Who was with you?"

Nancy's eyes brimmed with tears. She angrily brushed them away. "*She* was there. Caroline. I was in another room. A bedroom. The wardrobes were fitted along one wall, all with floor-to-ceiling mirrors. I saw my reflection. Except it wasn't *my* reflection at all. It was *hers*. It was *hers*...." Nancy broke down into gut-wrenching sobs.

Alli rushed over to her and put her arms around her. Nancy leaned against her. Ric handed her a tissue from a nearby box and Nancy blew her nose. Mike watched them steadily. Alli caught sight of him and wished she could read his expression, but it was like that of a statue. Stony, cold, disassociated from what was going on. And it didn't fit. It didn't fit at all.

Nancy shifted, trying to straighten up. Alli let go her hold and Nancy took a deep breath. "I called out and saw her mouth move in perfect time with my voice. There could be no mistaking it. As crazy as it sounds, I was in her body. Her young body as it would have been in 1968. I looked down at myself, and so did the reflection, but where I saw my twenty-first-century jeans and t-shirt, the reflection was wearing a white off-the-shoulder top, with ruffled sleeves and a wide cotton skirt. Real gypsy, Bohemian style. It was weird watching *her* hands stroke *her* soft skirt, when it was *my* hands, stroking *my* denim jeans. She stared wide-eyed back at me. And I knew the fear and confusion I read in her eyes were actually in mine. Then I flipped back again. I haven't been back there since. Everything else has happened in this house."

Alli swallowed. "Is there anywhere specifically in the house that seems more...active?"

"That room you and Ric found. That's pretty bad. But things happen everywhere."

Mike stood. "Have you seen Caroline again? Have you seen her in this house?"

Nancy sighed heavily. "I know I've seen her once. I may have caught glimpses of her out of the corner of my eye a few times as well. The worst, by far the worst.... That was enough to last me a lifetime."

"What happened?" Alli asked.

"I saw her...hanging there. Dead. Hanging in the hallway. Her neck was broken but she was alive, and she stared at me. 'Help me,' she mouthed. Then blood poured from her eyes...." Nancy collapsed against Alli, sobbing her heart out.

Alli held her. "Nancy, you can't stay here. It's making you ill. We've all experienced odd things since we arrived, and we've not even been here twenty-four hours yet. You've been living with this for months. You can't go on like this."

Ric touched Nancy's shoulder. "Alli's right, Nan. I've never seen you like this. You're so strong and confident normally. Always in control. This has got to you big time. You've got to let it go. Let's all pack, leave this place and get ourselves rooms somewhere a few miles away. We can spend the rest of the weekend enjoying ourselves. Maybe Mike and I will even agree to consign our differences to the past. What do you reckon, Mike?"

Alli glanced over to the tall man who wore that strange expression again. "Nice thought, Ric. It's too late though."

Ric's face paled. "What is?"

"It's too late for us to leave. That's what Nancy meant when she said we couldn't go now. Isn't it, Nancy?"

Between her sobs, Nancy nodded.

"Why?" Alli asked. "Surely it can't follow us. Ghosts or demons or whatever we're dealing with here, they're ingrained into the fabric of a building, aren't they?"

Mike moved closer. "It may start out that way. Usually does, or so I believe. This is different. As Nancy knows, in this case, the haunting has progressed from the building. Anywhere we go now, any of us will take a part of the evil with them. And splitting up will only make us weaker as individuals. I was going to leave. You were all with me. I got as far as opening the door and what happened? Alli had that strange turn and...I didn't tell you...the handle slipped out of my hand and the door closed. I tried to open it again, but it had locked itself."

Alli stood and advanced toward Nancy. "And you knew all this stuff was happening *before* you invited us here? Surely you couldn't, Nancy. Surely you wouldn't do that. Bring us here under false pretenses, knowing what you were condemning us to?" At that moment, Alli had trouble keeping her hand from striking Nancy a stinging slap across the face.

Nancy looked from one to another, tears still streaming down her face. "I didn't know for sure. I thought...I hoped. Like I said before...I hoped that if you were all here, it would leave me alone. It would see there were more of us to fight it. I wouldn't be battling it by myself."

Seeing the woman so distraught and desperate in front of them took Alli back to the first time Clarissa and her nasty little band of bullies had taunted her.

They had called her 'fat', 'ugly' and chanted her name, "Allegra Sinclair, Allegra Sinclair. How la-di-da." They had insulted her mother's Italian heritage, using words that would have seen them excluded from school. It had mattered so much, so very much at the time, in her first term at that horrible new school.

Nancy had come up and put herself between the other girls and Alli, even though she was small and thin, half the size of the athletic, muscular Clarissa. Through her tears, Alli had seen Nancy clench her hands behind her back until her knuckles turned white. The girl was petrified yet still she stood up to them. Seeing her chance to escape, Alli had run off, leaving Nancy to her fate. Only later had she thanked her and sympathized with her over the swollen eye she had sustained at the business end of Clarissa's right hook.

Alli had deserted her then, and again when she left the school. Could she really leave her to this? She softened her tone. "Nancy, if only you'd been honest with us. If you'd told us what was going on—"

Nancy's mirthless laughter chilled her. "Oh yes, and you would have come like a shot, wouldn't you, Alli?" So, she remembered what had happened at school too. "And how about you, Ric? Mike? No, this was the only way I could get you all here."

Alli couldn't argue with her. "Surely you know people who are...I don't know...more receptive, or better able to deal with this kind of phenomenon. With all your financial resources, you could have called on professionals. Trained people with special equipment...."

"Oh yes? And run the risk of letting charlatans into my home? Or worse still, people hell-bent on stealing from me. As for friends.... You know, Alli, it's odd, when you come into a lot of money, you suddenly have all the friends in the world. People love you – people you haven't exchanged more than a half dozen words with on social media are flocking like mad to remind you of all the wonderful times you shared together."

"*We* hadn't exchanged any words. Not until you sent me a friend request and this invitation."

"That's exactly my point. You had no preconceptions of me, although we had known each other at school. As for Ric, we knew each other well enough through work, didn't we? You never asked anything of me, and I always knew I could trust you, Ric. Simple as that. Same with you, Mike. None of you ever used me. It seems a crazy kind of logic now I come to try and explain it, but it made perfect sense when I decided to do this. I thought if I got you here, we could work it out together, find a way of settling this house, laying its ghosts once and for all and allowing Caroline to rest in peace." Nancy gave a little cry of anguish. "What have I done?"

"Come on," Alli said. "There's no point in a load of 'what ifs' and self-recrimination. We are where we are, and we have to find a way to sort this out. I can't believe I'm saying this, but I think we need to go back up to that attic room. It's where I had my first brief experience and, maybe it's because Caroline's ashes are there, I don't know. I do feel closer to the heart of things there. If we have to confront this…whatever it is, then best to do it where we're most likely to get a result."

Mike laid his hand lightly on her arm. "You're taking one hell of a chance. You do realize that."

She saw an expression in his eyes she couldn't read. There was a tenderness there that attracted her, but, alongside that, another aspect she couldn't make out. Whatever it was it would keep. "Mike, right now, I haven't a clue what I'm doing. You seem to know more about this stuff than the rest of us. Tell us what you would do."

Mike said nothing. He continued to stare straight at Alli. Finally, he spoke. "I'm all against having a full-on séance. You never know what's going to come through. We didn't intentionally contact whatever entity it was that killed my friend, but we opened up a portal and a demon took advantage of it. Whatever is in this house is quite enough, we don't need anything far worse."

Alli said, "When I was in that void…that black space, I told you about the strange…entity I suppose I should call it. Right before I came back to you, it spoke. It said, 'My world. My rules.' Have you any idea what it might have been?"

Mike shrugged and broke eye contact. "Maybe it's the entity that haunts this place. And make no mistake, I think we're dealing with far more than Caroline Rand or Lucius Hartmann. There seems to be a presence in this house that's far older and deadlier than any of that. I could be wrong, of course, but your recent experience, Alli.... The Laurel Canyon connection I could understand. That was Caroline's world, and Lucius's too. This entity you encountered doesn't seem to fit with it and it feels like it belongs in another world entirely. One much darker. Of course, there's no way of knowing unless it reveals more. We'll need to contact it through a Summoning. That means someone will have to channel its energy."

"Not me," Ric said. "No way. Sorry, I'm not up for that."

Alli looked across at Nancy. She seemed to have recovered slightly but it was clear she wasn't in any fit state to put herself through any more. Mike would be needed to perform the ritual, or whatever was required. That left one person.

"Okay, I'll do it," Alli said.

Mike glared at Ric. "And you're going to stand by and let her?"

It was Ric's turn to shrug. "If that's what she wants."

"You're unbelievable, do you know that?" Mike lunged toward him. Ric took a hurried step back.

Alli put herself between them. "This infighting is getting us nowhere. Let's go up to that room and get this over with before I lose my nerve."

Mike nodded.

They all trooped upstairs, Alli leading the way and Ric bringing up the rear. Alli opened the door at the top of the stone staircase. Its creak seemed louder today. Her heightened state of nerves no doubt.

The cold, oppressive darkness of the place seemed even stronger than before. Mike pressed the light switch, and the bulbs gave off their flickering glow.

"You could do with better lighting, Nancy," he said.

Nancy didn't reply. She took hold of Alli's arm. "Are you sure you want to go through with this?" she asked.

"Not really, if I'm honest, but we have to.... What's the term you used? Lay the ghost?"

"Do you actually have any idea what you're doing, Mike?" Ric asked. His voice dripped with sarcasm.

Alli turned on Ric. "At least he's giving it a go."

"It should be me," Nancy said quietly. "It's my mess."

"No," Alli said. "You've been through enough. Anyway, it's been decided. Mike will direct the proceedings and I'll channel this…whatever it is. What do you need me to do, Mike?"

"To the best of my knowledge, and based on what I've read—"

"What you've *read*?" Ric's exclamation reverberated around the room, bouncing off the stone walls. "So, you really haven't a clue?"

"Feel free to chip in whenever you like," Mike said. "Provided, of course, it's with a sensible suggestion. Until then, shut the fuck up."

"You're putting Alli's life in danger. Possibly all our lives."

"Then step up, Ric. Take Alli's place. I'm sure she won't mind, will you, Alli?"

Alli could feel her resolve weakening. "Oh, for heaven's sake, Mike, ignore him and let's get on with it."

Ric turned away.

Mike faced her. "Thanks. Now we all need to sit down in a circle so that we can hold hands. Forget everything you've seen in the films. I'm going to use a method called a Summoning. It's a form of channeling that should, hopefully, only bring us the spirit we want to talk to and, when it does, if all goes well, it will speak through Alli."

A lack of chairs meant they had to kneel in a small, close circle on the floor. Mike took Alli's right hand and Nancy took her left. Ric reluctantly took Mike and Nancy's hands in his.

When they were settled, Mike spoke. "Okay, in a few moments, I'll call out to the spirit in this house. Alli, you may experience a tingling, maybe a feeling of disorientation. Try not to fight it. Try to let it in. If it becomes too much though, squeeze my hand tightly and I'll send it away. We'll stop. Do you understand?"

Alli took a deep breath. Right now, she wanted to stop before they started. The mere thought of being taken over by some supernatural entity was too much to take in. "I understand, Mike."

"And are you ready if I start now?"

Another deep breath. Every fiber of her being screamed, 'NO'. "Yes."

"Then let's begin. No one is to break our circle. No one is to let go of the hands they are currently holding. Is that understood?" A general chorus of 'yes' greeted this.

"Right."

Alli could feel him tense beside her. He took a succession of deep breaths, in and out, rhythmically. She concentrated on them, and found the repetition soothed her.

Mike said, "I am speaking to the spirit that resides within this house. Spirit, I respectfully summon you and you alone. Please come forward. We need to speak to you. There is one among us who has of her own free will agreed to be your mouthpiece for the duration of our meeting with you. Spirit, we ask that you speak to us only through her. She is here, to my left. Her name is Alli. Spirit, can you hear us?"

Alli felt nothing. "Should we close our eyes?" she whispered.

"Perhaps," Mike said. "Yes. That might be a good idea. It will help us all to focus."

Alli closed her eyes. Immediately, she sensed a change. She could feel Mike lightly holding one hand while Nancy's more needy clutch grasped the other. Mike called out again. At first, she heard his words. Strong, clear, exactly as before. Then they seemed to fade into the distance. The plaintive opening chords of 'Lady Gossamer' floated to her from a long way away, growing closer.

Closer.

Whoever was singing and playing was in the room.

Caroline Rand. Her distinctive voice sweet, clear and pure.

"She flies through the heavens on gossamer wings...."

Alli didn't anticipate the strident male voice that spoke in her head. *Allegra. Allegra Sinclair. I am talking to you. You must reply. You must do exactly as I command....*

She swallowed hard and focused on sending a mental response. *You may speak through me, Spirit, but you will not command me.*

An unpleasant tugging sensation pulled at her insides. A feeling, not of pain, but extreme discomfort. A sense of things being rearranged. Not her organs – but her nerves, or simply her sense of awareness of what was real and unreal being ripped apart so that she would not know whether to trust her instincts or work in defiance of them.

Allegra Sinclair. You no longer have control of your mind. You no longer have a soul. All that made you what you are is now mine. And what I take, I do not return.

CHAPTER NINE

"Hey, Alli. Good to see you again. It's been months."

Alli opened her eyes. It took a moment to realize where she was – and that she was standing up, holding a front door open. A door that was at once familiar and unfamiliar. She was back. Laurel Canyon. The little timber-framed house she knew must be hers. There, Stetson in hand, and hair sun-bleached, stood a smiling John Denver.

"You could ask me in if you like," he said.

"Oh, sorry. I was miles away." He would never know how true that was. Alli stepped back to let him in. They strolled together into the living room and John sat on the settee.

"Fancy a drink?" Alli asked. "There's beer in the fridge." How she knew that, she had no idea.

"A cold beer would be great. It's mighty hot out there."

Alli departed for the kitchen. As she knew it would, the fridge revealed a pack of six bottles of Budweiser, well chilled. She pulled out two, deciding a cold beer wouldn't go amiss for her either. She called to him, "Do you want it in a glass?"

"Hell no, straight from the bottle is fine."

Alli brought the Buds in. He said he hadn't seen her in months, and he was treating her like an old friend. Certainly not someone who had frightened the living daylights out of him last time they had met, when he said he had seen his death in her eyes.

"Thanks, Alli," he said, accepting the beer.

Alli sat down opposite him. "How long has it been?" she asked.

"Must be...nine months? You've been away, haven't you? Cass said she hadn't seen you in a while either."

"Yes. Away. I've been away. Just got back. How is everyone?"

"I don't know. I need to do some catching up while I'm in town. Thought I'd start with you. Well, Cass actually. I called in for drinks and ended up eating lunch." He puffed his cheeks out. "Man, that lady sure knows how to cook up a storm. Roast chicken like you've never tasted it." He laughed and Alli joined in.

They chatted. Mostly about his new recordings and songs he had been writing. Alli replenished their beers and gradually drifted into a happy place in her mind. Nancy, Canonbury Ducis and England in the twenty-first century seemed so far away. This was her reality.

"So, that's my news up to date. How about you, Alli? What have you been up to since last year?"

Reality hit her with a bump. It was now 1969, but what season was it? The entire year had been so eventful. History lessons at school had taught her that much. Altamont, when that fan was murdered at a rock concert. Had that happened yet? No, that was in December surely. That was what rounded off the whole bizarre and terrible year. The year when the Summer of Love really ended. Woodstock…that was before Altamont. August. She was sure it was August. The weather had been unseasonably awful. Rain, mud. Had that taken place yet? It was hot outside. It felt like summer. This was California though so it could just as easily be spring. Woodstock and the legendary Yasgur's Farm were thousands of miles away in the east, where the climate was much cooler. California bathed itself in almost year-long sunshine. Did John perform at Woodstock, or was he booked to appear there? He surely would have mentioned it if he had. It was a big deal at the time, as well as leaving its legacy to history. And then. Summer 1969. Much closer to home. This home. The Manson murders. When were those? Before or after Woodstock? Alli struggled to remember. August. That was it. Same month as Woodstock. So many thoughts rushing through her mind simultaneously. Alli expected her face must be a picture of utter confusion.

John was certainly looking at her searchingly. A bemused frown creased his forehead. "Everything all right?"

"Yes, sorry. The beer's gone straight to my head. I haven't eaten yet today."

He laughed. "You should get on over to Cass's. She's got plenty left over."

The thought was appealing, but John was still waiting for an answer. *Be vague.* "Nothing exciting happened to me really. Visiting relatives and old friends back home. I stayed longer than I intended. Then, back I came."

"What are you getting up to here then?"

That was a great question. She lived in this lovely house. How had she paid for it? In this world, what did she do to earn a living? There were no musical instruments around, no signs that she was a writer or an artist. "I'm sort of between phases in my life." That sounded suitably woolly and even appropriate for the times she was living in. Seeing John nod and his expression soften, she latched on to it. "I may start writing. Poetry." Where did that come from? She had never written a poem in her life.

"Oh wow. I didn't know you were a poet. Far-out."

"Well, I'm not really. Not yet anyway. Hey, everyone has to start somewhere, don't they?"

"They sure do. You have to let me read some of your stuff when you're ready. You could be the next Rod McKuen...or Leonard Cohen. Hey, maybe we could work on a song together."

"Oh no. I'm not ready for.... You write such great lyrics. You don't need me. I'd cramp your style."

"Never say never," John said. His expression grew serious. "Hey, did you hear about Caroline?"

"Hear what about her?" What did happen to Caroline in 1969?

"Her last two singles flopped. There's talk of the record company dropping her."

"That's too bad. I had heard that things didn't go so well after she came over here. I suppose she just couldn't top 'Lady Gossamer'."

John shook his head, his frown lines deepening on his forehead. "The album received mixed reviews and only made it into the Top Thirty. It peaked at twenty-eight I think and then disappeared without trace. How did it do in England?"

"I'm afraid I don't know. I've been a bit out of touch with the... scene...recently."

"No offense intended, but the real sales…the big money…as far as the record companies are concerned, are in the U.S. You have to make it here."

"I know you're right. I think she did okay in Europe though."

"Really? I heard she bombed in Germany."

Alli improvised. "No, I meant 'Lady Gossamer'."

A sudden, furious knocking at the front door made Alli jump. She could hear Cass's voice, muffled by the timber.

John and Alli both leapt up. "She sounds frantic," Alli said, already at the door and wrenching it open.

Cass was out of breath, white-faced, her eye makeup streaked down her cheeks. "Oh, thank God you're here. I took a chance…. I knew John was coming over and I saw your window open."

Alli fleetingly wondered when she could have done that. She couldn't remember.

"What is it, Cass?" John asked.

"Get me a drink, will you, Alli? A stiff anything. I don't care what."

John steered Cass into the living room and Alli made for the kitchen. She returned seconds later with three glasses and a bottle of Scotch. Cass was still breathing heavily when Alli returned again with a bowl full of ice cubes. She sloshed generous measures of the fiery spirit into the glasses, chucked some ice in and handed them around.

"Okay," Cass said, after taking a draining gulp. Alli refreshed her drink.

Cass nodded her thanks and drank again. "It's Caroline."

"What happened?" John asked. "Did the record company drop her?"

"If only that's all it was. Yes, they dropped her. They dropped her like their hands were on fire from touching her. Ripped up her contract. She took it hard. Real hard."

"When did this happen, Cass?" Alli said. Cass's hands were trembling, as was her lip. Fresh tears spilled over her eyelids and streamed down her cheeks.

"Yest…yesterday. But that's not it. Oh God…we lost her. That poor kid. We lost her."

Alli's heart jumped. That couldn't be true. It must be a mistake. "You don't mean...she's *dead*?"

Cass turned her eyes to her and nodded. "She took her own life. I was at home. She could have called me. Come over. Asked me to go over. I would have gone. You know that, don't you, John? You know me. I would have gone like a shot. I would have stayed with her as long as she needed me."

John went to her and put his arms around her. She sobbed into his shoulder while he stroked her hair.

Alli's mind was racing. Caroline *couldn't* be dead. She simply couldn't be. "When did this happen?" she asked, a massive lump in her throat making it awkward to speak.

"Probably yesterday evening. Around nine o'clock maybe. She was seen on her porch at a little after eight and they found her at around ten this morning. Someone walked in and...they found her hanging there. We'll know more when they've done the...the.... Oh God, John, they're going to have to cut her open. That poor sweet child, that beautiful girl and they're going to have to cut her open."

"She can't be dead," Alli said quietly. Cass stopped in mid-sob.

John looked at her as if she had suddenly sprouted another head. "What do you mean, she can't be dead? Cass?"

Cass shuffled into a more upright position. "She was found hanging by her neck from a crossbeam in her living room. A stool was kicked over. She was barefoot, dressed in a beautiful hand-embroidered cotton dress. There was no note.... She *killed* herself. I'm sorry, Alli. I'm having a hard time understanding this too. We all are."

"She can't be dead. Not yet. It isn't her time. It isn't her time...."

The room darkened. The protesting voices of Cass and John faded away, became mere echoes. A rushing sound sped toward her, filling her ears like the severest tinnitus until she could hear nothing else. Alli lost all sense of space and time. All sense of her own body. She seemed to drift between worlds. Wave upon wave of despair flooded over her, cocooning her spirit which no longer seemed to possess a body to protect it.

On and on. On and on....

And that voice.... "My world. My rules...."

★   ★   ★

"Alli. Alli, come back to us." The voice was Mike's. She had no idea where he was or if she imagined it. It faded and another presence took hold of her. The voice that turned her world black.

Now, you see the power I command. The ability to change history. I control her. She is mine and always will be. Her spirit is mine and her soul is mine to command.

It was inside her. Wild images all formed in her head, but she had no part in their creation.

She sent her thoughts out to it. *Who are you? What are you?*

"Alli!"

Alli opened her eyes. She was back in the attic room. Nancy, Ric and Mike were all standing over her. They seemed to tower above her. She realized she was still on the floor. No longer kneeling, she had slumped sideways. Mike helped her stand. "Thank God you're okay. We've been so worried."

"You suddenly collapsed," Nancy said. "We couldn't find a pulse. I tried. Ric tried. Then Mike…."

Alli took a deep breath. Her heart was palpitating, and dizziness crept over her in waves. Mike steered her toward a chair, and she flopped down in it.

Nancy handed her a glass of water and she sipped it gratefully. Rarely had tap water tasted so good or been so welcome.

"What did I say, or do?" Alli asked. "Before I…."

Ric took the initiative. "Nothing that made a great deal of sense. Mostly you babbled away in some language none of us could understand. Your voice sounded gruff, as if a man was talking. Then you suddenly slumped over."

Memories drifted back to Alli. "I was back in 1969. Spring or maybe early summer, I think. I was in my home. I mean the place that feels like my home when I'm there. Cass came over. She said Caroline was dead…hanged herself. Exactly as she did here, but more than fifty years ago. She may have even died at the same time of day.

In the evening. They won't be sure until the autopsy is performed. Cass was particularly upset about that. The fact they would have to cut Caroline open."

"But you told them she couldn't be dead, right?" Ric said.

Alli nodded. "I said it wasn't her time to die, and that's when I zoned out of there. Then, before I came back here, I had a really strange encounter. It's not the first time…. This time I felt it made more of a connection. Maybe that's when I was talking. Speaking in that language you couldn't understand. We should have taped it."

Ric held his phone up. "We did. Or, to be more accurate, I did." He fiddled with the app for a few seconds. "Okay, here we go."

White noise sputtered out of the phone.

They all listened, waiting.

"What's the matter with it?" Mike asked, impatience dripping from each syllable.

Ric stopped it, checked it, started again.

Still only white noise echoed around the room. The recording stopped. Ric examined his phone. He pressed 'play' again and a recording of his voice filled the room.

"It's working all right," he said. "I don't understand it."

"I think I do," Alli said. "I reckon it wouldn't matter how many recordings we would have attempted. Nothing would have come through. The entity, or whatever it is, doesn't want that, so it won't happen. Lucius Hartmann won't let it happen. Or that…I don't know what to call it."

Mike stepped forward, positioning himself between Alli and Ric. "Lucius Hartmann. I am addressing you directly. Please come forward and speak to me."

The silence grew thick and oppressive. Alli hardly dared to breathe.

"Lucius Hartmann—"

The crash took them by surprise. The air grew thick with fine, gray ash.

"What's happened?" Alli looked around.

Nancy cried out. "The urn. Caroline's urn."

It lay on the floor, the top some distance away. It rolled silently, back and forth, in a slow rocking motion while its contents were whipped up by a breeze that extended no farther than the limits of the ash. Within seconds, the wind stopped as if someone had thrown a switch. The urn came to a halt, at the precise same time as the ash stopped floating in the air, instead descending and coating everything within reach in a fine mass. As they watched, the ash seemed to evaporate. They waited. Nothing else happened.

One of us has to make the first move. Alli took a deep breath and struggled to her feet, her legs shaky and her movement uncertain. She reached for the urn, surprised to see the top firmly secured once more. It weighed quite heavy in her hands as she shook it.

"It feels full. How is that even possible?" she said, her voice hardly more than a whisper.

"How is any of this possible?" Mike asked.

Suddenly Ric gave a cry and pitched forward. Mike broke his fall. He lowered him down onto the floor. Ric shook himself and looked up at the trio of faces who were watching him, their expressions mixed.

"What are you all staring at? What happened?" He looked around.

"You passed out for a second," Mike said.

Ric shook himself. "It's so bloody oppressive in here. This house.... It's...."

"Cursed," Alli said. "We've shilly-shallied around the subject, believing one impossible thing after another.... I've zoned in and out of here, finding myself transported back fifty years to a place I've never been to, surrounded by people who are purely legends to me. Every one of whom is dead now. All of them attached to Caroline Rand in some way. The Caroline Rand I've just been told died in 1969, when we all know she couldn't have. She lived another fifty years. Or was that really her? Maybe someone else took her place for that half century. I know I didn't dream what I saw, heard and experienced. We all know Lucius Hartmann was Caroline's Svengali—"

Mike interrupted her. "You know what? I don't think I like to use the term Svengali about Hartmann. I think that gives him too much power. I think he's just a tinpot dictator. A puppet master with delusions of grandeur. An upstart—"

"*Enough!*" Ric leapt to his feet too fast for any human, other than a supreme athlete. He advanced toward Mike, his face too close for comfort.

Alli wondered how Mike could hold his position. Ric must only be a few inches away from him. Much too far into his personal space. "Be careful what you say, Mike. Be very careful. One step too far and...." Ric backed off. "Just be careful. That's all." Ric physically slumped. He began to heave, clamped his hand against his mouth and beat a hasty retreat down the steps. The noise of dry retching sounded from below.

"Shouldn't we go and see if he's okay?" Nancy asked.

"You're the hostess, Nancy." Mike opened his hands expansively. "Feel free."

"It's all right," Alli said. "I'll come with you, Nancy. I don't really see any further point in being up here."

"True." Mike followed them down the stairs.

There was no sign of Ric. Not in his room, or any of the bathrooms. From outside, came the sound of a car engine starting up.

"No way!" Alli raced to the front door and wrenched it open, momentarily surprised that it let her. The others joined her in time to see Ric shoot off down the drive in a screech of tires and shower of gravel.

Mike pounded the door. "The idiot. Come on, let's get back inside. We need to decide what to do next."

The atmosphere outside felt strange; the air smelled wrong. Difficult to pin down. An old smell that didn't belong in the outdoors of the Wiltshire countryside in summer. The aromas that washed over Alli were more like the greasy, smog-laden stench of a city center before any attempt had been made to curb carbon emissions. It stank and burned the inside of her nose and throat. It was good to return to the pleasantly scented hallway.

Mike shut the door and it clicked.

"Locked, of course," Mike said. "The house has spoken. Here we stay."

Alli tried the handle. It didn't budge. It wouldn't even turn.

"You needn't try the kitchen door or the windows," Mike said. "They'll be locked too."

"How can you be so sure?" Alli said, aware that Nancy was following the conversation the way a person watches a tennis match.

Mike shrugged. "Isn't it obvious?"

"Not completely."

"We're not in charge here, surely you know that by now. The house is in charge. It dictates what will happen."

"You realize how that sounds," Alli said.

"Do you have a better explanation?"

"Not really."

"We can only wait and see what happens next. It's clear none of us have any say in it."

"Well, some of us, one of us…. Me, that is. I'm not giving up. We're here to help Nancy reclaim her home. I know I'm sent to Laurel Canyon in my mind, or some other way, for a reason other than a pleasant, and sometimes not so pleasant, diversion. There are answers there. I'm determined to find them, and Caroline Rand's the key."

"Oh, she's that all right," Mike said and immediately looked away, as if he wished he hadn't said that.

"What do you mean?" Alli asked. "What do you know that you haven't shared with us?"

Mike looked back. His face had paled, and he appeared uncertain. "Nothing. You're right. This was her house. She has to be the key."

"Come on," Nancy said, and the suddenness of her intervention made Alli jump. "Let's go and have a drink. Brandy in the living room."

Mike was already crossing the threshold, with Nancy close behind. Alli brought up the rear. Once inside, she glanced up at the portrait. The original pose was back in place, as if it had never changed.

What are we missing here, Caroline? And when did you really die?

Come back to me…. Come back. Help me…. Alli didn't expect Caroline's voice in her head. She gave a start.

Mike noticed. "What is it, Alli?"

Alli shivered. Her whole body felt cold, as if the temperature had suddenly dropped ten or more degrees. "I felt her. Caroline. I heard her voice. Here." She tapped the side of her forehead. "She told me to go back."

"Maybe that's it," Nancy said. "If Alli goes back to her in 1969, maybe she can get some answers."

"There's no guarantee where I'll end up, or rather when. Maybe I'll go back to 1968 again. I have no control over this."

"No," Mike said. "But I wonder if Caroline does. Or at least a little. Especially now she's summoned you."

"It was more like a plaintive plea."

Mike waved his hand dismissively. "Whatever it was. Can you project yourself back there? Maybe concentrate on a feature that's become familiar to you there. That house you think you live in. Or Cass's place."

"I'll try, but it's always just *happened* before."

"It's happened when there's been a catalyst," Mike said. "Like the portrait changing, or…. Let's try summoning her. Caroline, I mean. Let's see if we can get her to come for you."

Nancy, Alli and Mike sat around a table, their hands touching. Mike's hand felt warm against Alli's. From deep within her, she felt a twinge of desire. *This is hardly the time.*

Mike called out. "Caroline Rand. We respectfully summon you and you alone to come to us through this woman, Alli. We need to talk to you. Please, Caroline, please come forward."

Alli's eyes were firmly closed. In the darkness behind her lids, nothing stirred. Mike called out again. She felt nothing, no strange sensations of drifting, and no sight of the black void, for which she was thankful. Once again, Mike called out. Once again, Alli felt nothing. Mike paused for longer than before. Then he spoke to her.

"Do you feel anything at all, Alli?"

"No, sorry."

Mike sighed. Nancy squeezed her hand.

He called out again.

Nancy squeezed her hand tighter. Then tighter still.

"Ouch. Nancy, stop it, please. You're breaking my hand."

Alli opened her eyes. Beside her, Nancy stared at her in horror, cradling her hand. Alli tried to rub some life into her own.

Mike studied the two of them. "What just happened there?"

Nancy spoke first. "I had to let go of Alli's hand."

"You were squeezing too hard."

"No, she wasn't, Alli," Mike said. "I saw the whole thing. I didn't close my eyes as you two did. I kept them open to see if anything materialized. The first couple of times I called out, you two had your hands loosely clasped. Then, straight after I called out for the last time, Nancy, your hand shot away from Alli's as if someone had wrenched the two of you apart."

Alli looked down at her throbbing hand.

Mike's voice held a slight tremor as if he was fighting to control his emotions. "Alli, no one was holding your hand, but I saw your knuckles whiten. I saw finger marks imprint themselves on your wrist and lower hand. I saw your fingers clench together as they only could if someone squeezed them."

"So, who was it? Who was squeezing my hand?"

CHAPTER TEN

A doorbell rang.

Alli opened her eyes and took a moment to realize where she was. The wood paneling, polished floors, ethnic rugs. She was back there, in her house in Laurel Canyon. But when?

The doorbell rang again and Alli pushed herself off the sofa, her head heavy with sleep.

On the doorstep, Caroline Rand smiled at her. Alli took a step back, catching her breath.

"I don't usually have that effect on people," the smiling woman said. "May I come in?"

"Yes…yes…of course." Alli held the door open for her. She took a quick look outside. There was no one else there. She closed the door and followed Caroline into her living room.

"Can I get you a drink?"

Caroline shook her head. "No, I'm fine, thanks. I only dropped by to see if you would be at this festival they're all talking about. If it happens, it'll probably be out at some farm in the Catskills. Woodstock or somewhere. I've never heard of it. By all accounts, that area is becoming quite the east coast version of Laurel Canyon. Dylan's moved there, Hendrix…. Anyway, it sounds out-of-sight. If it happens, of course. It'll be sometime next month probably. Think you might come along? I think I might, and maybe I'll do a couple of songs if they'll have me." She was babbling, practically wringing her hands. Every muscle seemed stretched taut. Alli didn't know her well enough to get too personal. Besides, she was still trying to get a handle on the timing. From what Caroline had just said, it had to be July 1969. "Caroline, what's the date today? I've lost track."

"What? The date? It's the eighth."

"Of?"

"July. It's the eighth of July."

"The year?"

"The year? Are you serious? It's 1969…." Her voice trailed off.

"Of course it is. Sorry, I'm a bit jet-lagged, that's all."

"I get that sometimes. Usually when I'm flying from west to east, though."

"Oh, I always have to be different. I get it both ways. So, how have things been while I've been away?"

Caroline gave a deep sigh. It was as if someone had stuck a pin in a balloon she had been struggling to keep inflated. Now it would all come out. When Caroline spoke, her voice trembled. "Not good. My record company…." She broke down sobbing.

On impulse, Alli joined her on the sofa and put her arms around her. As she did so, a shock raced up her arms. She gave a little gasp. Either Caroline didn't hear her, or didn't feel the same sensation, or both. She didn't react. Maybe she was too caught up in her own grief.

Finally, Caroline drew herself free, sat up and blew her nose on a tissue from a box on Alli's coffee table. "I was so sure I had made it, you know? Everyone tells you success is fleeting in this business. But I really thought I had a bit longer before they threw me over."

"I had heard a rumor."

Caroline froze. "When? They only told me an hour ago."

Alli's mind went into panic mode. What the hell time was it? When had Cass found out and come to tell her and John about Caroline's suicide? Had the chain of events changed again? And there was Hartmann and…the face from the void loomed into her mind. That face had been so distinctive, and surreal. Not truly human.

"Alli? Please tell me. Who told you and when? Was it today?"

"You know…I'm really not sure. I don't believe anyone told me for certain. I think someone may have speculated. Because of the record sales? Sorry, Caroline. That's the best I can do. I can't remember." Alli wasn't lying when she said it was the best she could do. As for the rest…. "But you have friends, contacts." She knew she was fudging. She needed to stop

Caroline asking awkward questions she knew she couldn't answer. "And you have such a beautiful voice. Someone will sign you up." Anything to prevent the disaster that might be in her imminent future.

"Maybe…. I don't know what to do. It's come as such a shock. Perhaps I'll cut my losses and go back to England while I can still afford it. That's what Lucius wants me to do and he has been so good to me. I must listen to him. At least my records are still selling there."

Alli felt an unpleasant crawling sensation on her skin at the mention of Lucius's name. He might not be here, but his influence still held Caroline in its clutches. She must tread carefully. "It's always an option. But it's not the only one. There are other record companies. Some great small ones. The big ones don't care enough." That wasn't a lie. Her parents used to tell her that.

They had been signed with companies in both the U.S. and Britain, and always maintained they got better deals with the smaller ones. "They have to try harder," her father said. She racked her brains for some names that might resonate with Caroline. Maybe Alli could make things better, by giving her hope that all was not lost. Perhaps this is what she was meant to do – the reason why she kept coming back here. Supposing she had been sent to prevent Caroline's imminent suicide? That would make some kind of warped sense. Caroline could die tonight or in fifty years. Maybe her choice now, at this moment in time, would signal the difference. And if Alli could come up with just the right record company, it could offer a ray of hope to her at the precise moment she needed it most.

A name floated to the front of her mind.

"Lee Hazlewood," Alli said. It sounded like a triumphant pronouncement, and in a way, it was.

"Lee Hazlewood? The guy who wrote 'Boots' for Nancy Sinatra?"

"Well…not strictly *for* her but…. Yes, the guy who wrote 'These Boots Are Made for Walkin'' and a string of other hits, and he worked… works with Ann–Margret and Frank Sinatra and a host of others." She prayed she was right. In the back of her mind, she could see her father talking to her mother about this guy who had completely revitalized Nancy Sinatra's career by his genius as a songwriter and record producer.

Her parents had wanted to work with him but, for whatever reason, it never happened. More memories drifted into her mind and she warmed to her subject. "He has his own record label. LHI – Lee Hazlewood Industries. You must have met him at some point." Mentally, she crossed her fingers.

"Once or twice. I went to his house. His girlfriend invited me this one time. Lucius took me. I don't think he cared for Lee much. He's a very forthright person. Lee, I mean. Lucius didn't take to that."

I'll bet he didn't. Nevertheless, Alli kept her cool. "There you are then. Why not give her a call and see if you can't set up a meeting with Lee."

A smile lit up Caroline's face, then disappeared as fast as it had appeared. "I need to talk to Lucius first."

Alli snapped. "Why? Why do you need to talk to Lucius first? This is *your* career, not Lucius's. What kind of a hold does he have over you anyway?" *Apart from being the father of your child, and being the man who took her away from you at birth.*

Caroline raised tear-filled eyes to hers. "You wouldn't understand, Alli. I couldn't explain it to you. But I promise I will talk to Lucius about it."

"Caroline, he isn't even here. He wouldn't know if you spoke to LHI or not, would he?"

Once again, the hesitation, as if Caroline longed to tell her something she couldn't quite bring herself to.

"I'll think about what you've said, Alli. I promise I will." Caroline stood, wiped the last of the tears away with the back of her hand and made for the front door, when she stopped and, on an apparent impulse, hugged Alli. Once again, that shock of contact coursed through Alli's body, seemingly unnoticed by Caroline. "Thank you so much. You've no idea how much you've helped me. I felt so...desperate."

"Glad I was here." *I only hope it's enough to keep you from doing something irrevocable today.*

Caroline opened the door and stepped out. She stopped and faced Alli. "Promise me you won't go anywhere."

"I can promise I'll try not to. Sometimes it's not up to me though, I'm sorry."

"Oh, I know. I don't know how or why, but I know. Give my regards to Canonbury Ducis."

Caroline half ran down the driveway and out of sight. Alli raced to the edge of her property and looked up and down Lookout Mountain Avenue. The road was empty. She turned back.

★   ★   ★

"Alli."

Mike's voice drifted into her mind and she opened her eyes.

She was back. Exactly as before, Nancy and Mike held her hands. Now they broke contact.

"You were there, weren't you?" Nancy said. "I could feel it this time. I swear you touched her. Caroline, I mean. I felt a shiver...no, more like...."

"A mild electric shock?" Alli asked.

"Yes, exactly like that."

Alli nodded. "When I hugged Caroline back then, I felt the same sensation. It raced through my body. Caroline didn't seem to notice it though."

"So, what happened, Alli?" Mike asked.

Alli told them all she could remember. They both listened in total silence. When she had finished, Nancy spoke. "Thank God you stopped her from killing herself. You gave her a reason to carry on. I think. If you hadn't, all of this...." She spread her arms expansively to include the house. "Well, let's say it wouldn't be mine because Caroline's life would have ended that same day. You were meant to be there, Alli. I don't know how it's possible, but you were."

Mike nodded. "It seems that way. Without you, Caroline would have killed herself and none of the rest of her life would have happened."

Alli looked from one to the other. Had she saved Caroline's life? And, if that were true, had she actually done her, or the rest of them, any real favors? It was a horrible thought but if she hadn't been able, by whatever means, to travel back there and apparently avert the course of history for

Caroline Rand, none of them would have been facing whatever was in that house. Alli had the urge to talk to someone who had lived through these times; someone who knew the world she was dipping in and out of. The answer was obvious, but did they actually know Caroline Rand well enough and, more especially, Lucius Hartmann? It was worth a phone call at the least.

★　　★　　★

The phone rang continually. Alli's parents evidently weren't home, and she didn't have any cell phone numbers for them. The last time she had checked with them, they said they didn't see any need for them. Part of retirement was to cease being at everyone's beck and call, they said. They had good neighbors. A proper little British ex-pat artistic community. Everyone looked out for everyone else as they all lived in their comfortable bubble away from the real world. No need for anything other than a landline. They didn't even own a computer of any type.

Alli was musing on this seemingly idyllic existence when the unanswered line was automatically disconnected, and she replaced the receiver.

She joined Nancy and Mike at the dining table, where the photo albums were spread out. Nancy looked up as she entered.

"I thought we might look through these and see if anything might help."

"Good idea," Alli said. She grabbed an album and started turning pages. There were some beautiful studio shots with every famous name imaginable behind the lens.

"These must be worth a fortune," Alli said as she turned over yet another perfectly lit black and white shot of a stunningly beautiful Caroline, looking so much more sophisticated than the emotional wreck Alli had comforted such a short time, and five decades, earlier.

Nancy sighed. "I love this one. It was taken by Lord Snowdon."

Alli and Mike leaned forward to look at it more closely. In this one, Caroline's eyes conveyed so much.

"She looks so sad there," Alli said. "As if her heart was breaking. I wonder when that was taken?"

"There's no date," Nancy said. "Apart from a few portraits in one of the albums, there are no dates anywhere. They all seem to have been taken within a couple of years though."

"By the looks of her, hairstyles, fashion and so on, I would gauge that these were almost all taken in 1968 and 1969, possibly 1970. I doubt if any are much later. Or earlier." Mike flicked over more pages until he reached the end of the album. He added it to the increasing pile of viewed material. "It's strange that there are no family shots. Nothing from her childhood or later in her life."

"So, we're no further on, really," Alli said, finishing her album and adding it to Mike's. She picked up the next one.

This was slightly different. Same era, but in these, she recognized—

"Wait a second. This is Cass's house. I remember this. I mean...."

Nancy and Mike peered over her shoulder. Mike touched her arm. "We know what you mean, Alli. Good grief. This is like a catalogue of Laurel Canyon's greatest stars." He pointed out one after the other. "Jim Morrison, and I think that's his girlfriend, Pamela. He wrote songs about her.... Janis Joplin. Peter Tork. Mama Cass and Papa John. Oh, and Papa Denny Doherty. No Michelle though. George Harrison was there?"

"Yes. I nearly fell over him," Alli said.

Nancy gave a squeal. She jabbed her finger at the photograph. "There she is. That's Caroline."

Exactly as Alli remembered her. At Cass's party sometime in 1968.

"Oh, and look," Nancy said. "There's John Denver. I always liked his songs. He had a lovely voice, and...."

All three of them stared hard. Alli's heart thumped painfully.

"It's you, Alli. Sitting next to John Denver. It's you."

CHAPTER ELEVEN

It felt almost like her zoning-out episodes. The woman in the photograph was in profile, but unmistakably her. Probably if she concentrated hard enough, she could even remember what John had been saying to her at the time. Maybe he had been telling her about Caroline. This was the first time Alli had met her – the time when she zoned out while looking at her disintegrating face....

"Alli?" Nancy touched the back of her hand. "Are you all right?"

Alli forced herself to look away from the photograph. "I'm okay. It's just the shock. Seeing myself...."

Mike put his arm around her shoulders, and she found it comforting. "There's no doubt now," he said. "You were definitely there. The science of it escapes me, but you were there. In the late Sixties—"

"Laurel Canyon in 1968." It didn't matter how many times she said it, it still didn't feel real. Yet, when she was there, she couldn't think of anywhere she would rather be.

Mike pointed to the photograph. "That's Cass Elliot's house. And all the people in that photograph are dead."

Nancy squeezed her hand. "All except you, Alli."

"All except me."

"Are there any more photos of you in there?" Mike asked.

Alli turned the pages. Apart from a few shots of a drunken Jim Morrison draped all over an equally inebriated Janis Joplin, and a shot of a garden, the rest of the album was empty.

"Maybe this is the last one and she never finished it," Nancy said.

"Maybe." A thought had struck Alli. "You know, these pictures had to come from somewhere. Someone brought them back here, to this house. That much hasn't changed. Caroline *must* have survived that night because this house is still hers. She came here, bought it, lived in it. Okay, there may not be any pictures of her after 1968, or '69, but these albums didn't magically create themselves."

"They certainly didn't," Mike said. "Maybe she got that second contract."

"Surely she must have done," Alli said. "She continued to have hits in Britain and Europe, didn't she?" Strange she couldn't remember any of them though. "Were there any records of hers here when you moved in?"

"Just the one. That first album, *Madrigal for the Lost Temptress*. Apart from that, the place was empty except for the portrait, those photograph albums and the other stuff in that room upstairs. The rest of the place had been cleared out, on her instructions. I never saw any of it."

"And you've been through everything in that attic room?"

"Yes. You've seen it, there's nowhere you could hide anything. The whole place is well hidden enough as it is."

"That bothers me. Why would she have that place sealed up? And how did her ashes get there? Did the builders say how long they thought the false wall had been up?"

Nancy shook her head. "And I never thought to ask them. Maybe there's another way in."

"We need to check that…. I still don't know how that urn could have been put there. No one else has been in this house except you and your builders, right? Could they have moved it up there before you found it?"

"I can't think why. As far as I know they never met her."

"Hang on. There was a cleaner or housekeeper, wasn't there? The woman who found her?"

"Yes. Mrs. Creeley. Audrey Creeley. She'd been with Caroline for years, or so she told me when I called her that time."

"Could you call her again and ask her about the urn?"

Nancy frowned. "I could try but, as I told you, the last call didn't go well. She practically hung up on me when I suggested she might come and work for me."

"Nevertheless," Alli said, "she knows this place better than any of us. If there are any hidden entrances, she'd be the one who would know."

Nancy nodded, stood and went over to a small desk. She rummaged for a moment and came up with a small notebook. "Here it is. Caroline's address book." She flicked through it and alighted on a page. "Got it."

She went over to the landline and picked up the phone, pressed the numbers and waited.

"Hello? Is Mrs. Creeley there, please? It's Nancy Harper from Canonbury Manor. I'd like a quick…. I'm sorry? She's…. Oh, I see…. I'm so sorry to hear that…. Please accept my condolences." She disconnected the call and replaced the phone.

Alli ran her hands over her face. "She died, didn't she?"

Nancy nodded. "Last week apparently. She was out shopping, had a heart attack and was dead before she hit the ground. At least, that's what they reckon. I feel awful now. I called right in the middle of her wake."

"They'll appreciate you weren't to know." Alli stood. "Come on, let's see if we can find another way into the attic room. Those ashes didn't get there by themselves."

★   ★   ★

The house is letting us out. It wants us to find this. Alli couldn't still the silent voice in her head. She wanted to rail at whatever was playing with them and enjoying itself at their expense. Her anger boiled inside her, but one look at her companions stopped her letting it out. They would simply think she had gone right over the edge. They hadn't even remarked on the unlocked main door and now, here they all were staring up at the front of the house.

Nancy pointed upward. "That window is my bedroom. So, the entrance to the room is around here." She paced a few yards to one side.

Alli noted the landing window, Nancy's bathroom window and the next one along, which belonged to the guest room she was using. The pattern of windows was repeated on the story above. "The stairwell is between the rooms. There's no apparent external access," she said, thinking out loud. "Unless…. What about the cellar? You do have one, don't you? A house this age…."

"Oh yes, there's a cellar all right." Nancy shivered. "I've never been down there. The surveyor said it was waterproof and everything was solid, and that's all I needed to know. Cellars creep me out."

"Sorry, Nan," Mike said. "We need to know a bit more now."

They trooped back into the hall. As the front door swung shut, Alli heard the familiar click of the lock. *That's all we get.*

In the kitchen, Nancy turned a key in a door in the corner. She reached round and switched on the light, illuminating a steep flight of stairs stretching deep into the darkness. Alli positioned herself at the top. "Are there lights down there or do we need flashlights?"

"I'm not sure. We'd better take our own, just in case."

Mike and Alli waited as Nancy rummaged in a tall cupboard, eventually producing three flashlights. "One each," she said, handing them out and leaving one behind. They weren't large but at least the bulbs worked.

"I seem to be going first," Alli said, trying to make light of it when inside her stomach was turning to jelly.

They made their way down. It was a typical cellar. Low ceilings, exposed timbers, spiders' webs, signs that the faded dirty walls had once been whitewashed. At the bottom, Alli stepped onto a flagstone floor. There was no sign of damp although the air smelled fusty, typical of a room that had been shut up and deprived of fresh air for too long. "Everyone okay?" Alli's voice echoed off the walls.

"Fine here," Mike said.

"I'm okay." But Nancy didn't sound it.

Alli found another wall switch and pressed it, illuminating a further section of the cellar. Now they could see how far it extended, way into deep shadows on two sides. They were at one end, practically in a corner.

"Man, those shadows are dark," Mike said.

"Thanks, Mike," Alli said. "I was trying not to think about that."

"Sorry."

"It's so quiet down here," Nancy whispered.

"Like a grave." Mike's impersonation of Christopher Lee might have been intended to lighten the atmosphere, but it failed.

A sudden crack echoed around them, as if someone had stepped on broken glass.

They listened. Alli strained to hear. Nothing. Only silence so heavy it weighed her down.

Nancy pointed into the farthest darkness. "I think it came from over there."

Alli switched on her flashlight and stepped toward the shadows. "Is there someone there?"

A sudden breath of air ruffled her hair. "Did you feel that?" she asked as she shone her flashlight around.

"No," Nancy said. "Nothing."

"Me neither," Mike said.

"It felt like someone opened an outside door." Alli flashed her light in the general direction she thought the air had come from. Broken bits of furniture, old paint tins and a rotten wooden ladder lay strewn across the floor. A sudden darting movement made her catch her breath. She shone the light again. A pair of eyes reflected in the beam.

Nancy screamed. Mike let out a whoop. Alli burst out laughing. She couldn't help herself. "It's only a mouse. A tiny little mouse."

"I can't stand the things. Get it away from me." Nancy's hysteria was getting out of hand.

"Go back upstairs to the kitchen, Nancy." Mike sounded exasperated. "We'll take it from here."

Nancy's rapid-fire footsteps raced up the steps. She slammed the door shut.

"She had better not have locked that bastard," Mike said. "Come on, let's look for another entrance and get out of here. It's spooking me, even if that was only a mouse."

Alli nodded. "Let's start over here. It shouldn't take long. Simply a matter of following the house round."

"Keep up close to the wall."

Alli didn't need telling. The thought of wandering into the middle of that space in front of her sent icy fingers of fear coursing through every nerve in her body.

The surveyor had been right. The walls were in excellent condition considering the property's extreme age. There were signs of patching-up jobs, replastering, and then….

They both saw it at the same time.

The door was easy to miss. It had originally been painted white to match the walls. On closer examination Alli wasn't at all sure it hadn't been deliberately and prematurely 'aged' to match its surroundings. Even the door handle had received a generous dollop of emulsion.

Mike reached out tentatively and turned it. It creaked a little as if a good oiling wouldn't go amiss. He tugged and the wood gave a little but otherwise didn't budge. "I think it's just warped," he said and tugged again. This time the door shifted on its hinges. One more tug and it shuddered open, the hinges groaning and paint cracking, flaking off and floating down like confetti.

Mike looked at Alli. "I will, if you will," she said.

He nodded.

Their footsteps echoed on the worn stone steps as they ascended. Evidently this route had been in much more frequent use at some time in the house's history.

"Maybe this was the servants' entrance," Alli said. "Back in the days when servants should neither be seen nor heard, especially those who worked below stairs. Those poor old scullery maids, laundry maids and kitchen staff. You can imagine them trudging up and down these stairs, lugging heavy buckets of hot water and God knows what else, backwards and forwards, day in and day out."

The more steps they climbed, the more out of breath she became. They opened a door on the first floor and found themselves in the back of an empty wardrobe.

"It's like Narnia," Alli said. "How bizarre. Surely it can't have been like this when this staircase was in regular use." She shone her flashlight on the inside of the wardrobe door, pushed it, but it was locked. No hope of getting out that way. "Onwards and upwards," she said.

They reached a ceiling of sorts. "It looks like a trapdoor," Alli said, shoving at it.

"I reckon this will be the floor of Nancy's bedroom," Mike said. "Let me have a go." They switched places in the confined space and Mike pushed hard at the timbers. They shifted but not upward. They slid to the side until there was a space just big enough for one person to jiggle their way through. Mike went first. Alli followed.

"Recognize where you are now?" he asked.

Alli nodded, looking around her at the small room behind the door in Nancy's bedroom, with the flight of steps leading to the attic. "So, now we know how it was possible for someone to place Caroline's ashes where they are. We can only guess who was responsible, but my money is on either Mrs. Creeley or the solicitor. Let's go and tell Nancy."

They pushed open the door into Nancy's room.

Alli stopped dead. A woman sat on the bed, with her back to them. A woman with long blonde hair, wearing a hippy dress that Alli recognized. The figure slowly turned.

Sickly-sweet bile rose in Alli's throat. "No, this can't be happening."

The woman spoke. It seemed the words were drifting toward her and she was miming them. "Yet it is, Alli. You can see that. It *is* happening."

"Who the fuck are you?" Mike asked.

The woman smiled, revealing even white teeth. "You have to ask? I'm Caroline Rand. And this is my house."

CHAPTER TWELVE

"No," Alli said. "You can stop playing games, because I'm not buying this."

Mike put a restraining hand on her arm. "Alli."

Alli shot him a look that stopped him in his tracks. He let his hand fall. She turned back to the woman who sat silently, studying her every move with a strange smile on her face. Her eyes were vacant, devoid of any soul. Alli knew in that moment that her instincts were right. "You are *not* Caroline Rand. I don't know who – or what – you are, but you are definitely *not* her. Get out of here. *Now*."

The woman's mouth curled into an ugly grimace. One moment she was sitting, the next she was on her feet. Alli watched in horror as the body began to melt. An unpleasant smell of overdone meat and burnt fat filled the room, making Alli and Mike choke. Acrid blue smoke issued from every orifice of the creature in front of them. From far away, the sound of ribald laughter. It sounded like a men's stag night, inflamed with too much alcohol. Someone banged on the door. Nancy. She was yelling at them to unlock it, rattling the doorknob and hammering at the timber.

The vile vision ended in a smoking heap on the rug, then vanished. No trace remained, only a lingering smell of rancid burning flesh which evaporated by the second. On the wall, shadows danced and, for a second, Alli was sure she saw those reveling monks she had witnessed earlier. The laughter faded and was gone.

Eyes still streaming, Alli made for the door and turned the handle. It opened instantly. "It wasn't locked," she told a white-faced Nancy, who burst into the room.

"What the hell's been going on in here? How did you get in? The door *was* locked a moment ago. It wouldn't budge. What happened to you two? What was that awful smell?"

Alli glanced up at the wall. The shadows had gone, along with the smoke.

Mike wiped his eyes on his sleeve. "We found another entrance to the stairs up to the attic and it brings you out in a wardrobe in the room on the floor below. From there, it's a simple enough job to get up through the floor into the stairwell. When we came in here, there was a…creature… purporting to be Caroline Rand, sitting on your bed. Fortunately, Alli didn't believe her eyes and challenged it. She was right. Believe me, you wouldn't have wanted to see what it turned into."

"It was the eyes," Alli said. "Before whatever it was disintegrated, it felt like looking at a mannequin. You know, the ones in shop windows? They look beautiful, but they're just plaster and paint. This one was made of some other substance. I dread to think what."

Nancy sank onto the bed. "You haven't just been back *there*, I suppose. Back to 1968, I mean?"

Alli shook her head. "That'll happen when, and if, it happens, I suppose."

"I'm surprised it didn't happen when you saw the figure on the bed," Mike said.

"Because she…it…didn't belong there, I should imagine."

Mike and Nancy stared at her, apparently waiting for an explanation. Alli didn't have one.

"It's Sunday tomorrow," Nancy said. "And you two are supposed to be leaving on Monday morning. We don't have long." She glanced over at the window. "It's getting dark."

"A lot can happen in twenty-four hours," Mike said. "Besides, until we have this thing sorted out, I doubt any of us will be going anywhere."

"You're right," Alli said. "Whatever it is won't be content with simply letting us get on with our lives and, anyway, we can't leave you like this, Nancy. It wouldn't be right."

Mike sighed. "Let's face it, we're as caught up in this as you are now, Nan."

"Ric managed to get away."

"Maybe," Alli said. "But I have the strongest feeling he's not going to get off so lightly."

"I agree." Mike wandered over to the window.

There was an awkward silence until Nancy stood and made for the door.

"Come on, let's go down. The walls are closing in on me here. There's some chilled white wine in the fridge, and plenty to eat, plus it's a beautiful evening and we can watch the sunset. Let's try and…I don't know…relax a bit, if that's possible."

★   ★   ★

It seemed so normal. Unable to go outside, they sat by the living room window, sipping wine and watching the clear sky turning gradually from blue through to shades of pink, orange, yellow and red.

Alli looked out over the long lawn as the shadows deepened with the setting sun. The calming effect of the wine relaxed her. She closed her eyes, while the gentle hum of conversation between Mike and Nancy drifted into the distance.

"Alli. Alli."

The voice was soft, feminine, familiar. Caroline. And it wasn't in her head.

Alli opened her eyes. She was sitting outside, wooden timbers beneath her sandaled feet. Canonbury Ducis was far away, both in space and time. She recognized the porch of her home in Laurel Canyon. Next to her stood a small wicker table. On it, a tall glass of a liquid that looked suspiciously like the wine she had just been drinking in Nancy's home. Caroline was standing to the right of her, smiling.

"You're back, at last," she said. "You were gone some time. A couple of weeks."

Alli struggled for a plausible explanation. Caroline put up her hand.

"Don't bother. There's nothing to explain. I took your advice and met with Lee. One thing led to another and I have a new contract. Not with LHI though, another label. Dark Secret Records. Quite appropriate really, when you think about it."

Alli sat up straighter. "Appropriate?"

"Yes. You and I share a secret, don't we? About the times when you're not here."

What should she say to that? Alli looked down at her hands.

"Oh, don't look so worried, Alli. It's becoming much clearer to me now. I know you have a link to my life. Not my life here, in this time, but in another life. Perhaps it's an afterlife, or maybe, more accurately, an after-death."

"After-death? What does that mean?"

"Lucius told me. We all have someone we're linked to in a former life or in a future existence. Someone who forms our after-death. I believe you're my link to my after-death."

"I really don't understand any of that."

Caroline ran her fingers through her hair and smiled. "Don't worry. It took me a long time to get my head around it. You will though. One day. When the time is right."

Alli felt an uncomfortable prickle and changed the subject. "Is Lucius here?"

"No. He's back in England. He's in so much demand for his portrait work. Such an amazing artist."

"Has he painted *your* picture yet?"

Caroline smiled. "Yes." She looked away, staring off into the distance.

Alli took a deep breath. "Have you had the baby? I'm sorry, I never know exactly when I've returned here."

Tears formed in Caroline's eyes but, when she spoke, the words sounded false. Rehearsed. "Yes, I had the baby, and she's been adopted. It's for the best. I couldn't give her the attention she deserves and needs, and Lucius…."

"I know he's the father. I also know the child grew up and had a daughter of her own. She lives in your house. In Canonbury Ducis."

Caroline said nothing, then slowly nodded. "Yes. I understand. And there's another thing…." She shook her head and lowered her eyes.

"Another thing?" Alli prompted.

"Nothing. I…. It's nothing."

The fear in Caroline's eyes stopped Alli from pursuing the matter. What had she started to reveal?

The silence was only punctuated by the sound of cicadas, birdsong and a cat calling in the distance.

Caroline stood and went over to the wooden rail that ran all around the house. "I'm dead, aren't I? In your time, I mean."

Alli took a deep breath. There was no point denying it. "Yes. But you lived to a ripe old age."

"I mustn't ask too much."

"Probably best."

"None of it will come to pass if I do. That's the way it works. We're only meant to know so much and then, if we step over that line, the future is rewritten."

"I didn't know that, but I suppose it makes some kind of sense." Especially if someone had died, then not died, as Caroline had.

Caroline turned from the railing and faced Alli head on. "I was going to kill myself, you know. That day when the record company dropped me."

"I know," Alli said quietly. "I saw that version in one of my… episodes. Oh, I didn't see you kill yourself. Someone came here, distraught, with the terrible news. I won't say anymore. Thank goodness it didn't happen."

"You gave me hope. A kind of life raft, I suppose. That's when I realized who you were. Who you were in my life, I mean."

"I'm glad it worked out."

"Now we know who we are to each other, there's one more thing that must happen."

"Hang on a second. You might know who I am to you, but does that necessarily follow that I only exist to be your after-death? Don't I get a say in this?"

"Did I?"

Alli had no answer for that. "So, what is this 'one more thing that must happen'?"

"We must join."

"What?"

"Spiritually. You have to enter my mind and I'll enter yours. We join on a spiritual level."

"And what happens then?"

"We become one."

"I don't like the sound of that."

Caroline took a step closer. Alli stood and backed away, through the open glass door and into the living room. Caroline came closer, her eyes seeming to grow larger. She fixed Alli with a gaze she couldn't break away from.

"Stop this. Stop it now." Alli's pleas sounded hollow even to her own ears. She was fading – her consciousness becoming overwhelmed. Alli fought against the onslaught of Caroline's thoughts, consciousness, fears and anxieties as they swamped her own. She must resist the ideas that weren't hers, memories she had never made and.... A face appeared. One her Caroline-self recognized instantly.

Lucius Hartmann.

"Let go." The voice took on a hypnotic quality. "Let go, Allegra. Let Caroline fill your mind and your soul. Then you will begin to understand. You will be whole...."

Swirling shapes and colors, rich and vibrant in vivid purples, oranges, reds and yellows sailed past her. Alli 'remembered' an orphanage. Nuns in severe black habits, their faces stern and dictatorial. Beatings with a ruler. The pain sharp and intense across her knuckles. Her cries of anguish ignored. Then older, the same punishment but this time defiance replaced her tears. The nuns' long forefingers pointed at her, their voices admonishing her time and time again, the volume building to a cacophony, a dark vortex of sound, spiraling ever downward, deeper and deeper into the underworld.

And there was another presence down there. Its vileness, devoid of any soul, polluted the atmosphere, robbing it of all purity. An entity that fed on lost souls and gave back only misery and despair. Alli had encountered it before.

She filled her lungs with all the air she could scrape from the interminable descent. She opened her mouth wide. Wider than it had ever opened.

Alli screamed again and again...so loud the sides of the vortex rumbled, then imploded. The colors shattered into millions of tiny shards of glittering crystal. They showered down far below her ability to see.

Then she came to rest and gradually sounds drifted toward her. Birdsong, an owl hooting some way off.

"Alli? Alli, wake up."

Someone calling her. Yes, that was it. Someone was calling her.

She opened her eyes and looked around.

"Where am I?"

CHAPTER THIRTEEN

Darkness surrounded her, cloaking her in a shroud that was at once comforting and, within seconds, menacing. She fought it off. Struggled to breathe. Pushed hard, resisting its temptation to sink deeper into a cocoon of softness.

"Alli, Alli. Wake up, please."

The male voice seemed to sail in and out of her consciousness. Although it sounded familiar, she couldn't put a name to it. British accent. That's all she knew for certain.

"Alli."

That voice was different. Female. It sounded urgent and panicked. Where was she? *Who* was she? Alli. That was her name. But she had another name. It eluded her but she knew it was there, somewhere. Lurking just out of sight and earshot.

Caroline. That was it. Caroline Rand. That fit....

She sank deeper. The voices faded, then disappeared. The shroud closed in tighter around her. Someone had orchestrated this, taking over her mind until she no longer knew who she was.

An indistinct figure far in the distance seemed to beckon to her and she followed, not wanting to, but unable to stop herself.

As she drew closer, the darkness fell away, little by little. A dim light took hold, dispelling the gloom, growing brighter with every step she took. Music drifted toward her. A song she remembered. 'Different Drum'. Linda Ronstadt had sung the version everyone remembered, but this was.... A vision flashed into her mind, on stage. A girl with long blonde hair, singing that song. An audience dancing along to the beat. But the girl was *her*. And she was loving every second of it. Disembodied, she still felt an attachment to the body singing her heart out below her, while her consciousness floated above. Her voice sounded true and pure, not cracking a single note.

The backing band – four men, all long hair, bell-bottom jeans, two guitarists, a keyboard player and a drummer. They had played together for a year or more now. Printer's Devil's Due. That's what they called themselves.

She finished the song to rapturous applause and became aware of being watched from the wings. She frowned and turned her attention back to the audience. Instantly, the smile was back on her face as the band eased into the next song and the gentle strains of 'Lady Gossamer' whipped the audience into a frenzy of cheers. Alli felt the exhilaration flowing through Caroline's veins.

"Oh, you like this one a little bit?"

The audience cheered harder. Caroline glanced into the wings, where a male figure moved. For a second, a tangible stab of fear punctured her heart and Alli winced at the pain. Then Caroline remembered her audience, focused on them once again and smiled. "Thank you all for buying it. It's great to be back here in Sheffield. I've been away too long."

So, this was her home crowd? Or maybe Caroline said that wherever she went.

"Alli, wake up. Please, we're so worried about you."

The stage, the audience and Caroline vanished. Alli opened her eyes and stared around the room. "I know where I am. I'm in your house." She indicated Nancy. "You're Nancy and you're Mike." She pointed at him and instantly seemed to fall back into herself, feeling a presence drag itself out of her, leaving confusion and exhaustion in its wake.

The other two exchanged confused looks. Mike said, "Of course we are. Alli, what's happening? You've been so weird. Like now. It's as if you're someone else. You didn't seem to know who we were or where you were...."

Alli put her hands to her head. She felt muzzy, almost hungover. "I don't know. It was all so strange. I was looking down on myself. At least, I thought it was me. But it was Caroline. She was on stage. I'm pretty sure

Lucius Hartmann was watching from the wings, and she seemed scared of him or wary at least."

"He's still doing it, isn't he?" Mike asked. "Only now he's controlling *you*."

Alli shot off the couch. "What?"

"He's wormed his way inside you, Alli. I don't know how, or why, but he has."

"It should be me."

Nancy's remark took Alli even further off guard. "What do you mean, Nancy?"

Nancy's look was one of pure jealousy. What she had to be jealous of was anyone's guess. As far as Alli was concerned, she could take and keep whatever seemed to have the ability to manipulate her thoughts any time it liked.

"I mean, *I'm* the one related to Caroline," Nancy said in an almost petulant tone. "*I'm* her granddaughter. It should be me having the encounters and experiences in Laurel Canyon and in my house. Ever since you arrived, Alli, I've felt her slipping away from me. Away from me and into you."

She sounded like a fractious child. "I don't believe I'm hearing this," Alli said, resisting the temptation to take hold of Nancy and shake her. "*You're* the one who wanted this sorted out. You brought us here to get rid of the haunting and everything going on here. Do you think I want any of this? To have my mind and body taken over? To feel I'm being manipulated not only by some dead Svengali but by another entity even more evil? You got us all into this mess and now *you're* envious of *me*?"

"I should be the one Lucius wants to connect with. Not you. This isn't your legacy. It's mine."

"Dear God," Mike said. "Have you heard yourself, Nan? The man was a psychopathic control freak. Whether he made financial gain out of it or whether it was some almighty control trip, I have no idea. But you've seen how upsetting this has been for Alli."

Nancy laughed – the coldest, most cynical laugh Alli could remember hearing. "Upsetting? She loves every moment of it. All this attention.

Tripping off to Laurel Canyon and meeting the greatest musicians of the day. All the things I would give anything to experience. Plus, she gets to connect with *my* grandmother."

"*Enough*," Alli said. "Frankly, Nancy, you're lucky we both stayed. And that could change at any moment."

"No, it couldn't," Nancy said, her lips taut. "Have you looked out there recently?"

Outside, white mist swirled around, masking everything and giving off a faint silvery glow in the reflected artificial light.

"Switch off the lights," Alli said.

Mike threw the switch. It took a moment for their eyes to adjust.

"Can you see anything?" Alli asked Mike. "Anything at all, apart from this fucking fog?"

"Not a thing. It doesn't look right somehow." Its glimmering swirls were anything but natural. They seemed orchestrated.

"It isn't natural," Nancy said. She was standing inches away from Mike, who was next to Alli. All three stared out of the window at the mesmerizing mist.

"So, what is it then, Nancy?" Alli asked. "Since you seem to know all about it."

"If I said the mists of time, I wouldn't be too far from the truth."

"Stop all this beating about the bush," Alli said. "Tell us exactly what's going on."

"Very well. You've heard the term, 'suspend disbelief'? That's what you need to do now."

"I think we passed that point some time ago," Alli said.

"Maybe *you* did. Mike, on the other hand...."

"What?" Mike took hold of Nancy's shoulders and shook her.

"Let go," she said.

He let his hands fall.

"That's better."

Nancy's voice was changing, becoming deeper. "Caroline isn't dead. She is very much alive and in this house. In fact, she is in this very room with us now. You just can't see her."

"Is she inside me?" Alli asked.

"She was, and I think you know that anyway. Right now she's standing over by the door. Can't you see her?"

Alli and Mike both focused on the partially open door.

"I can't see anything," Alli said.

"Me neither."

"Look again and this time, suspend disbelief. Don't filter out. Allow anything and everything in."

Alli concentrated. Her mind was telling her there was nothing there but, in front of her, a figure of a woman was beginning to take shape. "Caroline?"

"I told you she was there," Nancy said, a note of sheer triumph in her voice. "Now, Mike, do you see her?"

"All I can see are shadows."

"Try again." Nancy's face had taken on an almost beatific expression.

Alli touched his arm. "She's there, Mike. She's standing right by the door and she's smiling. Oh...no...no...."

Caroline's beautiful face was aging, and she knew it. Alli watched, horrified, as the woman raised her hands, with their yellowed nails and gnarled, arthritic joints. She touched her face and let out a cry of animal pain. Her hair came out in golden clumps, turning dull gray as she let them fall to the floor, where they writhed like snakes before coming to rest. The tall, straight, young woman grew bent. She leaned heavily on the door frame and wept bitterly.

Inside herself, Alli felt a horrible tugging that twisted, cramping her stomach. She bent over, clutching the couch for support, and broke off eye contact with the dying creature who, mere seconds earlier, had seemed so alive and vibrant.

Nancy started to laugh. Her face was contorted and maniacal and her skin had turned yellowish-gray.

Mike reached out and slapped her hard, sending her reeling across the room.

At the door, the figure collapsed and disintegrated to white ash before disappearing.

Alli struggled to get on her knees. "Help me. For God's sake, Mike, help me." She sank to the floor, her gut slowly unclenching.

A few feet away, Nancy reached out, her hand as clawed and aged as Caroline's had been. Her long blonde hair faded to a dirty-white. Her clothes transformed into rags, torn and filthy so that she looked like an old woman who had lived on the street for decades.

"This isn't real," Alli said, but, inside her mind, the hellish voice she had heard before spoke so distinctly she wondered if it had been out loud.

This is my reality.

Alli's mouth dried until she was tasting sticky ashes.

Mike took a tentative step forward and reached out a hand to Nancy.

"*No!* Don't touch her." Alli had no idea why she cried out, only that she must stop him.

Mike dropped his hand.

The pleading, aged woman faded from sight and was gone.

"That wasn't Nancy," Alli said. "It was an illusion to scare us."

"Lucius Hartmann again?" Mike's lips set in a firm line. "Ever the master of ceremonies."

In her heart Alli could almost hear the artist laugh. "He does it because he can. It amuses him. It always did when he was alive and even more so, now he's dead. Death has released him. He's no longer bound by any conventional laws of nature. He's free to make up his own. Or he would like us to think he is. But there's someone far stronger than him. Someone who belongs to this house."

Mike stared at her, wide-eyed.

Nancy wandered in, looking disorientated. "What's going on? I found myself in the kitchen, but I don't know how I got there. We were in here, weren't we? Oh, my God, the picture...."

Alli and Mike spun round to face it. Alli stared in disbelief. She dashed over and picked up the shards of canvas and broken frame. "We were here. This isn't possible."

Mike touched the ripped and shredded painting. "It looks like someone took a sharp knife to it."

But the damage clicked off a different thought in Alli's mind. "Look at the pattern. It's like a large cat has clawed it and here –" she indicated some deep punctures "– teeth. Sharp canine teeth would do this." Alli dropped the painting as if it had burned her. "What animal could do such a thing? And how did it get here?"

"Another one of Hartmann's little games?" Mike said. "Not funny, Lucius." His voice echoed around the walls.

Alli shivered. Carpets, curtains, furniture, all should combine to muffle any such echo. Her throat closed up and she coughed. "Is it me, or has the air gone, sort of…thick?" She coughed again.

Mike wiped his eyes. "It smells like incense. Not the fragranced sort. The stuff they burn in censers in Catholic churches. Reminds me of my childhood." He broke off to cough violently.

Nancy put her finger to her lips. "Can you hear it?"

Alli listened. With the windows closed, they shouldn't be able to hear any noise from outside, but the noise of chanting drifted toward them from far away. "Is there a church near here? Or a monastery?"

"You're standing in it," Nancy said. "Don't forget Canonbury Manor used to be an abbey. It's only been a house for three hundred years or so—"

"It's getting closer." Alli hugged herself against the sudden chill that had filled the room. It seemed to have penetrated inside from that weird mist. She shivered, so cold, her mind felt numb. She couldn't allow this. *I have to concentrate.* First, she must warm herself. "I need to get a jacket from upstairs. Anyone fancy coming up with me?"

No answer. The other two stood almost statue-like. Frozen in fear? Alli couldn't hang around to speculate. Hell, her teeth were chattering and her breath misting. Somewhere, close outside the house, she had the sense of a large animal prowling. Imagination? Another of Hartmann's tricks? No, not Hartmann, whoever or whatever was really orchestrating things here.

At least the clogged air had dissipated, along with the smell of incense. But the thought of going up the stairs in this unnaturally quiet house was terrifying. Nothing for it, she *had* to do it. She sped past the clock, up the stairs and into her room.

Alli took her jacket down from its hanger in the wardrobe and thrust her arms into the sleeves before turning to leave the room and rejoin the others. She turned to the doorway, and froze.

In the hallway outside, shadows glided past, making their way steadily along the landing. The chanting grew to full pitch and she had the impression of monks in their dark habits, their hoods pulled over their heads, moving as one. The smell of incense wafted toward her as a swirling smoke shadow licked the landing walls, floated in through the open door and caressed the inner walls of her bedroom. It didn't touch her but left a cold draft and a stench of compost in its wake as it slithered out of the doorway and caressed the last figure in the procession. She could only see him in profile. It was enough to recognize him. Abbot Weaver.

He had stopped in front of the open doorway, his position fixed, aware of her presence. The waves of evil that wafted from him, tangible and spreading like tendrils through the space between them, made her shrink back into the room. Still, they spread. They were searching. Looking for…her? Surely, they could have taken her anytime they chose. She was exposed. Nowhere to hide from such an entity. Yet, as the figure of the abbot moved on, the tendrils left with him, curling their way out of the door.

Sure they had moved away, Alli dared to peer around her door. She could make out no words from the monks. Merely plainsong, a droning incantation repeated incessantly, echoing, becoming less distinct, but in no way resembling anything she had ever heard from any church choir. This was the obscene cacophony she had heard once before. It chilled her blood. Especially when she saw them turn into Nancy's room. Of course, they would be making for the entrance to the attic, or maybe down to the cellar.

Alli waited, dry mouthed, until the last of the shadows disappeared from view. Only the lingering aroma of frankincense remained. It should have been a reassuring, cleansing smell. It wasn't. And her unanswered question hammered again and again in her brain. Why hadn't the creature taken her? It seemed to be playing with her. Everything that went on here, everything that scared them at least, was a game to someone. *But who, and why?*

She made her way downstairs, pausing to look over her shoulder at regular intervals. Nothing followed. Only the faint tick of the clock, which seemed to grow louder the farther she descended.

Without warning, the clock chimed.

Alli almost missed her footing and her heart pounded painfully as she grabbed the stair rail. She took a second to steady herself.

Nancy and Mike appeared from the living room. Alli counted. Nine times it chimed. Nine p.m.

They waited until the final echo faded.

"The atmosphere's changed. Can't you feel it?" Nancy asked.

Mike didn't reply. His eyes wide, he stared around him, as if seeing things no one else could.

"What is it, Mike?" Alli asked, finishing her descent and joining them. "What can you see?"

"Nothing," he said. "I can see absolutely nothing."

And then Alli's world changed again.

She was alone in the living room. The door opened. Instantly, the atmosphere became charged.

The man who entered wasn't overly tall. He wasn't particularly prepossessing. He stood possibly five feet ten inches, with a not particularly fit build and graying brown hair, which was receding, giving him a high forehead. His moustache was salt and pepper in color, and he was smoking what looked like a black Sobranie with a gold tip. Instinctively she knew his identity.

Lucius Hartmann.

He fixed her with a penetrating stare, his eyes so dark, they were almost black. Maybe they *were* black. In contrast, the sclera shone brilliant white. Almost too bright. They stared deep into her brain. He seemed confused for some reason. As if what he read in her wasn't what he was expecting.

When he spoke, his voice was lightly accented. Romanian perhaps, or Czech? "Allegra Sinclair. You are from a musical family, I believe. They called you Allegra, though you prefer not to use it."

"I don't have their talent for music, and that name never suited me," Alli said, surprised at herself at the bold way she addressed this man. Yet, seeing him up close like this, he wasn't much to look at. Not tall, not possessing the sort of charisma his reputation would suggest. And his expression seemed to carry with it a perpetual sneer that was not so much intimidating as irritating. His voice grated on her.

"Where do your talents lie…Allegra?"

"I seem to have a gift for time travel," she said, concentrating on keeping her voice firm. She would show this…man…entity…no fear, even though her heart felt as if it were about to explode.

"Of course you do, my dear."

"What?"

"You don't really think this is real, do you? Perhaps your concept of reality and fantasy is a little compromised." Lucius waved his hand, and she was in the garden. It was nighttime, and she was alone, but at least that awful mist had lifted.

Alli clutched her jacket closer to her and looked around. In front of her, Canonbury Manor gleamed ghostly in the moonlight. Its pale sandstone reflected the silvery light. Inside the house, lights burned in the downstairs rooms.

She approached the building, up the short flight of stone steps to the parking area where her car stood, still alone. Where had Mike parked his? It didn't matter now anyway. She reached the front door and tried the handle. As she had suspected. Locked. Alli rang the bell, heard it echo inside and waited. No one came to answer. She rang again and banged hard on the door. Again nothing.

Alli made her way round to the living room. The curtains were open, with all the lamps and lights on, enabling her to see straight through. No one there.

She continued moving around the house, peering through windows, some lit, others dark. Finally, she arrived at the back door, which opened into the kitchen. Once again, she turned the handle. This time she was in luck. To her surprise, it turned, and the door opened, allowed her to enter, then issued an audible click as the lock engaged once more.

Alli switched lights on and passed through the kitchen to the main hallway. She called up the stairs.

"Nancy? Mike? Are you here?" She listened hard. She could barely hear the tick of the clock now. The time read twenty-five minutes after ten. She had lost over an hour.

Alli made her way up the stairs, her ears alert for any sound, however slight.

Nothing disturbed the eerie silence.

Nothing except the smell of frankincense....

It hung in the air. She could see gray-blue wisps of its smoke swirling above her head.

Alli reached the landing, the taste of tangible fear in her mouth, bitter and astringent. The incense made her eyes water. From the far end of the corridor, sounds of softly strumming acoustic guitars and people laughing drifted toward her. She moved slowly toward the source of the sound. It grew louder with each step she took.

She was outside a closed door she hadn't been through before. Whatever – whoever – was creating that music and laughter, was behind that door. Hesitantly, she put out her hand, willing herself to turn the door handle. She drew back and moistened dry lips. Someone was singing and she recognized the voice. Caroline Rand. Not 'Lady Gossamer' this time. Alli didn't know this song. Other sounds...clinking glasses, the occasional cough. How many people were in there? And, if she went in, which world would she be entering? Right now, with everything that had happened, anything seemed possible.

I have to find out.

Alli took a deep breath and opened the door.

The room was empty.

The walls were painted a soft creamy white, with a pale peach tone. The drapes were floor length and in a contrasting rust shade. The floor was polished hardwood. There was not one stick of furniture in sight. Evidently this was a spare bedroom Nancy hadn't done anything with yet except for redecorating.

Alli's sandals made a soft tapping noise as she stepped into the room. It still smelled faintly of new paint. No trace of incense. No sound of music from anywhere.

Alli half ran to the window and looked out over the gardens. The cloudless sky gave full vent to the silver light of the moon as it cast a glow, turning the grass a ghostly gray green. Deep shadows cloaked the bushes and trees whose uppermost branches stretched their twiggy fingers into the sky.

"A beautiful night, isn't it?"

Alli let out a gasp and spun round. She knew that voice. Lucius Hartmann again, but he was nowhere to be seen. The room was still empty. She ran out, raced down the stairs and threw open the kitchen door.

Nancy and Mike looked up, startled. They were drinking mugs of steaming liquid. Tea maybe.

Alli stared at them. "Is any of this real? Are *you* real?"

Mike stood and came over to her. "Come and sit down, Alli. You look like you've seen a ghost."

"Maybe I have. Maybe I'm looking at two right now."

"Whatever do you mean by that?" Nancy asked.

Alli hadn't a clue what she meant. She shook her head.

"I'll get you some tea." Nancy stood and went over to the kettle.

"Where were you both?" Alli asked. She knew her tone sounded sharp, unfriendly even.

"We've been here," Mike said, a bemused expression on his face.

"Why didn't you answer the door? I rang and knocked. You must have heard me."

Mike shook his head. "We've been sitting here for ages. You left us in the living room to go upstairs because you were feeling chilly. I see you got your jacket."

"Yes, but that was before...."

"Before what?" Nancy set down a steaming mug of strong tea in front of Alli. "Do you take sugar?"

Do I take sugar?

"No, I don't. Thank you," Alli added, trying to keep some kind of lid on her anger. "Look, I found myself outside. That was after Lucius Hartmann paid a visit."

The other two looked at her blankly.

"Then Hartmann…. I mean, I found myself outside. The kitchen door was unlocked so I suppose it was my time to come in. Needless to say, it locked itself straight after."

Mike gave no reaction. He sipped his tea.

"You weren't here, nor were you anywhere else in the house. I know. I checked the rooms. I called out to you. You didn't reply. Then Hartmann…." She couldn't go on. A voice was telling her not to. Her own warning voice. She found she didn't want to tell them about the monks, the entity she had encountered, Lucius's presence in the empty room. She didn't want to share any of it. The two people in front of her had become almost strangers in the past few minutes.

"We've been here around an hour now, I would guess," Mike said, glancing at the wall clock. "We wondered where you'd got to. To be honest, the time just went. We've been tossing ideas around. Trying to make some sense of what's happening here."

Alli struggled to restore normality to her voice. "And what have you concluded?"

"Not much, I'm afraid."

Nancy sat down at the island. "Come and sit with us, Alli. We need to keep together."

That was rich. Alli couldn't help herself. Anger swelled inside her. "I couldn't agree more. That's why I find your behavior so strange."

Mike banged his hand down on the table, rattling the mugs. "If we knew what the hell you're talking about it would help. What are we supposed to have done? We didn't hear you trying to get in. We didn't even know you'd managed to go outside."

"Neither did I until I found myself there."

"You've had another experience, haven't you?" Nancy said.

Despite her resolve to keep her most recent experience to herself, she had to tell them something. "Whatever lies in this house is bringing old memories to life and everything is linked together. Hartmann, what's been happening to the picture, Abbot Weaver, all of it. It's linked together. It has to be."

From the hallway, the clock chimed.

The three exchanged glances. "It's done that once tonight already," Mike said.

Alli and Nancy followed him into the hall. The clock struck nine and stopped. The clock face still read ten twenty-five.

Images began to form, seemingly born from the walls. These were different to the ones Alli had seen upstairs. For one thing, Abbot Weaver and his creeping entity didn't appear to be with them. Shadows danced all around them. Misty shapes moved past them, dressed in monks' habits. These shapes were ghostly, ethereal, their faces devoid of features, their hoods drawn over a black emptiness.

One of them swung a hefty, bejeweled censer. Clouds of purple-, blue- and charcoal-colored smoke filled the hall. Mike, Nancy and Alli coughed and spluttered as the smoke choked them. The monks ignored them, and carried on their way, out through the closed main entrance door at the end.

The air cleared the moment the last of them departed. Alli raced to the large window in the living room and peered out. No sign of the monks. But there was a faint shadow, shimmering. A familiar face.

"Caroline," Alli said.

"You can see her?" Nancy stepped forward.

"Can't you?"

Nancy shook her head.

Caroline was standing mere inches away. She put her finger to her lips and faded from sight.

"She's not there now," Alli said.

Nancy shook her head. "I don't understand why she still appears to you more than she's ever appeared to me."

"I'm sorry, Nancy," Alli said. "I don't have control over this."

"Come on," Mike said. "Let's go back and finish that tea."

Alli followed him into the kitchen.

And back fifty years.

CHAPTER FOURTEEN

Alli came to in the hall of Canonbury Manor. One glance told her it was in an earlier time. Not too far back though, judging by a canvas leaning against the stairs. The picture was all psychedelic swirls and a dreamy model, painted by Sara Moon, according to the signature. Probably destined to be hung in a bedroom.

She heard a slight snuffling noise coming from the kitchen and tiptoed to the door.

"Caroline?" she said.

The young woman looked over at her. She had been crying. Her cheeks were stained with mascara and her eyes red and puffy. Her stringy hair looked in need of a good wash and she had lost a considerable amount of weight, so much so that her dingy t-shirt hung off her.

"Alli. It's you. How did you know where to find me?"

"I didn't. You found me, I think. Anyway, here I am and here you are. And...." Alli was trying to take in her new surroundings. This was Canonbury Manor when Caroline first lived here. The kitchen was rustic by any standards. A large, old-fashioned Aga cooker took up a major part of one side of the room.

In the center stood a slightly battered, plain wooden circular table and four ladder-backed chairs, each with a seat cushion tied on with cotton ribbons. Caroline was sitting on one, a box of tissues in front of her. Alli pulled a chair back and it scraped across the flagstone floor. She sat and drew herself closer to the table, which was covered in a red-and-white-checked cloth. A washing machine looked as if it had been borrowed from a museum, and Alli had to remind herself that it was probably the latest thing in 1970 or whenever this was. A large, cream-colored refrigerator hummed to itself in a corner. It looked similar to one her grandmother had owned.

"Tell me what's happened, Caroline. Why are you here? Have you left Laurel Canyon for good now?"

Caroline didn't answer. She withdrew another tissue from the box and wiped her eyes, succeeding only in smearing her mascara still further. Alli waited. Finally, Caroline took a deep breath.

"The new recording contract was okay, but I couldn't get anything going in the States. Lucius told me he knew someone in London who could get me a better deal than the one I had with Dark Secret." A tear trickled down her cheek. "I shouldn't have gone against him, Alli. Signing contracts behind his back. He was furious, but I thought I could do it. I did what you said and made my own decision for once. Fat lot of good it did me. Lucius told me I had to come back to Britain. He wouldn't handle me if I stayed in LA."

"What about your manager? Isn't he looking out for you?"

Caroline shook her head. "I fired him. Lucius found out he was swindling me. He'd done me out of millions, apparently. Lucius has found this new guy. Arthur Sedgemoor. He's got loads of contacts and can get me the best record deal. I don't know what I would have done without Lucius. He's been my rock these past months."

Alli snorted involuntarily. "If things are looking up, how come you're in this state?"

Caroline shot her an angry look. "I'm just a bit...tired...that's all. I've been really busy these past weeks."

A whiff of sour, unwashed body swam past Alli's nostrils. "Too busy to take care of your personal hygiene?"

Caroline blinked reddened eyes at her. "I forget sometimes. I get distracted."

"Strung out more like. And I bet I know who keeps you like this. It would suit his purpose, wouldn't it? Lucius Hartmann."

"Lucius looks after me."

"Oh, come on. Wake up, Caroline."

"He does. He's the only one who doesn't steal from me. Oh, I know what people say about him – that he controls me. I've heard all the gibes and the jokes. They say I don't dare breathe without asking his permission, but that's not true, Alli. It isn't."

Alli felt a wave of pity for the pleading eyes. Who was Caroline trying to fool? Only herself.

"Look at you, Caroline. When did you last have a shower? When did you last eat? Where is this wonderful person who cares about you so much? Because from where I'm sitting, he couldn't care less."

"Don't say that!" Tears welled up in Caroline's eyes and spilled over onto her cheeks. "He's away now. Over in the States, looking after my interests and trying to get some of my money back from that swindler."

"And who's paying for that little jaunt? Him? Or you?"

Caroline broke eye contact and wiped angrily at the tears. "Lucius is the only one who's been here for me."

"He isn't here now."

"I told you…. He's the only one who cares. He helps me. Every day he calls me from L.A. If he didn't, I don't think I'd have the strength to get up in the morning."

"Caroline, listen to me. You don't need him. He's bad news. You need to break with him for good. You don't need him in your life. What has he got you on, pills?"

Of course, this was the era of pills. Pills to get you up in the morning, pills to keep you going, pills to bring you down at night because you were so hyper from the pills you'd consumed during the day. Highly addictive little pills. Barbiturates.

"How long has it been going on?"

Caroline shrugged. "A while."

"Why did you start taking that stuff?" Alli asked.

"I was feeling down one day. Lucius called a doctor."

"I'll bet he's not registered with the National Health Service," Alli muttered.

Caroline stared at her blankly.

"What are you taking?"

Caroline stood, wavering. It seemed like a tremendous effort to put one foot in front of the other. "I'm sorry, it's a bit early in the day for me."

Alli had no real idea what time it was here. Judging by the daylight, it had to be afternoon.

Caroline opened a reluctant kitchen drawer, took out a handful of bottles and returned to the table. She slid them across to Alli. Sure enough, none of the bottles bore a pharmacy label. She recognized some of the names from a misspent youth spent reading Jacqueline Susann's *Valley of the Dolls*. Of course, Ric had found a copy of it in the attic of this very house. Nembutal, Dexedrine, others she had never heard of. Bottle after bottle.

"Dear God, Caroline. People die from taking this stuff."

Caroline stared straight ahead. Alli wondered if she was even aware of her. She decided to take another tack. "These are not on a normal prescription. Who's paying for this shit?"

Caroline's eyes opened wide. "I am, I suppose."

"You mean you don't know? You never actually hand over any money?"

"No. Never."

"Don't you find that a bit odd?"

"Not really. I don't usually pay for things. Lucius takes care of all that for me."

"And before him, Harrison Grant?"

Caroline nodded.

"Have you any idea how much money you have?"

"Not really. Not now. I know that a few months ago I had nothing. Less than nothing. I owed the IRS thousands because of Harrison and I'm not the only one he swindled. He disappeared off to the Caribbean somewhere and I haven't a cat in hell's chance of getting my money back from him. Lucius says it's best to cut my losses and regroup over here."

The story sounded like an earlier copy of her own. For Harrison Grant, substitute Lincoln Wardrow. "So, you bought this house, then?"

Caroline nodded and gave a weak smile. "Lucius arranged it. It was a bargain. Of course, it needs work and it'll take a long time. But it's mine, Alli. Mine. The first time in my life I've ever had a home I can truly call my own. And my money's invested now...."

Alli had to remind herself that Caroline had indeed died a wealthy woman although, at this moment, looking at her, she found herself wondering how.

All roads led to Lucius Hartmann. Successful artist he may have been, but he had also taken total control over Caroline and her money, consolidating that by ensuring she remained in a perpetual drugged-up state so that she wouldn't ask awkward questions. Unless, presumably, he needed her for some other reason. Then he would sober her up. It all made sense. No doubt Hartmann had Power of Attorney over her legal affairs so any shady business deals would be transacted in her name and she would be none the wiser.

Alli was about to try and get through to her when, without warning, Caroline began to change. Her face took on a healthier glow, her hair seemed to fill out and it gleamed. Her clothes went from dirty and wrinkled to clean and pressed. Through the entire metamorphosis, Caroline seemed unaware. To Alli, while nothing outwardly changed, time seemed to speed up, hours, days, maybe even weeks passed. Or maybe no time at all. It was all so confusing. Like being on a fairground ride. A rollercoaster.

Once Caroline's transformation was complete, a frown creased her face. "I feel strange," she said. "I'm scared and I don't honestly know why. I love this house, but I don't understand it. I know that sounds crazy…. Look, come with me, I need to show you what I found."

The change in Caroline's appearance had been so sudden and unexpected, at least as unexpected as finding her here in that awful state. Another riddle. Unless…. What if this was simply another episode in her life that Alli was intended to witness?

Alli followed Caroline out of the kitchen into the hall. The stairs were the same as in the present, if a little creakier, and covered in a traditional wool stair carpet, worn threadbare in places.

Upstairs, paint had peeled off the walls along the landing. By contrast, Caroline's room was pleasantly chintz, with white gloss paintwork covering every inch of wood. Wallpaper in a gray Regency stripe adorned the walls. Floral bedcoverings and matching curtains completed the pseudo-eighteenth-century revivalist theme.

"It's through here," Caroline said, and opened the door to the attic stairs.

Up there, the room was familiar, up to a point. The walls were bare stone, with no psychedelic swirls and no Sixties paraphernalia of any kind. Instead, a stone ledge stood where Alli remembered the urn had rested on a cloth. Now a relic of a very different kind sat there.

A crucifix. Christ's body, pierced by vicious, protruding nails, but hung upside down.

"Gruesome, isn't it?" Caroline whispered. "I found it like this when I first discovered this room. Don't you feel there's a strange atmosphere up here?"

"There's a smell. Like decayed leaves," Alli said, and gagged. "It's making me feel sick."

"That's how I feel. It's not healthy up here, and I want to cleanse it. I spoke to Lucius about it and he suggested a party. Arthur didn't think it was a good idea at first. He said I would be better selling up and moving out. He said this house is cursed."

"Arthur had a point."

Caroline looked at her curiously. "I didn't know you knew Arthur Sedgemoor."

"I don't. I...heard of him recently."

A shadow flitted past, almost out of Alli's vision. She tried to ignore it, but she knew it was listening, watching, and its presence was threatening to her. Caroline seemed oblivious.

Alli cleared her throat. "Now Arthur Sedgemoor is your manager, you don't really need Lucius to be part of your life, do you?"

Caroline shook her head. "I couldn't possibly leave Lucius. He's my rock."

Given the transformation downstairs, Alli needed to know how aware Caroline now was. "What about the pills?"

Caroline moistened her lips. "That's all over with. Arthur told me about this amazing clinic, and I checked in while Lucius was in the States. Six weeks I spent there and now I'm clean and healthy, as you can see. Lucius was amazed when he got back. I didn't tell him anything about it. I wanted it to be a surprise. You should have seen his face." She laughed. "It was a picture."

"I'll bet it was," Alli said, as she tried to adapt to what Caroline had just told her. Down in the kitchen, maybe a couple of months of Caroline's life had slipped by in a matter of a few minutes.

"Anyway, Arthur and Lucius had a long talk and sorted out some differences. Arthur agrees with Lucius about the house now, so I'll throw that party and we'll make this home a happy one."

Alli seized her chance. "Caroline, don't you realize what Lucius is doing? Arthur was right to express misgivings about this place. He was right to tell you to sell up and leave. Now Lucius has got to him and—"

Something pushed Alli in the small of her back and she fell forward.

Caroline broke her fall. "Are you all right? Do you feel faint?"

Alli let Caroline steer her to a chair, as a sharp pain scythed through her lower back. "As crazy as this will sound to you, this house doesn't want me interfering. There's a presence here that works with Lucius to keep you under control. That's why you feel scared about this place, Caroline, and you're right to fear it. You have to leave here, and you have to sever all connections with Hartmann. Before it's too late."

Caroline dropped her hands from Alli's shoulders and stepped back.

"There's so much I don't understand…. It's as if there's a door closed in my mind and I can't open it. I…feel strange. As if I'm not really here. All I know is we're connected in some way, Alli. You and me."

The pain receded slightly but Alli still struggled for breath. "I feel it too. I get a strange kind of electric shock when I touch you."

"I feel…. I need to warn you about…. I don't know what. It's…. *No!*" Her cry was of an animal in pain. Torment. She staggered backward, grabbed her head in both hands and doubled up, strangulated cries issuing one after the other.

Alli reached out to her. Some kind of force field prevented contact. Her hand bounced off its invisible surface again and again. Alli fell to her knees, exhausted. All her energy had drained out of her in a second. All she could hear was Caroline's cries. The lights extinguished. The room grew dark.

Alli passed out.

★   ★   ★

Alli opened her eyes. She was lying on the floor. Caroline was busying herself, tidying the room as if nothing of Alli's last few conscious moments had happened.

Caroline caught sight of Alli, and a smile lit up her face. "Oh good, you're awake again. You must have been tired. One minute you were looking at the crucifix and the next you were flat out, asleep."

Alli sat up and shook her head, which felt muzzy, like a hangover but without the headache. "Don't you remember what happened?"

A puzzled look replaced the smile. "Just now? Nothing."

"You don't remember me warning you about Lucius? You screamed in agony. You can't remember any of it? You told me you had to warn me. What about?"

Caroline stared at her. "Wow, those were some powerful dreams you had. Mind you, I'm not surprised. This place is enough to give anyone nightmares. Lucius is right. This is the place to have a cleansing."

Why would Lucius suggest that?

"So, you're going ahead with this party then?"

"Of course. It's the best way."

"If you say so."

"Oh, it's not going to be a wild, drunken orgy. No, it'll be quiet, respectful, spiritual."

This was getting weirder by the second. "Lucius is suggesting you hold a spiritual party? What the hell is one of those?"

"A few of us – and we have to be serious about it if it's going to work – get together. Firstly, we burn incense to cleanse the air, then sage. We sing and chant, we paint symbols on the walls. We then perform a full cleansing ritual and, hopefully, all will be well."

"And if it doesn't work?"

Caroline's expression changed. It became serious, older and much more mature. She glanced over her shoulder as if expecting someone to be there. When she spoke, it was in hushed whispers. "I daren't think about that possibility. Things are becoming…difficult."

"Difficult in what way?"

Caroline's expression changed again, back to the late-Sixties hippy. She leaned against the wall and her voice returned to its usual volume. "I feel your skepticism. It's bad karma."

Alli ignored the sudden changes in Caroline's behavior. "Look Caroline, quite apart from what's going on with you, some really strange things have been happening, not only to me, to other people in this house. People you don't know. People you'll never meet—"

Caroline's laughter interrupted her. "I know all about that, Alli. I know the whole damn lot."

"What do you know?"

She leaned over Alli and her voice was barely audible. "I know I die in this house. Eventually. I know it passes to a descendant. My granddaughter. My only heir. If that were true."

Alli whispered her response. "What do you mean, 'if that were true'? Nancy Harper *is* your sole heir. Your daughter's daughter. Her only child."

"Really?"

Alli's mind raced. "I have Nancy's word for it. That's what she knows. She never knew of the relationship until your solicitor summoned her and read her your will."

"How easily we are deceived, Alli. How simple it all is to spin a tale, weave a spell, and then remove it, turn it on its head and then…." She snapped her fingers. "Gone. As if it were never there in the first place."

"I haven't a clue what you're talking about. Can you please explain?"

Caroline seemed to spot something behind Alli. She straightened, and a lighthearted smile lit up her face. "Say you'll come to my party, Alli. Say you'll help cleanse the house."

How could she refuse? For the first time, Alli sensed genuine fear pervading Caroline's entire presence, however ghostly or corporeal that might be. "Fine. When are you going to hold it?"

"Tomorrow. Go back downstairs. I'll join you in a few minutes. Then I'm going to call everyone I know. Everyone who will be sympathetic at any rate."

"And will Lucius be included?"

"I sincerely hope so. He's probably the only one of us who knows how to do this. I haven't a clue." She laughed like a young girl. There was an unnatural quality about her movements and her speech, as if she was trying too hard. Alli shot one final look at the room and grabbed the door handle for support. Dark shadows danced off the walls as a cloak of blackness descended on the ledge – the altar of this strange and forbidding room. Alli couldn't get out of there fast enough. She slammed the door behind her, its unnatural echo following her down the stairs.

The living room was quite different from how it would look in Nancy's time. Now it was dark wood paneling halfway up the walls, original oak exposed beams along the ceiling, heavy dark blue velvet drapes, fringed with long gold tassels.

Alli sat on a worn and sagging sofa, deep in thought. It wasn't long before Caroline joined her. Here she was as Alli had first met her. Vibrant, lively and beautiful, with no trace of the troubled spirit that had fleetingly passed through her in that attic room or of the strung-out barbiturate addict Alli had encountered in the kitchen.

Caroline grabbed the phone off the coffee table next to her, flicked open an address book and began dialing. The phone was answered nearly immediately. By Lucius Hartmann. Caroline told him what she was planning. "You will come won't you, Lucius?…. Yes, she will. She's here already. Isn't that a happy coincidence?…. Yes…. Yes." Her tone had grown serious. Now she seemed unable to look Alli in the eye. "Tomorrow then…. Yes…. 'Bye, Lucius."

She replaced the receiver. "Lucius sends his best wishes and says he's looking forward to seeing you again."

Alli doubted he had uttered one word of that but said nothing.

For the next hour, she sat more or less silently as Caroline called one person after another, including Arthur. Finally satisfied, she replaced the receiver and returned the phone back to the table. "That's eight of us. The rest can't make it, but that's quite all right. We have enough. It's a small room anyway. I think we have all we need. Three of them are bringing colorful paints and brushes and I have some too. Almost everyone has incense and Marla has sage that's been drying in a large bunch in her garage. She's going to tie some up for us and bring it along. Everyone's bringing food and drink, so we don't have to worry about that."

In the hall, the clock struck. Four o'clock. So, back in Caroline's day, the clock worked perfectly. Alli pointed toward the doorway. "Did you buy that clock, or did it come with the house?"

"Oh, it was here. Lovely old thing, isn't it? A bit noisy though. I can't work out how to turn the chime off. Maybe you can. It's very old."

"Caroline, I need to ask you about what you meant upstairs just now. About Nancy not being your grandchild."

"Grandchild?" She shrugged. "I don't know what you mean. I don't even have any children. Not yet anyway."

"But you *have* had a child. A baby girl. You gave her up for adoption. You told me, and I know it's true."

Caroline's eyes clouded over. "I never talk about that. Never." Her voice was rising, tinged with hysteria. "It was a mistake. It should never have happened."

Alli saw the fear in her eyes. "Caroline, listen to me. I need to know the truth. For some reason I don't understand, my life seems to have been taken over by events that have nothing whatever to do with me. Not only that, there are at least two other people involved, apart from your granddaughter, Nancy. People I had never met two days ago. People who only had an acquaintanceship with your granddaughter in common. We've all, in one way or another, been caught up in events that seem to span fifty years and more. Probably centuries more. Won't you help me? Won't you help your granddaughter?"

Caroline's breathing had quickened, and she was panting. She clapped her hands to her ears. "We can't have this conversation. I can't speak of these things. Stop it. Stop it now."

Once again, a black mist descended and Alli slipped into unconsciousness as Caroline's cries faded into the distance.

★   ★   ★

Alli opened her eyes to find herself on the same settee, wearing the same clothes. Caroline was nowhere to be seen, but the sun was shining brightly, pouring through the windows, as if it were morning, rather than late afternoon. Alli struggled to sit up, stretching stiff joints. Footsteps echoed from the hall and Caroline entered. She looked as if nothing had happened. Today she was wearing bell-bottomed velvet pants and a matching top with long sleeves. Her hair streamed down her back and she looked freshly washed, healthy and well rested, with no hint of any substance abuse.

"Ah, there you are. Good morning, Alli. Hope you slept well. I'd have given you a bed, but you were sleeping so soundly I didn't like to wake you."

"So, I've been here all night?"

Caroline looked puzzled. "Yes, of course. It's the party in a few hours, remember."

"So, what's your plan then?"

"Firstly, I'm going to get you some strong coffee. Then you can take a shower or have a relaxing bath. You can borrow my stuff and I'll lend you some fresh clothes as well. Come on, let's get that coffee inside you."

★   ★   ★

It was good coffee. Freshly ground and percolated. The kitchen smelled delicious. Orange juice and toast filled a gnawing hole in Alli's stomach and stopped the impending growls in their tracks.

Half an hour later, she was luxuriating in a deep, warm bath fragranced with some exotic bath oil.

Dried, perfumed and dressed in a flowing red kaftan, Alli made her way downstairs to the kitchen, where the chink of glassware and plates signaled Caroline was getting everything they needed for the party.

She smiled at Alli as she joined her. "I'll leave the serving platters out, along with spoons and so on. Everyone can help themselves whenever they want anything and have the run of the house. You never know, some kindly soul might even do the washing up." Caroline laughed.

Alli smiled. It all seemed so normal. A typical late-Sixties informal decorating party. Her parents had spoken of them. It was the ideal way to get your place done up without it costing more than the price of the paint. In this case, Caroline didn't seem to be even footing the bill for that either.

"I think that's it," she said, setting down a dozen wine glasses and surveying the kitchen table. All we need is guests, food and drink. I'll open a couple of bottles of wine an hour or so before they arrive, and there's chilled beer in the fridge. Everything's going to be fine."

Alli hoped so. But doubted it.

"Let's go up to the room. Make sure everything's…okay up there."

Alli nodded and followed her, her heart already beginning to thump harder than felt comfortable.

In the attic, the heavy atmosphere clung to the walls, the floor. And the….

"It may be an altar," Alli said, "but it's the wrong kind of altar. There's nothing holy about this."

The crucifix had been turned upright and leaned against the wall, on a piece of black velvet.

The expression on the Christ's face was twisted and unnatural. "It's depicting agony," Alli said. "But…."

"It's a mockery of agony."

"That's it, exactly. As if whoever created this hated the subject so intensely, he or she had to defile it."

"What I find so chilling is that it works better when it's upside down." She picked up the crucifix and Alli shuddered. She could no more have touched that abomination than she could have created it in the first place. Caroline seemed to read her thoughts.

She brandished the artifact. "It's only a lump of wood. It can't do any harm."

"If you truly believed that, Caroline, you wouldn't be holding this exorcism party this afternoon."

"Exorcism party? I like that. Henceforward that shall be its name." She held the cross aloft. Alli shrank back from her. There was an odd glow in Caroline's eyes. Aberrant. Her whole face distorted, her eyes became elongated, her lips twisted, her skin gray. Only for an instant until she lowered the crucifix. As soon as she replaced it on the altar, her features returned to normal.

"Probably best not to tempt fate," she said quietly.

"You didn't see your face just then," Alli said.

"What do you mean?"

"Maybe I imagined it…. Never mind. It doesn't matter. A trick of the light, that's all." How could she describe what she had seen? At best Caroline wouldn't believe her and at worst…. But any closer relationship between Caroline and whatever evil existed in this house didn't bear lingering on.

"Come on," Caroline said. "We've done all we can here. We need our guests to play their part."

Alli followed Caroline down the stone steps. As she descended, she wondered how much longer she was intended to stay here, in this time. This was by far the longest she had spent away from her own era.

Down in the hall, Caroline led her past the first few portraits and stood in front of the one nearest the door.

"Here he is, in all his glorious splendor." She read the familiar inscription set into the bottom of the gilt frame. "Hippolytus Weaver. The last abbot of Canonbury. I should get it restored. There are things in the painting that look like symbols of some kind, and, I may be wrong, but they don't look Christian to me. There's a set square and compasses. No great secret there, that's a symbol of Freemasonry. As for the others…. Lucius told me I'm being fanciful, but Arthur pointed it out. Look. There." She tapped her finger on an indistinct figure in the bottom left-hand corner. "Doesn't that resemble a ferocious cat? Those fangs look like a saber-tooth tiger."

Alli forced herself to get closer to the painting and peer closely at the shapes Caroline had indicated. She could see it now. As she peered more closely, she could distinguish another figure lurking in that picture, and it wasn't as easy to make out. Except that it looked familiar.

Despite her reservations about it, Alli touched her finger to the painting right where she had spotted the figure.

"Can you see that?" she said. "That face. I've seen it before."

Caroline looked closely. "Oh yes, I see it. That's weird. It's…it doesn't seem attached to anything. I mean, it's a face, but a face without a body."

Alli withdrew her finger and rubbed it. It was tingling unpleasantly as if it had been stuck in a tub of ice and was now thawing out. She looked down at it, and saw her fingertip was blistered. She rubbed it. Pins and needles set in. "What the hell?"

Caroline looked back from the picture. "What's the matter?"

Alli stuck out her finger.

"Ouch. That looks painful. It looks like…no, it can't be."

"Frostbite. I've never had it, but I've seen pictures. It feels like it too."

Caroline touched her hand and the now-familiar burst of electricity shot up her arm.

"Come on, let's get that hand warmed up. Your finger's freezing cold, and it seems to be spreading."

Caroline ran hot water into a bowl in the kitchen sink and Alli sank her hand into it. A stab of excruciating pain shot through her. Mercifully, it quickly settled to a deep, jaw-clenching throb.

"Any better?" Caroline had a first aid kit open and was examining a tube of antiseptic cream.

"A bit. I think I have to do this for about half an hour or so. Then it'll need to be wrapped in a bandage. Probably best not to use the cream though."

Caroline returned the tube of cream to the box. She rummaged for a moment and held up a hygienically wrapped, cotton bandage.

"That's perfect," Alli said, between clenched teeth.

An hour later, with her finger neatly bandaged, Alli sipped a cup of strong tea. The doorbell rang and Caroline looked up at the clock. "That's the first of them. Come on."

Alli followed, taking care to keep her still-throbbing finger out of harm's way. She was grateful for the deep pocket in Caroline's voluminous kaftan.

At the door were three unfamiliar faces. Hardly surprising, with the shortness of notice there wouldn't have been any point in contacting her celebrity friends. They all had full diaries for months ahead.

Caroline made introductions but the names slipped by in a blur. In passing, she picked up a Susannah, and a Del or Belle. The other name was lost in a cacophony of four voices all speaking at once. At least two of the guests had the cut-glass accents of British aristocracy and, no doubt, the double-barreled surnames to boot.

"Oh, I say, what a grisly collection of clerics," the sole male said. He removed a long, thin black cigarette from his mouth and peered at Abbot Weaver. "Not a fellow one would wish to trifle with. I'm not at all keen on the look in this chap's eyes."

Well, he might sound like King Charles with an extra-large plum stuck in his throat, but at least the man had perception.

Caroline steered him away from the painting. "Alli and I have just been talking about him. That picture is distinctly odd." The doorbell rang again. "Lucius!"

"I met these reprobates outside, so I guessed they were with you." Lucius was all smiles as he crossed the threshold and clasped Caroline to him. He kissed her chastely on both cheeks before letting her go so she could greet her remaining two guests. One of them, Marla, Alli guessed, handed over a garden basket containing bunches of carefully tied dried sage.

The other guest was an unprepossessing-looking young man with a floral shirt, cord jeans and a firm handshake.

"Arthur," he said, shaking Alli's hand. "Arthur Sedgemoor. Caroline's manager. Pleased to meet you."

Alli stuttered her name, desperate to talk to him about a hundred and one things. He looked at her curiously, probably because she was wearing some stupid expression. Then he shifted his gaze to stare around at his surroundings.

Everyone moved to the kitchen and Caroline collected incense from her guests, who busied themselves pouring drinks and putting food out on the serving dishes. Alli stood apart from the chattering group and watched Caroline. She seemed carefree, happy.

Alli hadn't realized Lucius had also separated himself from the others and now stood right next to her. Too closely. Alli surreptitiously moved a few inches sideways. Lucius followed. This time she stood her ground.

He took a deep draw on his Sobranie. "You have returned from your time, then?"

Alli would not show the trepidation that saturated every pore. "It would appear I have precious little choice in the matter." None, as it happened, not that she was about to admit it to him.

"And have you worked out what is going on here? Why you keep coming and going from this time to your own? Why you can seemingly travel across, not just time, but space as well?"

He's enjoying this.

Alli took a deep breath. Her injured finger gave a vicious throb. "Why? Do you have any suggestions?"

Lucius smiled. "You have spirit. That is always good. Spirit and courage. Those are qualities that will serve you well in life, as long as you don't abuse them."

The unexpected, if somewhat backhanded, compliment threw Alli off kilter. She tried another tack. "What do you know about Abbot Weaver?"

"Ah, so you've seen his portrait."

"He seems…. Not what he is portrayed as."

"Oh, I think he is exactly as he is portrayed. If you know where to look."

"You mean the symbols? The Freemasonry stuff…and the face?"

Lucius grabbed her arm and turned her to face him. "You saw a face? In the painting. Did Caroline see it?"

"Yes, of course."

"What did it look like?"

"Why don't you see for yourself?"

"Show me." She was too shocked to protest as he virtually frog-marched her out of the kitchen and into the hall. No one else seemed to notice. They were all too absorbed in themselves.

Taking care not to touch the picture, Alli pointed in the direction of the ghostly image. At least, the ghostly image as it had once been. "It was there. Ask Caroline. She saw it. It injured my finger. I mean touching the picture right where it was damaged my finger. There was another too. A cat, or maybe some sort of tiger."

Lucius stared from the picture to Alli and back again. He was frowning.

"Clearly they're not there now."

"But they were."

"I don't doubt that. The fact that they aren't there now is not good. Not good at all."

"I've seen that face before. In fact, at first I thought it was you."

"Me?" Lucius laughed. "Oh no, my dear Allegra. I can assure you it's not. The owner of that face is far more powerful than me. Far more." He touched the place where the cat-like figure had been. Then he strode back into the kitchen.

Alli gave one last glance at the painting and a chill flooded her body.

Caroline's voice rang out. "Come on everyone, time to go up to the room and begin our exorcism party!"

Alli winced. She wished Caroline would go back to taking this seriously.

Marla spoke up. "Exorcism party? I love that." She waved a smoking sage brush too close under Alli's nostrils, making her cough.

"Oh, sorry."

Alli doubted it.

The group grabbed paint, brushes and drinks and trotted happily up the stairs, following the basket-toting Caroline into her room and up the stone stairs.

"This is a bit spooky, Caroline."

"Oh Del, this is nothing. Wait till you see upstairs," Caroline called down.

"It's *really* creepy up there," Arthur said. He stared at Alli in a way that made her feel uneasy. There was an intensity in that gaze that didn't belong there. Not only that, he too was sporting a small bandage. In his case, wrapped around his left hand.

Alli nodded toward it. "Accident?"

Arthur touched his injured hand with his other one and winced. "Scalded myself." He looked away quickly. Too quickly.

They crammed into the small room. Alli did a double-take. The atmosphere was so thick with evil, she could have cut through it.

The crucifix was once again upside down. The Christ figure gazed upward in a twisted grimace.

Del picked it up and set it down immediately, withdrawing his hand and wiping it on his denim bell-bottoms. "Oh, I say, that's a bit gruesome."

"Very…Gothic," Marla said as she surveyed the room, while waving her sage brush.

"Come on, let's get these walls cheered up." Caroline pried open a tin of daffodil-colored paint. Two of the others did likewise and, within minutes, splashes of green, pink and yellow adorned the stone.

Out of the corner of her eye, Alli saw Arthur creating great swirls of purple.

"I shall proceed with a little more caution and precision," Lucius said, producing a tube containing sticks of charcoal. Alli stood back, admiring the speed at which the artist created floral swirls, reminiscent of William Morris, especially when he began to add some stylized birds.

A couple of the others paused to watch the professional at work.

"Lucius painted me," Caroline said. "Months ago. But he hasn't let me see the portrait yet."

"All in good time. There are still some finishing touches to make."

"Should make for a great album cover," Arthur said. Lucius shot him an angry look and once again Arthur looked away. This man had real trouble looking at people in the eye. "Not that it's up to me. That's for the record company to decide."

"And I'm quite sure they would hate the idea," Lucius said, his voice chilling the air around it.

Arthur's next brushstroke nearly knocked Del over.

"Hey steady on, old chap."

Arthur mumbled an apology. He seemed brittle. On edge. For a second his eyes locked with Alli's. She read terror in them. Sheer, naked terror.

Alli remembered the conversation about Arthur's death on those rail tracks. Suicide? No, that had been murder. She didn't know how, or even properly why, but she had never been surer of anything. Somehow, Lucius Hartmann had reached out from beyond the grave and murdered him.

A low hum, so faint Alli wondered if she was really hearing it, resonated around the room. One by one the guests stopped what they were doing. No one spoke. It seemed to be trapping them all. The effect reminded her of a couple of instances when Nancy and Mike had seemed to freeze. Even Lucius stood, statue-like, paintbrush in hand, eyes glazed like the rest of them. Only Caroline and Alli seemed unaffected.

"What's happening?" Caroline squeezed past the immobile bodies of her friends and stood next to Alli.

"I don't know. Oh God. Look." In the far corner, a flickering light danced off the wall. The candle-like flame grew stronger yet, instead of illuminating the room, it grew darker as, one by one, the guests faded from view.

"Alli, I need to tell you…." Caroline's voice faded.

"Tell me what?" A loud buzzing sounded in Alli's ears. The room grew black, except for the solitary flickering flame. She could no longer see anything, only its wick, shining white and yellow. The rest of the room was plunged into a black murk. She couldn't even see Caroline anymore. Alli called to her, but her voice merely echoed off the stone. She *must* speak to her. She couldn't lose her now. The buzzing grew louder. Alli felt faint. She must sit somewhere, anywhere. Her legs wouldn't hold her up any longer. And then they didn't. She sank to the floor, unconscious.

The last face she saw belonged to Lucius Hartmann. He was smiling.

*   *   *

The voices were American, indistinct, growing closer. Alli's return to consciousness felt like traveling a vast distance along a narrow tunnel. Warmth bathed her cheeks, the smell of jasmine soothed her spirit, and the gentlest of breezes caressed her skin. Such seductive sensations, like being cocooned in a comfy blanket. She didn't want to lose the moment, but she must find out where she was. *When* she was. She opened her eyes, caught sight of her hand and saw the skin had healed. No bandage. How much time had elapsed on this occasion? Was this before or after her previous experience?

No one paid Alli any attention. They were in her house in Laurel Canyon. The conversation was muted. Nearby, Mama Cass, dressed in black, dabbed at her eyes. John Denver looked serious and sad. He wore a black suit, white shirt, black tie. Looking around, everyone seemed to be dressed in similar fashion. Everyone she had ever seen on her previous trips back there. All the dead Laurel Canyon music royalty and, in the center of the room, in pride of place, a shiny mahogany casket.

Alli leapt off the sofa where she had been lying, alone. "Who's died?" She hadn't meant to sound so abrupt. It sounded so callous. It didn't seem to matter because no one had apparently heard her.

"Hey. Please tell me. Who have we lost?"

Again, no reaction. The assembled group continued to talk with each other, glancing over at the coffin now and again, wiping away stray tears.

Alli made her way over to the casket. A photograph frame stood on top of it. Instead of a picture, there was an inscription handwritten in elegant black calligraphy. "Allegra (Alli) Sinclair. Our Friend. Until we meet again. R.I.P."

"*What?* I'm not dead. I'm here. Can't you see me? I'm right here."

Alli tried to grab John Denver's arm, and stared incredulously as her hand passed straight through it. She went right up to Cass and touched her. Once again, nothing. Her hand passed right through.

Out of the corner of her eye, someone moved. She spun around.

Lucius smiled at her. "They can't hear you or see you. To them you died yesterday. You hanged yourself in this very room, from that beam." He pointed upward.

Alli looked up. The sturdy timber gave no indication of the grisly task it had apparently aided so recently.

"So…I'm dead?" It didn't sound real.

"Oh, one day no doubt you will be. As will we all. For now, it depends on which reality you are in. Or which reality *they* are in. They are, of course, all dead. You know that anyway. Yet back in the time we're in now, they were alive and you, dear girl, well, you didn't exist at all. You weren't even born. They knew of no relatives of yours, so they claimed the body for themselves. It will be cremated later today, and your ashes will be scattered in each of their gardens. Rather sweet, isn't it?"

He made the word sound anything but sweet.

"So, what's your role in this, Lucius?"

His eyes opened wide in mock surprise. "My role? I have none. I am merely an observer. An onlooker, if you will. A servant…of sorts."

"And Caroline? I don't see her here."

"Caroline is back in England. Time has moved on since you were last here in Laurel Canyon. As you know, she bought Canonbury Manor." He laughed. "I bought it in her name at any rate. She has quit America for good and will never return here. Meanwhile, you stayed on for a short while longer. You were a good friend to all these people, although even now, they still can't work out exactly what it is you did. Listening to them this afternoon has been most entertaining. The speculation…." He clapped his hands together. "One said they thought you were an entrepreneur, another that you were a business adviser. Most disagreed with that. They said you were far too decent to be involved in anything as sordid as business, or finance. They can't work it out at all and have totally bypassed the obvious explanation."

"And what is that, exactly?"

"Why, the truth of course. The plain, unvarnished truth that you are from the future. Cass came the closest when she described you as an enigma. Someone who never seemed to quite belong here in this space."

"I don't understand when I'm supposed to have bought this house, or with what money, so I'm not surprised they don't get it. You love this, don't you? It's some crazy little game to you. I don't know how you're doing this, and I haven't fathomed out why yet but, so help me...." Just then, if there had been anything she could have used as a weapon, Alli was sure she could have killed Lucius.

He laughed. "My dear Allegra, I am merely one of many."

"What do you mean?"

Lucius waved his hand nonchalantly. For the first time, Alli noticed he wore a ring. Made of gleaming gold, it looked antique, and its vivid violet-blue stone glinted. How had she never noticed it before? Yet, that didn't matter when compared to the unrequited anger that seethed within her. She looked back down at the coffin and struggled to compose herself. It wouldn't be a good idea to show her feelings too openly. It would give this man power over her and he already had far too much of that. She took a deep breath. "What happens now? Do I stay here as some sort of ghost or do I go back to my own time?"

"I can't answer that."

"How about you? You're supposed to live out your life to a grand old age and die sometime in the 1990s."

"Then that's probably what will happen, unless it changes."

"And that could happen?"

"Our future is never fully determined."

"Surely it's already happened."

"Not now it hasn't. Not here, now, in 1970."

Alli felt as if her head were about to explode. "It's too much to take in."
Lucius smiled. "Then don't try."

"Lucius." Cass came and stood between them, oblivious to Alli's presence. "I didn't see you there. So good of you to come. Such a sad business. None of us knew she was so depressed, so desperate. I wish she'd come to me. I wish…." Cass broke down and leaned heavily on Lucius. He put his arm around her and steered her to the sofa Alli had been sitting on when she came to.

Alli sighed. Lucius was right. None of what went on here conformed to any laws of nature as far as she knew. She gazed around the room, at the solemn faces. When, or if, she returned to her own time, would she read of this in someone's memoirs or biography? Would she provide a footnote in history? Already, life was changing for the people who lived their hedonistic lives in Laurel Canyon. In August of 1969, the terrible Tate-LaBianca murders had taken place. People had begun locking their doors for the first time, buying guard dogs. And guns. One by one, those assembled here would move out. Some to gated, secure mansions in Beverly Hills and elsewhere. Some would leave the West Coast altogether. None would ever be the same again. All would die too young, many from the excesses of what they were doing now.

Alli wished she could touch them, speak to them one more time, but Lucius said she was never supposed to have been here. So why was she? There could be only one link.

Caroline Rand.

CHAPTER FIFTEEN

Alli woke on the floor of the small upstairs room. Alone. The freshly decorated walls showed all too clearly who was the true artist and who were the enthusiastic amateurs.

Lucius Hartmann's work was precise, decorative, like a small piece of exquisite wallpaper. It was far more complete than when Alli had last seen it before everything went black.

Votives flickered on the ledge where the crucifix still stood upside down. On the floor tall church candles stood to attention in brass candlesticks.

She froze at a sudden movement in the corner of the room. A huddled figure uncurled itself and, with the grace of a large cat, stood on four legs, its body cloaked, impossible to determine. The image of that terrifying tiger-like creature in the painting sprang into Alli's mind.

Alli shrank back against the wall, trying to make herself as small as possible, knowing full well it was futile. The creature had seen her. If she could get up and make a run for it, she would, but how? Her legs turned to jelly and it would catch her before she even got to her feet.

She sat and waited, praying to zone out to some place of safety. Cass's house. Her own nearby. But that route must surely be closed to her now? She had never wanted to leave Laurel Canyon. Now she could never return. All that was left lay here and now. Or in the future.

"Alli."

Never had she been more relieved to hear her name called.

Caroline appeared at the doorway. "What are you doing up here alone? Everyone's gone."

"Can't you see…." But the figure had vanished. Alli struggled to her feet, her legs numb. Dizziness overtook her and Caroline took hold of her as she staggered.

This time their touch gave her a sensation so powerful Alli couldn't breathe. She felt herself falling, sliding downward. At first, all she could hear was Caroline's voice, calling to her, becoming increasingly agitated as she didn't...couldn't...respond.

Help me. Into her head, came an image of Caroline, her face melting, skin peeling away from her skull.

Help me.

Images flashed through her mind like some film on fast forward. She saw a small child. The child grew into an adult. Caroline.

Caroline working in a boutique...dancing in a nightclub...singing in a theater...on a television show...then another and another. The images came at her faster and faster, melding together.

They stopped. Like a carousel coming to a sudden halt.

Alli opened her eyes. Somehow, she had made it downstairs into the bathroom. She looked in the mirror. Caroline's face looked back at her.

That's me.

CHAPTER SIXTEEN

Alli put her hand to her head. She was in the hall and one glance told her she had returned to her own time. She stared straight ahead at the picture of Abbot Weaver. It had changed.

The colors looked fresher and richer than she remembered. The eyes even more mesmerizing, the twist of the supposed holy man's mouth even more cruel and the eyes…. Those eyes.

Alli searched the picture for the shadowy face and the tiger-like creature, but they weren't there. She touched the finger that had been so recently injured. It seemed totally unscathed.

Alli stared hard at the abbot's left hand. That ring. The exquisite detail. The distinctive iridescence of the violet-blue stone. She had never noticed it before on his finger. But she had seen it on someone else.

Lucius Hartmann.

Alli had a sudden urge to speak to her parents. If they knew anything, she must hear it from them.

She dashed into the living room and picked up the phone, relieved to hear the dialing tone. Alli punched in the numbers and waited. It only rang twice.

"Dad?"

A sharp intake of breath relayed down the phone.

"Allegra? It's been…a long time. How are you?"

It might have been a business colleague for all the lack of familial warmth in his voice. Alli felt prickles up her spine as she so often did on the increasingly rare occasions she exchanged pleasantries with her father, and this call had to be much more than that.

"I'm keeping fine, Dad. How are you and Mum?"

"Well, thank you. Enjoying the scenery and gentle way of life. The peace and tranquility. It's what we need at our age."

Why did Alli feel as if she had just been chastised for intruding on it by her mere presence on the end of a telephone? She brushed the sensation aside. Paranoia. A result of all that had been going on.

"I'm glad to hear you're both happy. Listen, Dad, I need to ask you...."

She heard a voice in the background. Mum.

"It's Allegra," her father said. She couldn't make out her mother's response.

"What is it?" her father asked Alli, and she could hear the impatience in his tone. She ignored it and carried on.

"Many years ago, probably in the late Sixties, early Seventies, did you ever come across Lucius Hartmann?"

Her father's voice exploded down the line. "*Hartmann?*"

In the background, Alli's mother cried out.

"What is it?" Alli asked. "What do you know about him?"

"Why are you asking?" her father demanded. "Why do you want to know about that...man? He's been dead thirty years."

Alli had never thought to hear panic in her father's voice, but she heard it now. "I'm staying at a friend's house for the weekend. Her grandmother was Caroline Rand."

"Caroline *Rand*?"

Alli's mother gave another cry of anguish. This time, she voiced her fears. "Dear God, what has the girl got herself into?"

Panic was beginning to rise inside Alli too. "Dad, please. Tell me what you know about Lucius Hartmann."

On the other end of the phone, a furious exchange of words between her parents had Alli straining to hear. She could make out nothing that made any sense.

Finally, her father came back to her. "Allegra, whoever that friend is you're staying with.... She isn't who she says she is."

"What do you mean? She's Nancy Harper. We were at school together."

"That's as may be, but she isn't Caroline's granddaughter."

"How do you know that? Besides, she *must* be. Caroline left Canonbury Manor to her *because* she was her granddaughter."

"No, Allegra. Canonbury Manor didn't belong to Caroline. It belonged to Lucius Hartmann. He used Caroline's name and money and was the vilest excuse for a human I have ever met. He belonged to a sect called the Cabal of Seraphragius…. We…. Just a minute…. Where are you calling from?"

"Canonbury Manor."

"Oh, dear God." Her mother had given way to hysteria and her sobbing almost drowned out her father's voice as he tried to calm her, while holding on to the phone.

"Dad?"

"Look, Allegra, I can't talk now. I have to deal with your mother. Call back later. And get out of that house. *Now.*"

The line went dead.

★   ★   ★

In the kitchen, Nancy and Mike were eating more of the party leftovers and sipping chilled white wine. They looked up as Alli entered.

"You've been a while," Mike said.

"I've been talking to my father about Lucius Hartmann."

"Find out anything useful?" Nancy asked through a mouthful of vol-au-vent.

Alli remembered her father's warning about the woman who sat here, munching happily away. She must be careful. "Only that the mere mention of his name sent my mother into a fit of hysterics, and my father issued dire warnings about him. He said we should get out of here. Now." She looked for any reaction on Nancy's face. Any hint that the woman was, indeed, not who she claimed to be. Not a flicker. The lack of reaction in itself bothered Alli. She should be concerned. She shouldn't be tucking into a plateful of food as if nothing was wrong.

"Anything else?" Nancy asked.

Alli decided to withhold the rest. "He told me to call back later when he had calmed Mum down."

"Does she often have hysterics?" Nancy asked and took another bite of vol-au-vent.

Alli shook her head. "Not frequently." In fact, never before, as far as Alli could remember. Nancy didn't need to know that though.

Mike sipped his wine. Nancy reached for another savory. All so domestic. You wouldn't think anything was wrong, though everything possible about this place was wrong. She would give it an hour and then call her father back. She had to know everything he did about Hartmann, Caroline and, it appeared, Nancy.

Meanwhile…. "Nancy, that picture. The one of Abbot Weaver."

Mike put down his glass. "Is that the guy whose eyes never leave you? Even when you're not looking at the picture, it's as if they're on you the whole time."

"That's the one," Alli said. "The last time I zoned out, I found myself back here with Caroline. She had only recently bought this place and that picture was exactly where it is now, but it was really grimy and dark. You couldn't make out much detail. There's a lot of symbolism in it. Some of it's Masonic stuff and when I saw it with Caroline, there seemed to be an animal…like a tiger or large cat, and a face. They're not there now. If they ever were. He's wearing a ring. The abbot I mean. I read somewhere that bishops' rings were usually set with amethysts, which are violet in color. This stone is much bluer than that."

"I noticed that ring," Mike said.

Alli nodded. "Of course, it could be artistic license, except I'm sure I've seen it before. On Lucius Hartmann's finger."

"Are you certain?" Nancy asked.

"I could always be wrong, but, yes, I'm as sure as I can be. It's quite distinctive and not as clunky as a lot of ecclesiastical rings you see."

Alli took a sip of wine and fixed her gaze on Nancy. So far, the woman had given no tangible sign of being anything other than who she claimed to be. Alli decided to push a little farther. "As I've said before, whatever is in this house is much bigger than Lucius Hartmann. Bigger, older and it goes far deeper into dark places, and I mean *dark* places." What was it her father had called it? The Cabal of Seraphragius? Is that what was connected to this house? He had seemed terrified of it. But if it was so powerful, it probably wouldn't be a good plan to reveal her knowledge of it yet. Not until she was sure her father was wrong and that she could trust Nancy – and Mike for that matter.

Alli cleared her throat. "I would lay odds that Lucius – whatever and wherever he is now – is scared of it because it's so powerful it can even get to him." Alli thought back to her last conversation with Lucius, when he had admitted to being some kind of servant or minion to a higher authority. "In fact, I reckon it's using him too."

There was no time for Nancy to react. A loud crash from the hall sent Alli, Mike and Nancy rushing out.

The clock lay face down, the discordant clang of its chimes echoing all around them.

Nancy cried out, "Look, up the stairs!"

A grayish mist billowed down from the top. They were back. The ghostly procession of chanting monks, the accompanying smell of incense growing stronger every second as they descended. They seemed not to be taking steps downward but carried by the mist. They reached the bottom, and Alli, Nancy and Mike parted so they would not be caught up.

As they moved past, the monks showed no sign of being aware of their presence. Then, as the first of them drew level with Abbot Weaver's portrait, the mist engulfed it.

Alli felt she was being watched. She looked back up the stairs.

"It's Lucius."

Nancy and Mike followed her gaze.

Unlike the monks, Lucius made it clear by his reaction that he was only too aware of their presence. He glared at Mike, as he touched the ring on his finger.

"You do not belong here," Lucius said, his voice an echo sounding in Alli's head. She guessed the others must be sharing a similar experience, judging by the bemused expressions on their faces. "Only Allegra should be here."

"This is *my* house," Nancy said. "Alli is merely a guest here."

Lucius threw back his head and let out a guttural, harsh laugh. It barely sounded human. He stood within a few feet of them and raised his hands.

The chanting had stopped, the monks no longer there. The mist swirled around the abbot's portrait. Lucius threw it occasional glances. He inhaled deeply, as if drawing energy from it.

Lucius took a step forward and an icy cold descended over Alli like a shroud. He didn't seem to be moving of his own volition. He proceeded with awkward, jerky steps as if someone was placing one of his feet in front of the other. No bravado now in those eyes, which cast a terrified gaze ahead of him.

"What the hell...?" Mike's whole body began twisting and writhing, as he tried to free himself from an invisible grip.

Nancy and Alli leapt forward and grabbed hold of his arms, trying to drag him away from whatever held him so firmly in its grasp.

Anger raged within Alli, but it wasn't her anger. It seemed to be coming from the invisible force that held Mike. Nancy's face twisted into a mask of hatred. She bared her teeth. No, not teeth. Fangs. Like the creature's in the picture. She clawed her hand and struck out at Alli. Deep scratches tore down her arm. Sharp pain stung as blood filled the abrasions and fueled Alli's own rage. She cried out and struck Nancy with her injured arm. Her blood streaked across Nancy's face. Nancy tried to bite her but missed. Mike was still trapped. He roared like some caged beast.

Then it was over. He went suddenly limp. Alli let go and, as she broke all physical contact with Mike, her anger evaporated.

"Nancy, let go of him. Let go. Now."

Nancy's eyes flamed. Alli could see nothing left of the woman. Nothing human in those feline eyes that burned with an unnatural bloody fire. But then, she too wrenched herself free and the madness left her gaze. She staggered backward as she caught sight of Alli's wounded and bleeding arm.

"Alli, I'm so sorry. I don't know how I did that. *Why* I did that.... What's happening to me?" Her voice disintegrated into a wail, like an animal in distress.

Alli's heart clutched at the sight of that white face and scared eyes. Despite her misgivings about her, she had to comfort the distraught woman. "It's not you, Nancy. It's that—"

But Lucius had gone, and mist no longer concealed the portrait.

Mike sank to his knees and passed out.

★　　★　　★

The two women settled Mike onto a sofa in the living room.

"At least he's sleeping now," Alli said, clutching her arm. The bleeding had stopped but the scratches needed cleaning and bandaging. They stung and burned like crazy. And the surrounding skin was black.

"That looks awful. Like…."

"Frostbite. It happened to me before. Then I touched a face in the painting of the abbot. This time…."

"I have a first aid box in the kitchen." Nancy's voice was small, barely audible.

Alli forced a smile. "Thanks." She followed Nancy into the kitchen, where she washed and dried her arm, patting it gently with a soft towel. Nancy bandaged her wounds.

"I can't understand what happened to me, Alli. I am so, so sorry. It was as if I wasn't in control of my actions anymore. I wasn't myself…."

"It wasn't your fault. What I saw when I last zoned out…. It scared even Lucius Hartmann."

A shuffling noise came from the doorway. Mike. Disheveled and looking as if he hadn't slept in a week.

"Hey guys. You need to see the picture. The one of the abbot."

Nancy and Alli followed him into the hall.

Alli stared up at the picture. "It's glowing."

An orange radiance had spread over the painting, transforming the features of the abbot. The one-dimensional image took on substance. It filled out, swelled, expanded until it could no longer be contained within the confines of the gilt frame.

The transformation was complete.

The abbot stood before them, a living, breathing creature of flesh, blood, bone and sinew.

The evil within him hung over the hallway. It spread its tendrils into the walls, the timbers and every fabric of the building. The house groaned as it shifted on its foundations. Alli felt as if she were on a ship's deck in heavy seas. Nausea welled up inside her. Nancy heaved. A few yards away, Mike had closed his eyes and his skin had taken on a greenish tinge.

The abbot stood, unmoving, unaffected by the rolling motion around him, his face expressionless. His eyes held Alli, his mouth crueler than the artist could ever have captured in oil. His skin had an inhuman shimmer, betraying a body that was more than merely mortal. Of flesh he might now be, but this creature wasn't human.

Alli found her voice. "What are you?" She was relieved to hear that she sounded firm and not the scared child she felt inside.

He made no sign of having heard her, but she knew he had and that he understood what she had asked.

The house settled itself once more. Nancy took deep, cleansing breaths, and Mike's cheeks gradually took on a healthier color.

Still the abbot stared at Alli. He didn't utter a word. Into her head, a series of images played out while the tendrils swirled across the ceiling, apparently unnoticed by Nancy or Mike.

Alli saw herself as a child, watching her parents perform at a concert in a festival hall she didn't recognize. She barely remembered the event, and everything seemed so big. She must be seeing it from a child's perspective. She felt a swelling of pride at her father's note-perfect guitar solo. Her mother was playing a keyboard. They were backing an internationally renowned male singer but Alli only had eyes for the two people in the backing band.

The image faded and the abbot was gone. Nancy and Mike helped each other stagger back to the kitchen. They could barely get one foot in front of the other.

Alli dashed into the living room and picked up the phone. A bizarre thought had struck her, partly initiated by her father's words when they had spoken earlier and partly by her role in the events unfolding in this house. At first it had seemed too crazy to contemplate, but the more the thought persisted, the more pieces seemed to find their place in the jigsaw. She must make the call now or she would lose her nerve, talk herself out of it. Tell herself she was overreacting. Fabricating.

She dialed the number.

"*Pronto.*"

Her mother's voice.

Alli took a deep breath. "Mum? It's Alli."

A sharp intake of breath at the other end. At least she didn't sound hysterical anymore. In fact, when she spoke, she sounded calm. Too calm.

"Hello, Allegra. How are you?"

An odd question considering how her last call had ended. "Fine, Mum, fine.... Look, I need to ask you.... I need you to be totally honest with me, okay?"

A pause. The silence was deafening.

"What do you want to know?" There was fear, coupled with a dash of resignation in her voice.

Alli pressed on. "There's no easy way of asking this, so I'm going to come straight out with it. Was I adopted?"

She would deny it, probably rant a bit. Nothing happened. More silence. Alli bit her lip. "Mum?"

A deep sigh, like a rush of wind down the phone. "I'm here."

"Well, was I?" The question seemed redundant after her mother's reaction, but Alli needed to hear the answer, plainly and simply, however much it hurt either of them.

"Yes." It was a whisper, as if her mother was scared to say it out loud.

Hot tears pricked Alli's eyelids. "Then why? Why didn't you ever tell me? Lots of kids are adopted. They grow up knowing who they are. They don't have a problem with it, so why did you never tell me?"

Sounds of gentle sobbing. Despite their differences and the anger that threatened to burst out of her, Alli felt a wave of compassion for this woman who, for her own reasons, had decided to keep Alli's true identity a secret. "Mum, I don't mean to upset you, but I have to know. How did it all happen?"

Once she started, her mother's words came out in a rush, like a river bursting its banks. "Your father and I wanted a child so desperately and we couldn't have one. We were very young, but there was never going to be a possibility because I didn't develop properly. I was born without ovaries so I could never have children. I began to obsess over having a baby. Your father was happy to go along with it.... Oh, it sounds so foolish now.... We decided we wanted our child to be just that. *Our* child. I faked a pregnancy. We told everyone I was expecting. My parents would have been the only ones to have known differently and they were both dead. Someone...we had met in the business…recommended an adoption agency. Normally, the process can take months, years even, and I didn't want to wait. It all seemed perfect. Too perfect, I know that now. I'll never forget the day we brought you home. I had no idea how to look after a baby and no one except the midwife to show me. Your father had to go away on tour almost immediately, leaving me all alone with this little squalling infant. I made mistakes, but I loved you so much." The sounds of heart-wrenching weeping poured down the line.

Tears flowed freely down Alli's cheeks. "If I was so special to you, how come you ignored me most of my childhood? How come I grew up never feeling good enough? I hadn't your musical talent. I thought that was *my* fault. Now I can see it wasn't. I wasn't your blood child, so I couldn't inherit your skills. How cruel is that? Have you any idea how I've felt all these years? Never feeling good enough, or worthy of your love, or your time and attention?" It was all coming out now. All those years of frustration, of self-doubt and insecurity. Once the floodgates had opened, Alli couldn't close them.

On the other end of the phone the weeping turned to great, heavy sobs.

"I'm sorry, Allegra. I'm so, so sorry."

In the background, Alli heard another voice. Male this time. Her father. Then his voice. Angrier than she had ever heard him.

"What's the meaning of this, Allegra? How *dare* you upset your mother like this?"

Her mother's voice, fainter than before. "She knows everything."

Her father's voice exploded. "*Everything?*"

"The adoption. Only the adoption. I swear."

Alli froze. It all fell into place.

"Dad?" She knew her voice sounded like a frightened child's. "Why did you do it? It was Hartmann who recommended the adoption agency, wasn't it? And you knew he was part of the Cabal of Seraphragius, whatever that is. So, what does that make me?"

Only her father's breathing interrupted the silence on the other end of the phone.

"Dad, please. You must tell me."

This time, her father cleared his throat and spoke into the phone. "Very well. Now you know. You have all the answers you are going to get from us. There is no reason for any further communication between us. Please don't call here again. We can't help you anymore." He cut the call, leaving Alli staring into the dead receiver.

Her hands shook as she replaced it on its cradle. In one phone call, her whole life toppled like a house built of balsa in a hurricane.

Without warning, a furious thumping sounded at the front door. Pushing her own shock aside, Alli rushed out and met Nancy and Mike in the hallway. From outside, a familiar male voice sounded.

"Let me in. For God's sake, is there anyone in there left alive?"

"It's Ric," Nancy said. "Ric, the door won't open."

But the handle turned. Nancy stood back as the door opened and Ric, bedraggled and dirty, crossed the threshold. The door swung shut and locked itself.

He half collapsed into Alli's arms. She, Nancy and Mike manhandled him into the living room and eased him down onto a sofa. He had only been gone a day, but his body gave off an odor of someone who hadn't seen the inside of a shower for over a week. His hair was matted and his eyes dull and lifeless.

"I'll fetch you a glass of water," Alli said, leaving the others to settle him down.

In the kitchen, Alli ran cold water, selected a tumbler and filled it to the brim. She stared out of the window across the gravel pathway and over the front lawn. Trees swayed in a light breeze, a Red Admiral butterfly fluttered past the window. Everything seemed so peaceful. Bucolic. The English countryside in summer. Life out there at least was going on as normal. Her life would never be the same again. She felt numb, too shocked to think about what had just happened; what she had just learned.

The scent of jasmine drifted toward her nostrils. Laurel Canyon jasmine. It didn't belong in Canonbury Ducis. At least not this corner of it at any rate. There wasn't even a window open. They were still locked.

Goosebumps rose on Alli's arms. Any moment, she would find herself back there.

Except this time, she didn't. The scent of jasmine evaporated.

Alli took the water into the living room to find Nancy quizzing Ric about his time away. Mike was sitting across from him. Nancy stood adjacent. Alli handed the glass to Ric, who nodded his thanks and tried to raise it to his lips. His hand shook so badly he spilled some down his dirty tie-dyed t-shirt.

"It's so hard to remember," he said, having managed to take a sizable swig. "I was angry. Furious at you, Mike, over that girl. It was too ridiculous for words. The whole thing was over years ago, but I couldn't let it go. I felt I *had* to hang on to my anger at you for some reason. I'm sorry."

Mike waved his hand dismissively. "Don't apologize. I felt the same way. I even wanted to kill you at one point. It was so hard to keep my hands from your throat."

Ric nodded. "I behaved like a total prick. I know I raced out of here. I had the weirdest sensation inside my head and stomach. I felt propelled. I mean literally. As if I had some kind of bizarre helicopter rotors, spinning around…. You know that feeling when you travel at speed over a hump-backed bridge? That sensation of your insides taking off? It was like that. I couldn't stop if I wanted to. I had to keep going. I got to the car and realized I'd left my keys in my room, but then the car door unlocked by itself and I could see the keys in the ignition, so I must have been mistaken. Except I never leave the keys in the ignition. Besides, the car wouldn't have locked without them." He paused, glancing from Nancy to Mike and back again.

"Go on," Alli said.

"I remember diving into the car, turning on the ignition and tearing off down the driveway. Then it's a complete blank for a while. I seemed to be in some kind of limbo. Now and then I heard music. Sixties music, and it all felt perfectly natural because, after all, here we all were at a 1969-themed party. Jefferson Airplane, Caroline Rand, Grateful Dead, Jimi Hendrix…. I heard them all. Some were definitely on record, others sounded live, but I couldn't *see* anything. And that's when the voices started." Ric looked at Alli. His eyes seemed to have a little more life in them now. "I heard Lucius Hartmann. He spoke about you, Alli. He said you belonged with *them*."

Alli's heart lurched. "What does that mean? Them?"

Ric shook his head. "I've no idea. I don't even know whether he could see me, whether my body was there, wherever *there* was, or whether it was purely my mind, or spirit. But he clearly said, 'Allegra is doing well. It won't be much longer, and she can join us.'"

Alli swallowed hard. Ric's gaze never left her. He seemed to be staring *into* her. She caught Mike staring at her too. He averted his eyes as soon as he realized she had spotted him, but Nancy…. She kept right on. Her eyes fixed on some point in the center of Alli's forehead.

Ric plowed on. "I came to in the pub down the road a few hours ago. The landlord was kind. He assumed I'd been taken ill. My car was parked in his car park although I had no recollection of driving there. I must have been in a real state. He wanted to call for an ambulance, but I assured him I just needed to rest for a bit. He guided me into the main bar, brought me a Scotch and I knocked it straight back. A few of the locals were drifting in for their afternoon pint and a chat. They all stared at me. Not surprising, considering how I was dressed and behaving. I had managed to explain to the landlord about the party and he proceeded to explain to each of them, and that didn't bother them. It was when he told them where the party was being held that their expressions changed."

"What do you mean?" Alli's voice cracked. She tried to moisten her lips, but her mouth had dried. She felt a ringing in her ears and Ric's voice seemed to be coming from farther away. She struggled to concentrate.

"Canonbury Manor is cursed, or so I heard. Nothing good ever happens here. The landlord told me that Caroline Rand made millions when she lived here but no one really knew where her money came from. Certainly not, it would seem, from record sales. When the landlord had managed to convince his regulars that I was a harmless, probably eccentric, victim of whatever was wrong with this place, they started to trot out their tales and theories. Each one seemed wilder than the last, as if they were trying to outdo each other. Everything from Satanic rituals back in the eighteenth and nineteenth centuries, through to human sacrifice, apparently at the instigation of some abbot who lived here at the time of the Dissolution."

"Abbot Weaver," Nancy said.

"That's him," Ric said. "Abbot Hippolytus Weaver. For once Henry

VIII did everyone a favor getting rid of him. He burned at the stake for heresy, but, evidently, he had some loyal followers because what was left of him was brought back here and is buried somewhere on the premises. He was part of a cult called...some weird name. I got the landlord to write it down so I wouldn't forget." He produced a scrap of paper from the pocket of his jeans.

Alli took it from him and opened it. She fought hard to keep her face and voice free of expression. "The Cabal of Seraphragius." She handed the paper back to Ric. "I have to say, Ric, the locals seem remarkably well informed about this...stuff. This isn't your usual village banter, is it?"

Ric looked at her questioningly, as did Nancy and Mike. All shifted uncomfortably. "I mean, I would expect gossip about this house, but cults? The very name Seraphragius is hardly one you come across every day, is it? Do you think they're involved in it as well?"

Ric shook his head slowly. "I...I've no idea."

Nancy came to his rescue. "Never mind about that now. Ric, what did they tell you about this cult?"

Ric slid the paper back into his pocket. He shot Alli one last glance and picked up his story. "Apparently way back in history, there was an obscure mystic called Seraphragius of Sidon and he had a strong affinity with cats. Oh, not domestic ones, if indeed there were any then. No, his affinity was with the tiger and its ancestors. Especially a mythical arctic white tiger. It was said he could even manifest as one if he chose to. He lived in God knows when BCE and Weaver somehow found some records of his teachings. Those who follow Seraphragius are supposed to reap great financial reward and can live many lifetimes so they can enjoy it. Eternal life through rebirth, but different from reincarnation because each successive rebirth knows where he or she has come from. Maybe not immediately, but they discover it at some stage. They develop a symbiotic relationship between the giver of their life, themselves and Seraphragius, who, naturally, as the head honcho, gets to live on and on through each of them. The wealth possessed by the cabal is supposed to be in the billions by now. They own property, international companies.... You name it."

Nancy shivered. "I wish to God Caroline hadn't left this place to me."

"That's another thing," Ric said. "When I told them you'd inherited it, they agreed with each other that wasn't possible. The house can't belong to her. It belongs to that cult, courtesy of…. I'll give you three guesses."

Ric's voice echoed through Alli's head. The ringing in her ears became a low, steady hum. No one around her seemed to notice even though she felt sure she was swaying. "Lucius Hartmann," she said.

"Hole in one," Ric said. "The cabal is alive and well, or at least it was when Lucius was around. Judging from what the locals were saying, it didn't die with him either. At various points in Caroline's later life, people would report seeing strange things. Lights flickering, moving around outside as if people were carrying lanterns."

The buzzing in Alli's ears intensified. She could no longer hear Ric. His mouth moved, but no words came her way. She let out a cry as a sharp pain stabbed behind her eyes. She could barely see the others through a mist that had descended over her eyes. No one came to her aid. No one noticed.

She was falling deeper into nothingness. All around her, surges of blackness broke like waves across the shore and disintegrated. Down, down she fell.

And stopped.

Alli blinked hard and gradually shapes emerged. The ringing in her ears was replaced with echoing chants. Little by little her vision returned.

She felt cold stone beneath her outstretched hands and found she was lying on some sort of slab. She raised herself, expecting her head to swim with the motion, but felt surprisingly calm. Her senses took in her surroundings. The room itself looked like some sort of underground mausoleum, minus the coffins. Apart from the raised marble slab, there was no furniture and the place was lit by massive torches set in iron fixtures secured to the walls. Had she slipped back even farther in time than the 1960s? It seemed probable. She swung her legs over and put her feet to the ground, trusting herself to stand. Ahead of her stood a massive wooden door. Oak by the look of it, with robust iron bands and a massive lock. No key.

Alli made her way over to it, a little unsteady but growing stronger with each step. She turned the handle and, amazingly, it opened.

Outside, a long corridor stretched in both directions. She paused to listen. In the distance, the sound of a party in full swing but the noise seemed to be coming from both directions at once. She could stay where she was, or investigate, hoping to find a way out.

Alli hesitated, looked back into the room where there was no likelihood of escape, and made her decision. She pulled the door closed behind her. It made no sound.

She crept up the corridor, careful to keep glancing over her shoulder. Not that it would have helped. There were no more doors. Nowhere she could dive into if she needed to escape attention. She had to press on.

The laughter, clinking glasses and shouting grew closer. Whoever they were, they knew how to enjoy themselves.

At the end of the corridor, there was only one option. To the right, a solid wall, to the left….

Alli gasped. A massive great hall, crammed with people dressed in clothing that belonged in history books of the medieval period, lay ahead of her. She stood in its entrance, apparently unnoticed by the revelers – men and women, engaged in drinking, eating and sex. Everywhere, men with women, women with women, men with men. They rolled around in the food on the tables, on the floor, against the walls. Naked bodies, half-naked bodies, tumbling over each other, food, drink and probably more smeared over their skin, which gleamed greasy and sweaty in the light from hundreds of candles.

Was this a nightmare? Would she wake up in a moment? But Alli knew it was all too real.

A loud clanging as of a giant bell being struck repeatedly silenced the crowd in an instant. It seemed to sober them and they quietly disentangled themselves, rearranged their clothes or threw on robes that lay in a pile at the far end of the room. They ignored the devastation of the room and stood in silence, bowing their heads.

The clanging stopped. Alli hardly dared breathe.

A shining orb of brilliant white light pulsated on the wall at the bottom of the room. It grew brighter, larger, took shape. A collective sigh echoed around the room, along with one word.

"Seraphragius...."

Alli watched in wonderment as the orb revealed its identity. A pure white, enormous tiger with dazzling blue eyes and massive, curled canine teeth paced the floor. The assembled threw themselves down, prostrate on the floor, heedless of the muck.

Only Alli remained standing. She couldn't move. A force held her there. As frozen as the icy lands this creature must have come from.

The tiger locked eyes with her and stood as still as she was.

Lucius Hartmann touched her shoulder. "So, Allegra, now you see. The Lord Seraphragius. You are honored. He doesn't reveal himself in this form to just anyone. This shows how special you are to him. To all of us. You will return now to your own time, but you will say nothing of this encounter."

★   ★   ★

Alli opened her eyes, back where she had been before she had zoned out. It was as if she had never been away. In fact, no one had missed her. No time seemed to have passed. Should she say anything? Maybe later. For now she must listen, see if she could learn anything that could help her make sense of the experience she had just lived through.

Nancy was speaking. "But if the house belongs to *them*, where does that leave me?"

"Good question," Ric said. "I don't have the answer to that, but it may be worth finding out more about that solicitor you saw. Wouldn't surprise me if he isn't one of them. The Cabal of Seraphragius, I mean. From what I've heard, nothing happens purely by chance or serendipity when they're involved. The fact that you're here, believing this is your house, is because for some reason it suits them."

Nancy sat down abruptly on the nearest chair. She stared down at her hands, clasped in her lap, but Alli was aware of a curious expression on her face. One of resignation.

Ric carried on. "It was a bit difficult to know whether it was all true or whether a certain amount of embellishment had gone on. When I asked if any of them had ever met Lucius Hartmann, the older ones nodded and a couple of them crossed themselves. And there's her cleaner. Mrs. Creeley—"

Nancy interrupted. "Yes, she died. I rang during the wake."

Ric gave her an odd stare. "You can't have phoned during the wake," Ric said. "Mrs. Creeley is alive and well and living in a village nearby. The landlord of the pub spoke to her yesterday. Only briefly. He said she seemed scared." He looked straight at Nancy. "'She said, "Good morning" and scurried away like a frightened rabbit.' His exact words. A frightened rabbit."

"Ric. *No!*"

Nancy's face was white. Mike sat next to her and put his arm around her. "Don't say any more, Ric. You're upsetting her."

To Alli's amazement, Ric started to laugh. "*I'm* upsetting *her*. That's rich. That's really rich."

Tears streamed down Nancy's face. "No more, Ric. Don't say any more. Please. I…I can't bear it."

"Maybe I'm paranoid," Alli said, "but it does seem an awful lot of people kill themselves, or at least attempt to, when they've come into contact with Lucius Hartmann. Let's face it, with the question mark over Mrs. Creeley's death, and Arthur Sedgemoor…we can't even be sure the story about her finding Caroline's lifeless body, hanging from a rafter, is true. For all we know, Caroline could have been dead for years."

"Or she could still be alive."

The words were Ric's.

"Indeed, she could," Alli breathed.

"You can't seriously believe that?" Mike said. "What about the solicitor who contacted Nancy? The will, probate, all that legal stuff? There was a death certificate produced at the time. No way. You can't fake a death like that. Not in this day and age. There are too many hoops to jump through."

"Really?" Alli said. "I would have thought that would be easy for an organization such as the Cabal of Seraphragius." After all, with what she had witnessed mere minutes earlier, it seemed the Lord Seraphragius was capable of pretty much anything. "Besides, Lucius even managed to conjure up a version of my own death."

"What?" Mike exclaimed. "What do you mean?"

"It was a sick illusion designed to demonstrate the power he has, or rather, given what we know now, plus what I learned today from my father...." She caught sight of the curious faces around her, Mike's surprise, Ric's bewilderment and Nancy's impossible to decipher. No, now was not the time to divulge all that had passed between her and the people she had believed to be her blood parents, any more than she was going to tell them about her latest encounter. She took a deep breath. It was hard controlling her voice and her emotions after such a traumatic experience, but she must hold on. "Suffice it to say, this cabal has its roots in evil and it's evil for its own sake and for personal gain. Thanks for coming back and telling us this, Ric. It's helped."

Ric nodded, but still looked confused. "I can't think how." He exchanged questioning looks with Mike. "I'm off to have a shower."

Mike followed him but was back in less than a minute and sat down. He seemed lost in thought.

Alli gazed around the room. Nancy had drifted off into a troubled world of her own. She was frowning and appeared to be trying to understand something she found incomprehensible. *Aren't we all?*

Mike was chewing the skin around his thumbnail. Sensing Alli looking at him, he stopped, and lowered his hand.

"What is it, Mike?"

Mike shook his head. "I never...not in a thousand lifetimes...I never thought I would suggest this, but I think the only way we're going to get anywhere is with a full-blown séance. Oh, I know we tried a Summoning, and that was as far as I was prepared to go then but now...."

"What exactly is the difference between what we did before and a séance?" Alli asked.

"To a cursory glance, probably not a great deal, but with the Summoning, we were locking on to a specific entity, whereas this time it would be open house. Pretty much, anyway. That's where the danger lies."

Alli blinked. "And that's what you did when...your friend...?" She felt her stomach muscles clench.

"Yes." Mike lit a cigarette and inhaled deeply before letting the smoke drift out through his nostrils. "We're getting nowhere, and it seems clear that we need to break this deadlock. The trouble is all the protagonists are dead. Dead in the usually accepted sense of the word at any rate. We can't call them up on the phone. We can't pile in one of our cars and drive over to visit them. To communicate with them, we have to do it on their terms or else none of us are going to escape from this. All we have is question after question and a force that infests this house and holds all the answers. At least we have numbers on our side and, if we're careful and avoid all the bad practice that happened…." He lowered his eyes. "There are certain rules and the last time I was involved in a séance, we broke them. That won't happen this time. I'll make sure of it."

Alli nodded slowly. She knew he was right. There was no alternative, however dangerous. Then she had a thought. "Did you try the kitchen door? It worked for me earlier."

Mike shook his head.

Alli stood. "I'll go."

"I'll come with you." Mike followed her out.

In the kitchen, all seemed quiet and normal. Alli took in the neat surfaces, apart from the central island where their unwashed coffee cups remained, along with a few crumbs. She made her way to the back door and turned the handle. It was shut fast.

Back in the living room, Ric had showered and looked fresh and clean in a pair of jeans and a t-shirt. "Sorry it's not vintage 1969 but I've run out of those clothes."

"I doubt any of us have any desire to party now," Alli said.

Nancy shook her head so that her long hair fell over her face.

"Mike suggested we hold a séance," Alli said.

"*Mike* has?" Ric's eyes were saucer-like. "But—"

Alli leapt in. "We know, we know." The last thing they needed now was another fracas between Mike and Ric. "It's the last resort and Mike said he knows how to avoid the danger his friend found himself in."

"Is that true, Mike?"

"I believe so. Hey, that's the best I can offer. We were young and foolish then. Since that happened, I've read a lot about the subject. None of it has made me want to get mixed up in it again, quite the reverse, but at least

I've learned what not to do. And given what you've told us, Ric, I see no alternative." The last comment was delivered with a barb that wasn't lost on Ric. He flinched almost imperceptibly.

"So, are you with us?" Alli asked, as Nancy stood silently next to her. "We're trapped in here."

"Have you tried breaking the windows?" Ric asked. He picked up a solid-looking chair. Before anyone could stop him, he threw it straight at the large patio windows. The chair shattered before it hit them, reduced to kindling, scattered all over the floor.

The four of them stared at the mess.

"What the hell did you do that for?" Mike raged.

"I didn't even see it hit the glass." Ric sounded almost in awe of the force that had shattered the chair.

"It didn't," Alli said, her palms clammy. "It smashed against an invisible wall of some kind."

"That's what I saw," Nancy said, her voice a tiny whisper.

Alli knew she had to act, and it had to be now, before the séance. Who knew what changes that might induce? Especially after Hartmann's warning to her. But she must try and get hold of probably the last person who had seen Caroline alive. There was a telephone in her room. If she could get hold of Caroline's address book, which, right now was sitting next to the living room phone, she could make a call. "Before we start this, I need to go to the bathroom. Who knows how long we'll be and we've all had a bit to drink."

"Good idea," Mike said.

Nancy and Ric murmured their agreement, and, within seconds, they were trooping upstairs. All except Ric, who made for the downstairs bathroom.

As soon as they had left, Alli grabbed the address book. Once in her bedroom, she locked the door and dashed to the phone. She took it off its cradle and prayed there would be no resounding click anywhere else to give her away. She found Mrs. Creeley's number and dialed.

The phone rang out.

Come on, come on.

At the fifth ring it was answered.

"Hello?" The voice was female, not young.

"Mrs. Creeley?" Alli whispered.

"I can hardly hear you."

Alli raised her voice a shade. "Is that Mrs. Creeley?"

There was hesitation. Then, "Yes. Who's that?"

"You don't know me. I'm Alli Sinclair and I'm staying at Canonbury Manor."

Silence. Followed by an audible intake of breath at the other end.

"I need your help, Mrs. Creeley. I need to know what really happened to Caroline Rand and whatever you can tell me about the Cabal of Seraphragius."

"Do you want me to sign my death warrant?" The woman sounded terrified.

"No, of course not. Please. My life…. Other people's lives may depend on it. I don't have long."

"That much is true. No one mixed up with that lot has long. They mostly died out. The cabal. They lost the big house. Canonbury Manor. After the Great War. The owner sold it outside the cabal before hanging himself. That's the preferred method, you know. Suicide by hanging. That's what Miss Rand did. I found her. Before her there was Mr. Sedgemoor. He owned the house for a while, but he wouldn't do. Not when they had someone of the true bloodline to take over. So, he had to go…. That man. Lucius Hartmann. He found her. Miss Rand. He made sure the house went to her. Their only means of survival is to keep under the radar. Miss Rand was perfect for them, for years. They never thought she'd do it. Never dreamed she had the courage. But I knew. I…."

"Mrs. Creeley?" Loud scuffling came over the phone.

A roar. Like a tiger.

The woman's scream tore at Alli's insides.

"Mrs. Creeley? Mrs. Creeley?"

A click and the phone went dead. Alli tried again and again, but she couldn't get a line. Goddammit, she had been warned. Hartmann had *told* her not to…but she hadn't mentioned anything about what had gone on at that bloody orgy. Nor about seeing their vile deity in his feline form. Not a word.

But she had crossed the cabal. And Mrs. Creeley had paid the price.

Someone banged on her door. Mike's voice. "Alli? Are you all right?" He rattled the door handle. "Hey, what's happening? Who were you talking to?"

Alli replaced the receiver and took deep breaths. She must act normally, not invite awkward questions or suspicion that she was keeping anything from them. She forced herself to take steady steps to the door and turned the key, before pasting a smile on her face. "Sorry, I always lock my door. Force of habit."

"I heard you talking. Did you make a phone call?"

"I tried to. The phone's dead."

"Oh great. Not only can't we leave, we can't phone anyone either."

"Perhaps we should have thought of that earlier and called the police. To get us out of here."

"And say what exactly? 'Officer please come. We're locked *in*.' Can you imagine? Quite apart from the fact that if they had even bothered to come out here, the house would have let them come and go as they pleased until they left. *Then* it would have stopped us going anywhere."

"We could have gone with them."

He seemed to consider that for a moment. "Maybe. But it's academic now anyway. Come on, let's get this thing over with."

Alli followed him downstairs. In the living room, Nancy and Ric looked up as they entered. Alli made straight for the phone. It too was dead. Her lie had become reality.

CHAPTER SEVENTEEN

They sat around the circular table in the living room, their hands touching but not clasped, as Mike had instructed. It seemed to Alli as if everyone, herself included, was too scared even to breathe more than absolutely necessary.

"Close your eyes," Mike said.

Alli closed hers and a light breeze wafted around her as if someone had opened a window or door nearby. Should she open her eyes again? No. They must do this, and they must do it according to the rules, even if she wasn't entirely sure what they were, nor was she confident Mike did either. He seemed to be making it up as they went along.

He spoke. "We are here to ask the spirits of this house to join us in our circle. We mean you no harm. Caroline Rand. If you are there among them, please step forward. We're here to help. We will each introduce ourselves. I am Mike."

"I am Alli."

"I'm Nancy."

"And I'm Ric."

Mike called out again. "Caroline, we know you're troubled and that your spirit cannot rest. You have joined with Alli and asked for her help. We are all here to provide support so you can get that help. Tell us what you need."

Silence.

Mike tried again. "Any spirits surrounding Caroline at this time, please step forward. Bring her to us."

Another breeze. This time it hit Alli full in the face. "Woah, did you feel that chill?"

"I did," Mike said.

Judging by the noncommittal murmurs from the others, they were the only two.

Across the table from her, Ric started to laugh. It began as a nervous giggle, but soon developed into a full, almost hysterical belly laugh.

"Ric, for fuck's sake!" Mike said.

"I can't help it," Ric said. "I'm...not...doing it." He was gasping for breath.

Alli opened her eyes. Nancy screamed. Ric's chair flew backward, and he raised up a couple of feet off the floor, spread-eagled and suspended in mid-air, still laughing like a maniac.

He spun, slowly at first, then built momentum, faster and faster. Mike sprang out of his chair. He, Alli and Nancy tried to grab Ric's flailing arms but were beaten back by the force propelling him. The laughter turned to screams as Ric crashed to the floor. The rest of the group tried to help him up. His eyelids fluttered and there seemed to be recognition in his eyes, but his face had turned an unhealthy pasty shade of gray.

"Let's get him onto the sofa," Mike said. Alli helped him and, having sat him down, Nancy brought up his legs while Alli tucked cushions under his head. Beads of sweat formed on his forehead and his hands felt clammy and cold to her touch.

He fixed Alli with a stare that made her cringe. "He's coming for you. You know too much now. I...." He heaved a sigh that seemed to be wrenched out of him, then his eyes closed and he slumped to one side.

"Ric. Ric." Mike slapped his cheeks and Ric stirred again. This time when he opened his eyes, he stared vacantly around.

"What happened? We were sitting round the table."

"Don't you remember anything?" Alli asked. "A force of some kind grabbed you.... You told me someone was coming for me. Do you remember any of that?"

Ric hesitated. "No. I don't know. There's...." He shook his head. "It's gone now."

"One thing's for certain," Mike said. "We've started this. Let's finish it."

Nancy hung back.

"Oh, come on, Nancy," Alli said. "We can't stop now. Even *I* know you can't simply let these things go. We *have* to keep going."

Mike took Nancy's hand. "Come on, you know we all have to see this through. You're not on your own. You've got all of us here. Anyway, it seems to be Alli it's most interested in."

"Thanks," Alli said, with a wry smile. Mike winked at her. It was an unexpected warm gesture, friendly and natural at a time when everything else seemed surreal and impossible. Being with these three and going through this séance together was gradually reassuring Alli. They really *were* in it together. With the terrible revelations she had experienced in these past few hours, she had never been in more need of friends than now. And, at this moment, these were the only friends she had in the world.

"Let's get back to it," Mike said, and they resumed their seats.

"Okay, touch hands again and close your eyes as before," Mike said. "I'm going to try for Caroline alone this time."

"But that—"

Mike banged on the table. "Shut up, Nancy, the other way is too dangerous. You must see that."

Nancy said nothing.

Mike began again. "Spirits in this house. We are reaching out to Caroline Rand. Only Caroline Rand. Caroline, please come forward and speak to us."

Nothing.

"Caroline, we come with love to help you."

In the distance, music played.

"Can you hear that?" Alli asked. "She's singing 'Lady Gossamer'."

"I don't hear anything," Mike said. "Do you, Nancy?"

She shook her head.

"Only you are supposed to hear it," Mike said to Alli. "Looks like we made contact. Go on, Alli, speak to her."

Alli moistened her lips. "Caroline? It's me, Alli. Tell me what you need me to do so I can help you find peace."

She knew the others didn't hear the voice that spoke only in her head. Caroline's voice.

The cabal is here. They want you. Only you, Alli. It's always been about you.

The music stopped. The atmosphere changed. An unfamiliar male voice, with a slight East European accent, addressed her.

"Welcome to The Columbine, Miss Sinclair. You are expected."

Alli opened her eyes and stared into the smiling face of a man who was holding two menus. "Please follow me."

This was a restaurant like no other Alli had ever been in, not that she went to many. The ambience was peaceful, gentle classical music played in the background. Seating was secluded in high-backed semi-circular booths, constructed so no one except those sitting there could see their table companions. This was a place for people who valued their privacy and, judging by the sumptuous décor and rich fabrics, paid handsomely for it.

The maître d' led her through a tangled maze of enclosed booths from which a gentle thrum of conversation and the clink of cutlery and glasses gave the only clue to the popularity of this place. What had he called it? The Columbine. Not a name she was familiar with. And he said she was expected, but by whom?

The maître d' stopped at a booth and indicated where Alli was to sit. Opposite her sat Caroline, smiling, looking healthy and happy.

Alli sat and accepted the menu offered to her, noticing at the same time that her arm had healed and the bandage was nowhere to be seen. Caroline took her menu. They both laid them on the table next to them.

"It's so good to see you again, Alli," Caroline said. "I've been lonely without you around and I wanted to see you again before I left for England. This is it this time, I'm afraid. No more return trips for me."

"Really?" Alli asked. "How can you be so sure? You could have another major hit one day. Stranger things have happened."

Caroline laughed and shook her head. Her long hair fell over her shoulders. "No, not me. I'm going to live in a lovely house in Canonbury Ducis. You see, I didn't forget what you told me, and I'm helping to make it come true. I bought Canonbury Manor. It seems my investments have been paying off handsomely, thanks to Lucius's financial wizardry."

Alli's heart sank. "You do know Lucius belongs to an organization called the Cabal of Seraphragius? You have a picture of Abbot Weaver on the wall of your hall at the Manor. He was one of the leaders of it in Tudor times. As evil a character as you could wish to meet. He pulls Lucius's strings—"

Caroline's hand was cool, her grasp was strong, and her expression racked with fear. In a mere few seconds, she seemed to have aged, as if she had donned the mask of herself as a much older woman. "Don't speak of him like that, Alli. It's too…dangerous. I know about the cabal. I know what they're capable of…Lucius is…and Abbot Weaver…. They're… related. I can't tell you any more. They'll know. They're everywhere. Everywhere. Even here." Her voice had dropped to a mere whisper and Alli had to strain to hear her.

"But Caroline. I'm here to help you. You asked for my help. Begged for my help. I have to be honest with you. You must break free of Lucius, even if it means losing…." Alli's voice petered off. Caroline's expression said it all. She was already in too deep. To break free now would mean losing everything, even assuming she could do so.

Caroline picked up her menu. "The maître d' will be back soon for our order. We don't have long. Choose whatever you like. It's on me."

"I didn't come here to eat. In fact, *you* brought me here. Right now, in my own time, I'm sitting around a table with some acquaintances of mine. We're in your living room at Canonbury Manor and we're holding a séance. We called out to you to join us, to connect with us. And right at that moment, you spoke to me. Only me. And I found myself here, in this restaurant with you."

Caroline raised eyes brimming with tears and hopelessness. "Don't you see? It's too late for your help. It's always been too late for that. They chose me. I used to think it was pure chance that it was me Lucius met that day when Harrison Grant introduced us. You didn't know that, did you? Yes, good old swindling Harrison. He's one of them as well. Everywhere you look, pretty much everyone with power that I came into contact with at that time was one of the cabal. They made sure I was successful and then I decided I didn't need them anymore. I had made it, you see. Me. Caroline Rand. But I had been chosen, even before I was born. You want to know how you can help me, Alli? How you can *really* help me?"

Alli nodded, dreading what was coming next.

"Kill me. Kill me now before I go back to England. Once I set foot in Canonbury Manor they won't let me go, unless…. You see, the real power lies in that house. It's in the walls, the very fabric of that place, put there when Abbot Weaver brought Seraphragius's remains back from the Middle East and buried them beneath the foundations in some kind of vault. Then, when Seraphragius's descendant, Abbot Weaver, was executed, the cabal brought *his* ashes back to Canonbury Manor. The place was in ruins then, but they concealed them for a later generation to find. Now, they're in an urn in a small room in the attic. Maybe you've found the place?"

Alli nodded. "There's an urn, but it has *your* name and date of birth on it."

Caroline nodded. "Lucius's little joke. I am to join the abbot when I slip this 'mortal coil' as they like to call it. Of course, in your time, I already have, haven't I?"

Her face continued to age. Crow's feet etched their way around eyes that sank deeper into their sockets. Her hands clutched the menu – an old woman's hands – and when she spoke, her voice wavered. "It's far too late for me. I begged you to kill me a few moments ago in your time, but you couldn't kill me now if you tried. Empty words, Alli. Empty words." She clutched at Alli's hand. "I can sense his presence. It's growing nearer. When he comes, look at his face, Alli. Look and be warned."

"What is this place? Where is it?"

"You won't find The Columbine on any map. It's the most exclusive restaurant in the world. Perfect privacy, divine food, exquisite wines. Always a table when you want one. Always the company you want to keep. But it's expensive, Alli. Some might say beyond price. And you don't find it. The Columbine finds you."

The maître d' was back, a smile pasted on his face. He held a small notebook and pencil ready to take their order. Caroline closed up her menu. "Champagne, Pol Roger, I think. And the finest Beluga caviar for both of us."

"Certainly, ladies."

As he took the menu off her, Alli looked closer. The eyes. So distinctive, and the overall bearing of the man. Why hadn't she seen that before? And then…the flash of the violet-blue stone set in pure gold. Their eyes met and Alli sensed the recognition. A slight frown momentarily replaced the smile, only for him to paste it back on again. In a second, he swept away from their table.

"You saw, didn't you?" Caroline said.

"It's him. Abbot Weaver."

"And Lucius Hartmann. And countless others. They are all one and the same."

★   ★   ★

The notebook, Alli. Find my notebook. It's in that attic room…. The voice in Alli's head faded, to be replaced by Mike's voice, sounding anxious.

"Alli. Alli, please wake up. Please come back to us. Oh, God, don't let it happen again."

Mike was shaking her, but it took so much effort to open her eyes. Caroline's plea replayed itself over and over in her head. She must find that notebook. Alli forced her eyes open.

"Thank God for that." Mike let go of her shoulders and sank down into his chair.

"What happened?" Alli said. "Did I say anything? Did I make any sense? A lot happened to me, but it was in my mind."

Ric, Mike and Nancy exchanged glances. Nancy said, "You were talking about The Columbine…. It seemed you were in a restaurant or somewhere. You said Caroline's name and the cabal. That was about all that made sense."

The desire to track down that notebook of Caroline's – if indeed it existed – almost overpowered her. She wanted to share it with the others, but she could feel Caroline's spirit within her, urging her to keep it to herself; that it was for her eyes only. She must get away from the rest of them and find it.

"I'm sorry to be such a nuisance. I really need to lie down."

"Of course," Mike said. "We should probably all think about turning in anyway. It's been a long and…difficult day."

"Oh no, don't do anything on my account." She couldn't have the others upstairs while she was searching for the elusive notebook. She could only hope and pray Caroline would somehow guide her to its hiding place.

Nancy stood and made for the small tray of crystal decanters. "I vote we have a nightcap. I don't know about you, but I could do with one." The others murmured agreement and Alli made her way to the door.

"Fancy a little something to take up with you?" Nancy waved a brandy glass at her.

"Oh, no, no. Thanks. I won't need anything to help me sleep. I'm quite sure of that."

"Well, night, night then."

Alli avoided looking down the hall at the pictures. The last thing she needed was to see Abbot Weaver.

The hall clock stood, broken and leaning against the wall where Ric and Mike had heaved it earlier. Its hands stood stubbornly fixed at ten twenty-five. That time again. The very sight of it made Alli shudder.

As she mounted the stairs, Alli concentrated. Where would Caroline secrete an important notebook? Two places sprang to mind, both of which required her to go into the bedroom Nancy had adopted as her own. At the top of the stairs, Alli paused and listened. Only the merest hint of conversation permeated through from downstairs. She had to act now before Nancy also decided it was time for bed.

Relieved to see Nancy's door slightly ajar, Alli went in, glanced around, and made for the door leading to the small attic room. Adrenaline fueled her steps as she almost sprinted to the top and opened the door into the room itself.

As soon as she was in there, she wanted to get out. Surely, they had been through everything? It couldn't have stayed concealed. There was nowhere....

Her eyes locked on to something she hadn't noticed earlier. The cloth covering the altar was askew, probably from when they had come up here before. Alli approached it. There. Faint but discernible. A gap between the stones, which had been filled...but not with mortar. In color it was almost indistinguishable. Someone had gone to some considerable trouble to match the sandy color of the mortar with the object that Alli now touched. It seemed to be cardboard. When she scratched at it, flakes of sand floated down, coating the cloth. She needed to dig it out. Her nails weren't up to the job. Around her neck were hippy chains and a pendant with sharp edges. That might do. She took it off and pressed it into service.

Within seconds, she pried the object loose and held a slim volume, covered in a layer of fine sand and plaster dust.

Hearing noises downstairs, Alli scuttled out of the room, notebook in hand, and closed the door quietly behind her. She crept down the small stone staircase and managed to escape into her room before the others, who had come out of the living room, began to ascend the stairs.

She locked the door, sat down on her bed and began to read.

CHAPTER EIGHTEEN

Note to whoever finds this. The Cabal of Seraphragius exists. Don't believe those who say it is a myth.

And walk away from it now. If it isn't already too late.

Laurel Canyon, March 16th in the first year of my after-death.

My name is Caroline Rand.

I need to write my story down before it's too late. It could be all there will be to remember me by. I must relive every second as if it were happening again now. It won't be easy, for so little of it makes any sense. Oh well, here goes:

It feels strange here. I can hear voices, smell…incense, I think, but not mine. An unfamiliar scent. I can taste my mouth and it's stale, as if I haven't brushed my teeth in a while, like the morning after too much drinking and smoking. My body works. I lift my hand. Except it isn't my hand. My fingers aren't the same. Mine are long. 'Perfect for playing guitar' someone told me. Indeed, I can achieve the most complex chords quite easily.

I look through eyes that aren't mine. I know they're not because I'm shortsighted and these eyes can see things perfectly.

This is a lovely house. I recognize it straightaway. It belongs to Alli. At any rate, she lives in it. Maybe she rents. She comes and goes so often and at no notice. I had something to tell her, but I can't see her anywhere. Maybe she left and went back to England. To Canonbury Ducis. Such a lovely name. So quaint. Like somewhere Agatha Christie might have invented for Miss Marple. One day I'll buy a house there. I don't know how I know that. I just do.

I decide to go outside, thinking I might find her in her garden. It's such a pretty one. Like mine. We both have little natural streams providing a haven for frogs and dragonflies. The sun's shining and, as I slide open the windows and step out, the birds greet me with their happy, carefree songs. I inhale the fresh air, so different from the filthy smog-ridden city that lies so near and yet, mercifully, so far away from Laurel Canyon.

From the end of her short drive, I can see my house. It doesn't look right. There's a 'For Sale' notice, and a memory floats into my mind like a letter dropping into my mailbox. Is this a real one, or one planted, like so many of the others? The sign makes it seem real enough. I have no home. It must be sold to pay off the creditors. That swindling manager will, right now, be sunning himself on a South Sea island, spending *my* money and the creditors'. But it was my name on the contracts, so I must pay.

I hear a noise behind me. A man standing at the window looking out. He's dressed strangely. As if he were performing in a Shakespearean play. I saw *Henry VIII* once and this man looks like one of the clerics. The Archbishop of Canterbury perhaps. His sumptuous robes and abbot's hat look just like it. A jewel flashes on his finger as it catches the sunshine. Such a vivid blue, with hints of violet. I have never seen such a stone before. He beckons to me and I have to go. I can't stop myself.

I drift toward the window, my feet barely touching the ground. The frogs stop their croaking. The birds aren't singing. It's as if the world were holding its breath.

The strange man steps aside for me to re-enter the house and I catch sight of my reflection in a wall mirror.

Except…it isn't me. I blink and Alli blinks back at me.

"She is ready," the man says, and his voice has a deep resounding echo. It seems half a tone lower than his own voice and a fraction slower.

My muscles tense and my jaw locks. I can't move. The room grows darker, and shapes begin to move around. Gradually they become more solid and take on form. I hear them before I can fully focus on them. They are chanting. Ancient plainsong voiced by figures in plain monks' habits. Their hoods hide their faces. There must be a dozen of them, but I can see through them to the furniture and the wall beyond. Their gray-blackness draws closer as they move as one. Not walking as such. The closer they come, the stronger the smell of incense mingled with decay, a rotting smell that reminds me of long-dead, saturated leaves concealing an animal carcass beneath. Like that long-dead rat that scared me so much when I was a child and out for a walk one Sunday. I kicked at the deep carpet of leaves, releasing a foul smell. Then I saw the teeth.... I *think* it was my memory.

I close my eyes and pray. I beg for them to go away, plead to awaken and find myself in my own body again, with my own memories and not this strange melting pot of fact and fiction. Am I sharing Alli's memories as well as her body? If I call out to her, would she hear me and come to me somehow? If everything that is me is in her, where is *she*?

They're taking me, ghostly hands manhandling me. I open my eyes and look straight at the monk nearest to me. I stare at the all-enveloping hood. I try to lift my hand, but my arms are pinned down by other monks. They surround me. They lift me, their arms concealed beneath their robes. Except one.

I scream at the skeletal hand, the white bony fingers that clench around my wrist. I scream again as the monk dislodges its hood and it falls back, revealing more gleaming white bone. A skull with no eyes, only sockets. It wears a sickly, deathly grin and clacks its jaws together, making a sound like snapping twigs. I scream, scream and scream again. The monks lift me higher. They're laughing. They sound drunk and I can smell stale wine on their breath. How is that possible? It's like this is a celebration and I'm the cabaret act.

The robed man is chanting in Latin. Or maybe it's some other language. There's nothing holy about this. I scream myself hoarse. It doesn't matter. No one cares.

They hold me high above them and the wooden beams of the ceiling melt away. A swirling sky, gray and angry with clouds, thunders above me. Crack after crack of thunder rolls through the charged atmosphere. Lightning forks hit the ground and sizzle all around. The smells of electricity and burning grass swamp me. Still the man chants, and still the monks hold me aloft, laughing and echoing the foul mantra.

The sky parts and all grows black. The only light scythes in flashes from the lightning. No stars. No moon. Only blackness darker than any night. I fight to breathe. The air grows colder around me, and I'm shivering.

The man stops chanting.

The monks lower me. I feel cold stone beneath my back, still dressed, as I am, in my thin summer dress.

A mighty roar sends the monks scurrying back from where I lie.

★   ★   ★

Time has passed. How much, I don't know but I am bound by my arms and legs to the raised stone slab beneath me. I cannot move as an animal I cannot make out bends over me. Its hot breath stings my cheeks and its strong feral smell makes me choke. I retch at the odor of decay, and I vomit bile. The creature moves into my vision. A great beast with downward curving fangs like a massive white tiger. Its fur is coarse to look at, not gleaming. Dull, lifeless. The evil within the monster pours out of it. It lifts a massive paw and with one slash, rips open my tethered right arm.

I scream at the shock of it, then scream again with the pain. I know blood is pumping out of a severed artery. I know I am dying. Again. It comes almost as a relief. I stop screaming. My breath comes in short pants, my lungs unable to cope with the shock of the blood loss, the screaming icy coldness that replaces it, and the horror of what is happening to me.

The creature moves out of my vision and the stink of it fades.

One by one the monks reassemble around me and one of them unties my injured arm. He holds it up so that I might see the damage.

But there is none. Not one sign. They untie the rest of the ropes and the heavy iron rings embedded into the stone, through which the rope has been threaded, clang against granite. I realize I have been lying not merely on a stone slab, but on someone's final resting place. A granite sarcophagus.

But, in that moment, I am alive again. I can breathe and have no feeling of losing blood.

The monk speaks. "She is one with us and will be my acolyte." He throws back his hood and I see him.

I recognize him.

He is Lucius Hartmann.

★   ★   ★

The account stopped there. Alli idly flicked over blank pages until she came across another entry. Judging by the handwriting, this had been written much later, maybe decades after the first. It was recognizably the same hand as the earlier section, but this time, it was much more personal.

★   ★   ★

To Alli,

My Granddaughter.

You are reading this because you were brought here. The Cabal of Seraphragius ensnared me and, as my only living descendant, you have a right to know all of this.

Let me tell you about this house.

Parts of it are older than you can imagine. It hides many secrets. Maybe you have already seen the vault – the Unholy of Unholies. Some of the stone was brought back from Seraphragius's homeland, along with his mortal remains. His influence has grown up like a tree from its roots. This house is his and he is this house. Once human, now his spirit is pure evil. This is his resting place, if you can call it that. But he never rests. His spirit transfers itself from generation to generation.

His acolytes live to serve him. Some choose to, most don't. They are unwittingly born to it as I was. As Lucius before me – yes, we are related. Don't be shocked. It is a distant relationship and one I was unaware of until much later. Then there are the followers. Disciples if you prefer. Many of them are lured by promises of great wealth, which are indeed fulfilled, at a price. On their death, all their wealth reverts back to the cabal. And this house – Canonbury Manor – is their headquarters, established by the greatest of acolytes, Hippolytus Weaver. I am sure, that by now, you have encountered him. Lucius will have ensured that. You see, we all have our roles to play.

Legally, this house is yours. Ignore anyone who claims the contrary. You'll find the papers in the attic room. Open the urn. The lid has a false top. Unscrew it and you'll find the proof, all duly attested.

A word of warning, the cabal need the legitimacy of an owner who is corporeal, but they can't allow you to inherit it and live here of your own free will. You *have* to become one of them as they forced me to, on pain of forfeiting my eternal soul.

They have always known all about you. Every last detail. I expect you know now that you were adopted. This will probably come as a shock, but your adoptive parents were involved too. Not that they were members. Just a couple desperate for a child of their own.

The cabal paid Christian and Jessica Sinclair to adopt and take care of you. Struggling musicians, especially those who want children they can call their own, are very vulnerable. They tried their best to shield you but, in the end, they were powerless, and they knew it. Don't judge them too harshly. They went away because they were forced to.

But they did truly love you, Alli. I know they did.

★   ★   ★

Alli laid the notebook down. So much to take in. And where did it leave her?

After a while, she undressed and went to bed, her mind reeling. Finally, she fell asleep, but her dreams were swirling nightmares.

CHAPTER NINETEEN

Alli opened her eyes. Someone was in the room with her. Not just the room. Her *bed*. She tried to sit, but strong hands pushed her back. Strong, male hands. In the semi-darkness, a tall man knelt astride her. He had her arms pinned down. She tried to scream. Her vocal chords wouldn't work. An instant's panic, was she paralyzed? No. Asleep. Another nightmare. This one seemed too real. Behind the figure, the shadowy monks poured into the room. They chanted softly and stood against the walls until not an inch remained between them.

The man astride her touched his fingers to his lips and then to her own. He murmured in a strange language Alli didn't understand, but she felt soothed and reassured by his voice and her fear melted away.

He took his time, gently, tenderly. Like a lover. No hint or thought of violence. When he entered her, she wanted him. Yearned to feel him inside her. Hell, she desired him as she had only ever desired men she felt strongly attracted to.

He seemed familiar, even if she couldn't physically recognize him. His cloak concealed his arms and shoulders and a hood cast his face into dark shadow. She thought of Ric. No. And Mike had long dreadlocks and she was as sure as she could be that this man didn't.

When it was over, she felt at peace. The man kissed his fingers and placed them over her lips before he climbed off the bed. He covered her nakedness with the duvet. Then, without a word, stepped back into the shadows as the monks made room for him.

A central figure, neither human nor animal, stepped forward and Alli, still unable to move, felt her inner core quake. With a clawed hand, the creature performed a gesture, tracing a shape in the air. A star maybe, she couldn't be sure. A wave of exhaustion overwhelmed her, and she closed her eyes.

★   ★   ★

Dawn lit up the room through the chinks in her bedroom curtains when she awoke. Memories of the strange dream returned to her and she inspected the bed for any trace it could have been real. There was nothing. It had been the notebook. Caroline's words had invaded her dreams. Except that wouldn't explain her nakedness. She reached under her pillow to find her nightdress, neatly folded.

It had certainly been a night of strange illusions and, apart from the erotic encounter, Caroline had dominated. Sometimes she had been old, at other times young. The words she had written filled Alli's mind along with a host of unanswered questions.

So much had changed in the course of this short weekend. Finding out her parents weren't who she thought they were would have been cause enough for grief, but everything else? And what about Nancy? How would she face her now she had read Caroline's notebook?

She had become one with Caroline and some part of her lingered deep inside, no longer controlling any thoughts or movements, but still a part of her.

Alli felt changed and, in an odd and indecipherable way, empowered. She also had an overwhelming desire to get out of the house – not merely to escape its clutches, which in the circumstances was more than reasonable – but because she must go somewhere that she was being directed to. The problem was, she had no idea who was doing the directing this time. She could only hope it was Caroline.

Showered and dressed, Alli descended the stairs. She found the others drinking coffee in the kitchen. They smiled and greeted her.

"Did you sleep well?" Nancy asked, as she poured a cup of coffee and handed it to her.

"Fine thanks," Alli lied. She sat on a stool at the island, next to Ric.

Mike set his cup down. "We've been saying what strange dreams we had. Did you dream at all, Alli?"

Alli shrugged. "I expect so. Can't really remember."

"The odd thing is," Ric said. "We all seem to have experienced the same dream. All about Caroline and that Abbot Weaver."

"And don't forget Lucius," Nancy said.

"How could I ever forget him?" Ric laughed. "Are you sure you didn't have a dream about them?"

Alli shook her head. This conversation disturbed her, but instinct told her not to question it, merely to tread warily. "If I did, I can't remember. I slept heavily though. I think it was to do with that experience I had during the séance. It seemed to completely drain me."

"Ah, yes," Mike said. "It would."

Alli stared hard at him, looking for any trace of change in his attitude toward her. She couldn't find any. He seemed exactly the same. She tried to picture him in the hooded cloak, kneeling astride her, but there was no escaping that hair. It reached down to his waist. Even if he had tied it back, or pinned it up somehow, there would have been some trace of it. The cloak wasn't concealing enough to cover all that. Alli couldn't resist one comment though. "Isn't that a bit odd? You all having the same dream? I mean, was it exactly the same, down to the last detail, or did your dreams simply feature the same characters?"

"The same," Nancy said. "Right down to the last detail of what each of us was wearing and who said and did what."

Alli didn't like the hardness of Nancy's stare. It made her feel as if she knew Alli had read the notebook – and what it contained, how it undermined her own position.

That strange compulsion overtook her again. She had to get out of there right now. But would the house let her?

Alli slipped off the stool and made her way to the back door.

"Where are you going?" Mike asked.

"I don't know," she said. "I only know I have to go."

"Then we're coming with you."

To Alli's surprise, the kitchen door opened to the outside world. A breath of freshly scented summer air caressed her face as she took a step outside. The three duly followed at a slight distance. All Alli knew at that moment was she had a fierce compulsion to move in a certain direction

and right now that took her out of the house, across the gravel pathway
and into a grove of trees at the back of the house.

Not a word passed between them as the others trudged after her, along
a dirt path. She veered off between some bushes where they all had to
push their way through self-sown sycamore seedlings, tall switchgrass
and overgrown hawthorn. Alli snagged her clothes on brambles, and tall
thistles scratched her arms and feet. Then she saw it. In the distance, stood
an ancient summerhouse built of the same stone as the manor. What
wasn't obliterated by vegetation gleamed dully in the sunshine.

"We're here," Alli said, although she hadn't a clue how she could
be so certain. Other than Caroline's voice, which now rang in her head,
urging her on. "I know it looks as if no one has been here for a couple
of hundred years, but here is where we're meant to be, and this is where
we'll get our answers."

Through the tangle of brambles, vines and ivy, a sturdy wooden door,
the timber charred and blistered, drew Alli toward it. A mere handful
of steps led up to it, but with all the tangled undergrowth, trying to
find a foothold wasn't easy. At least the others helped, tugging at the
undergrowth to provide sufficient space to step. She had the oddest feeling
that, with every passing second, they were becoming more and more like
strangers to her.

Alli ignored the scratches on her hands and arms and the tiny rivulets
of blood that bloomed in their wake. The door handle was a large, rusted
iron ring. She tried to twist it. It wouldn't budge.

"I'll have a go," Mike said. Ric helped him. They made slow progress.
Finally, with a massive effort on both their parts, the handle turned, and
the door juddered reluctantly as they put their backs to it. It creaked,
groaned and finally gave way. How could this be where they would find
answers to anything, other than discovering a new species of spider? But
Alli knew she was right. Beside her, Nancy remained silent. What was
going through her head right now?

"Come on," Mike said, and Nancy and Alli struggled over the
remaining brambles into the echoing circular building.

Inside, enough remained of the delicate plasterwork to indicate that this had once been an elegant retreat back in the eighteenth century. Black mold crept up the once immaculate sand-colored walls but hadn't reached the fine white carved dado rail running around the room. Light filtered downward and Alli looked up, craning her neck to see a glass-paneled domed roof, partially overgrown with vegetation. A few panes of glass were missing, and a thin sycamore branch, in full leaf, had penetrated, plugging the hole. Beneath their feet, an accumulation of dead, dry leaves provided a makeshift carpet that rustled with every step they took.

"Now where?" Mike asked and Alli realized he was addressing her.

Alli looked around and spotted an apparent crack in the wall, only it seemed like a straight line and cracks were surely never so precise. She hurried over to it and traced it with her finger. Apart from the lack of a handle….

When Alli pushed at it, she felt it give. She tried again, and it gave a little more. The others joined her. One big, concerted shove and it opened. This time, with barely a murmur and no protesting groan from rusted hinges.

"We should have brought flashlights," Ric said. "Why didn't you warn us it would be dark here?"

"Because I didn't know," Alli said. "I had no idea we were even going to a building. I only knew when we got here that this is where we were supposed to be."

"Look what I've found." Nancy held up half a dozen tall candles in one hand and a box of matches in another.

"Where did you get those?" Ric asked.

Nancy pointed to a pile of leaves. "Over there. I saw something and when I kicked the leaves away, there were these candles and matches. I think they've been there for some time. The matchbox looks old. Pre-decimal anyway. Look at the price on it. Fourpence in old money."

"Before 1971 then," Mike said. "Wonder if they still work."

"There's only one way to find out," Alli said, and Nancy handed her the box. She held the candles steady as Alli took out a match and struck it. It took a few scratches of the sandpaper, but the leafy bed seemed to have kept the box and its precious contents dry and the match suddenly flared into life. She lit the candles one by one until the match burned her fingers. Nancy lit the remaining two from the others which had stopped sputtering and were now burning with a steady flame. She tucked the matchbox into the pocket of her skirt.

"Okay, let's go," Mike said. He pointed at Alli. "You first."

Alli held her candle in front of her, illuminating a small room with four doors leading off it. Which one should they go through? Should they try them one after the other and then decide which to pursue? The others were waiting. They were looking at her to lead, but she had no more idea of what they should do than they did.

She made her decision. "How about we open each in turn, have a quick look inside and then move on to the next?"

Alli could sense the others exchanging glances behind her back. No one said a word. She pressed on and started with the door nearest to her. It had a round, polished wooden handle, which turned smoothly. A rush of cold, stagnant air sent the candles flickering madly. A low thrum of chanting began, coupled with a rushing noise of something moving at speed toward them. A familiar feral smell.

"Fucking hell!" Ric exclaimed.

Alli slammed the door. They listened. From the other side, no more chanting permeated. A snuffling noise sent shivers through her body. "Let's try the next," she said, trying not to sound as panicked as she felt. The others nodded, their faces white in the candle glow.

The second door opened sweetly as well. This time, no rush of foul air, merely a waft of a summer breeze and an aroma she recognized all too well. "I think I know where this leads," Alli said. "Come on."

The others followed down a narrow corridor. Sunlight shone at the end, along with a trickle of water she knew came from a natural stream. Alli half ran, a wave of happiness and familiarity spurring her on. In a moment they were out. They blew out their candles and left them at the entrance, which they could barely see for the concealing bushes.

"Where is this place?" Nancy asked, staring around her in wonderment at the garden, the trees, the lush jasmine and...Caroline's little bungalow.

It was all here, just as she remembered it. The cicadas, the birdsong and, nearby, someone was softly strumming a guitar.

"This is Caroline's house, Nancy. We're in Laurel Canyon. Come on, I'll show you."

The others exchanged bewildered glances. Alli felt a dizzy wave of delirium, as of being home. She had thought she would never be able to return but now here she was. Okay, so it wasn't her own home, but she still felt a strong connection to it. Everything would be all right now. She was back. If she could only stay here.

When she looked closer, she changed her mind.

The unfamiliar drapes at the windows. The door, freshly painted in a dark green, a world away from the natural pine that had been Caroline's choice. The car in the driveway. A dark blue Chevrolet. Caroline hadn't owned one of those. Maybe a friend? Or maybe time had moved on.

Someone came to the door. A man, well-dressed and not pleased to see them. "What are you people doing here? This is private property."

"I'm sorry, sir," Alli began. "We meant no harm. It's just…a good friend of mine used to live here. This was her house."

He looked her up and down. "You mean Caroline Rand."

"Apparently," Mike said. The man looked at him sharply.

"Yes," Alli said quickly. "She lived here in 1969."

"Things have changed a bit here in the Canyon, since the Sixties," he said. "Did you live here then?"

"Briefly," Alli said.

"Bet you didn't lock your door then, did you?"

Alli shook her head. "I don't think anyone did."

"I have three locks on mine now. Three." He held up three fingers. "And I still keep a loaded shotgun to hand. Just in case. A .44 Magnum, under my pillow."

"The Manson murders," Alli breathed.

The man nodded. "You'll understand my reaction then. People around here are a bit suspicious of anyone dressed like you these days. Most of your type are long gone from here." He glanced at his wristwatch. "You'll have to excuse me. I have to get to work."

"Of course." Alli moved aside to let him out to his car.

He must have watched them until they had left his driveway and turned onto Lookout Mountain Avenue. Only then did Alli hear the car engine start. "Keep walking," she said. "Away from the house."

"We can't get back any other way," Nancy said.

"I know, but he's not going to be satisfied until he's sure we've sated our curiosity and are heading back to L.A."

"Even though we're walking," Mike said. "And, from what I've heard, no one walks anywhere in L.A."

"We can hardly steal a car," Alli said. "I have an idea. Let's go to my house. I mean the house I used to find myself in. I know where it is. Right around this bend."

The sound of the man's car drew closer behind them. He seemed to be driving at a walking pace. "Take no notice," Alli said. "Just look as if we're chatting happily without a care in the world." She gave a light laugh. Nancy giggled, a little too enthusiastically. Mike did a little jig, which had the advantage of giving him an excuse to turn around. When he twirled back again, Alli asked him, "What's he doing?"

"Calling someone. He's using one of those clunky car phones from the Seventies."

"Maybe this is the Seventies," Alli said.

"Probably the cops," Ric said.

The man's foot hit the gas and he was off and away, but Alli was sure he was staring at them in his rearview mirror.

They rounded the bend. "It's just here—" Alli stopped dead. In front of her, right where her beautiful little bungalow had been, lay a mass of charred timbers and blackened ground.

Nancy put her arm around her shoulders. "Oh, my God, Alli."

Mike and Ric crowded around her.

Into Alli's mind floated the memory of that zoning-out incident when she had seen the blackened ruins of a house. So, it had been hers. She stared at the cremated remains of her once lovely home – a home she had allowed herself for one beautiful second to believe she could return to and stay in – destroyed and gone forever.

Mike squeezed her arm. "I'm afraid it's all too common. Somebody told me once. In summer Laurel Canyon can be like a tinderbox. Fires were a common occurrence back in the Sixties and Seventies. Judging by the regrowth, this must have happened a few years ago."

"Difficult to tell," Ric said. "Nature has a way of taking back what's hers with incredible speed."

"We'd better get back," Mike said. "My guess is this place will be crawling with uniforms any minute, and we'll be picked up for vagrancy or some other trumped-up charge."

He had barely got the words out of his mouth before sirens wailed in the distance, drawing closer.

With no time for grief for what might have been, Alli pushed her thoughts aside and caught up with the others as they raced back to Caroline's former home. They dashed down the driveway back into the garden. Alli pointed to a clump of bushes. "Over there. I'm sure that's where we came out."

They dived into the undergrowth as the cars squealed to a halt. The sound of running feet. Then a familiar voice.

"I first saw them in my garden."

They were well hidden by the bushes and Alli peered around for sign of the entry that would take them back to the summerhouse. For some reason, 'White Rabbit' came into her mind yet again. The police were searching through the undergrowth on the other side of the garden. It wouldn't be long before they moved over in their direction.

The other three crouched down with her, so closely they were almost on top of each other. Alli could feel anxious breathing all around her. Then she saw it. A pair of small, beady black eyes blinking at her. A mouse. Alli nudged the others and pointed. The tiny creature seemed to be gnawing on something white. A bone? She hoped not. Nancy whimpered. Alli clamped her hand over the woman's mouth to stop her crying out. The mouse froze for a second, fixed Alli with its intense gaze, and took off, dropping its prize. A candle.

A police officer called out, "Over here!"

They didn't wait to be found. Like Alice's rabbit, they raced down their own hole. Alli grabbed the gnawed candle and they retrieved the rest at the entrance.

Hot on their heels, a uniformed police officer wielded a nightstick. He was so close, Alli could smell his sweat. He stared straight at her. He should have been able to see her, but his blank expression told her he couldn't make out anything except the bushes and plants. Only she and the others were meant to use that entrance, so only they could see it. Once over its threshold, they were invisible to anyone outside its confines.

"I could have sworn I saw movement here," the bemused officer said and moved out of vision.

"Well, there ain't nothing there now," another cop said, clearly annoyed. "Keep looking."

Alli and the others lit their candles and made their way back to the door.

"We've eliminated that exit. There's nothing for us there. Not anymore." Alli forced back the tears she so longed to shed. "Let's try the next."

"Two down, two to go," Mike said.

★   ★   ★

Alli knew the instant she laid eyes on the Aga cooker that this wasn't the right choice either. Her strange mixture of memories and insights told her this was merely a step along the way. A revisiting of an old haunt of Caroline's — and, after all, isn't that what had been happening? Alli revisiting episodes in Caroline's life?

"Where the hell are we?" Mike asked. "*When* are we?"

"Welcome to Canonbury Manor in the 1970s," Alli said, as they stood in the sunny kitchen. "We're back in the house as it was when Caroline first bought it and renovated. She had a new recording contract and Arthur Sedgemoor was her manager. She had money in the bank and the creditors were paid off. I met her here once. At least, I *think* that's when we are now. It all looks the same."

Mike said, "Let's look around. The trouble is, I don't know what we're looking for."

"Neither do I," Alli said. "I have to believe I'll know it when I see it."

Ric wandered out into the hall and, seconds later, called to them.

They trooped out. Ric was pale and shaking as he pointed at the painting of Abbot Weaver.

"It's alive. In the picture. The face...."

Mike and Alli approached the painting. In the bottom left-hand corner, a disembodied face, little more than a mass of swirling smoke, stretched and contracted. One minute, long and thin, the next...fat, its expression caught between an insane grin and a snarl. At once animal-like and human. And when it seemed more humanoid, it bore more than a passing resemblance to Lucius Hartmann.

Alli let her eyes travel upward to the abbot himself. His expression remained frozen. Caroline's words flooded back. "They're all related," Alli whispered. "One big dynasty, back through time, as far as you can go...." No one seemed to hear her.

Around them the house creaked. Alli forced her eyes away from the painting. "Old timbers. That's all," she said, trying as much to reassure herself as anyone else.

Mike looked at her. "Are you sure? I don't think so. There's a presence here. Can't you feel it?"

The clock struck. Nine clamoring rings. But the hands were still stuck fast at ten twenty-five and it was pitch dark outside. Surely it had been daylight a moment ago?

Ric stared ahead of him. "The stairs. Look at the stairs."

A figure stood silhouetted against a light that couldn't be there. A ghostly silvery-white light, as if the moon shone through a window. Except there was no moon. The figure was male, wearing long robes. Abbot Weaver had returned.

He slowly descended the stairs. The aroma of incense and decay grew stronger as he approached. At the foot of the steps, he stopped and pointed at Nancy. Beside her, Alli felt her tense up.

"You are not of Caroline," he said.

"I'm her granddaughter."

"It is time to put that matter right."

Nancy staggered forward, clutching her chest. Alli leapt to help her as did Mike, and Ric, who caught her as she fell.

The house shifted on its foundations. The figure on the stairs slid in and out of focus, alternating between Weaver and Lucius Hartmann as its fluid movements settled into a rhythmic thudding. The pulsating throb found its echo in the walls. To Alli's eyes it seemed the house closed in on them more and more with each beat. The figure on the stairs grew, seven feet, eight feet, more, until it towered above them. It stretched out its arms, the folds of its abbot's robes forming giant bat's wings, revealing creatures from the depths of hell.

It isn't real. None of it is real. Alli repeated the thought like a mantra. The creatures of the abbot's robes snapped reptilian jaws and clawed the air around them as if unaccustomed to it. Their huge black eyes blinked. Faces that had once been human sloughed skin and became bone, human skulls perforated with horns, bone spurs erupting from every joint.

"This isn't happening. It's an illusion." Alli's voice didn't sound like her own. It rang out across the maelstrom of writhing demons and their devil master.

The house throbbed louder, louder, louder.

The abbot laughed and the sound rose up from the soles of his feet and built to a crescendo.

Alli forced herself to stare him fully in the eyes, despite the pain, a horrible stabbing that felt like someone piercing her eyeballs with needles. But she could still see. The feeling was an illusion. Nothing more. It couldn't be real. She must stand her ground.

Her voice rang out, strong and unwavering. "Everything is an illusion. I do not fear shadows. I do not fear circus tricks."

The abbot ceased laughing. He lowered his arms, and the creatures were once more hidden, if they had ever been there.

He spoke. "This is not over." The face was expressionless, lips set in a firm line, and the eyes stared, exactly as in his portrait. The house ceased its relentless heartbeat and, with a final creak of timbers, settled.

The image of the abbot dissolved into shadow.

"Nancy?" Alli stroked her hand, shocked at how icy it had grown. "Can you hear me?"

Nancy moved her lips. "I see…nothing. I…don't…know…what… it means."

She went limp and Ric laid her on the floor. It was the action of a lover rather than a casual acquaintance. "I'm so sorry it came to this, Nancy. I wish I could have stopped it, but I couldn't." He gave an anguished cry, staggered, then fell, his body engulfed by darkness.

A roaring like a hide of tigers filled the hallway. Mike and Alli reeled from the cacophony. In front of them, holding what looked like a life-size ragdoll, stood Abbot Weaver and it was no ragdoll. Ric screamed as he threw him across the hall, sending him crashing against the stairs. From the unnatural angles of his limbs, it seemed all had been crushed. Then he whimpered.

"I…beg…forgive…me…Father…Abbot."

Abbot Weaver's mouth twisted into a snarl. He aimed a vicious kick at the body of his acolyte. "So perish all who betray our secrets. Watch and be warned." He raised his hand. An unnatural fire burst into life and consumed Ric within seconds. The smell of burning flesh assailed Alli's nostrils and bile rushed up into her mouth. She swallowed hard and repeatedly as the final scream, ripped out of the lungs of the dying man, echoed all around.

The abbot vanished.

"You saw that," Alli said to Mike. "Tell me I didn't imagine it all. He…that…*creature* killed them."

Mike sighed as if expelling every bit of oxygen from his body. "No, you didn't imagine it. I saw it too. Come on, let's try that other door."

How could he be so casual? Two people had just been murdered in front of them. "But, what about Nancy? And Ric…?"

Mike shrugged. "Look around. They're gone. There's no more we can do here." He strode into the kitchen.

Alli clutched her stomach as her insides seemed to coil and uncoil. Seconds later the unpleasant sensation had passed, as quickly as it had hit her.

Mike's tone had been callous, but he was right. There was nothing more they could do for Ric or Nancy. They had vanished as if they had never even been there. And the danger remained. Alli joined Mike in the kitchen. "Before we go, I need to go up to the attic and find something."

"What kind of something?"

"Caroline told me to find it," Alli said and started up the narrow staircase.

Mike followed her. At the top, breathless and panting from their exertions, they opened the door into the attic room.

Alli made straight for the altar and grabbed the urn. Without hesitating, she unscrewed the lid and set the vessel down, but not before she caught sight of the mingled gray and black ash. Caroline and Abbot Weaver. "They really did mix the innocent with the evil, didn't they?"

Mike said nothing, his mouth set as if holding himself back.

Alli fiddled with the lid until it gave, releasing the false compartment. The piece of paper, folded many times, fell into her hand. She set the lid down.

The document was a duly signed and witnessed affidavit, stating that ownership of Canonbury Manor was to pass to Caroline's natural granddaughter, Allegra Carmen Isolde Sinclair. It also directed Alli to 'dispose of the property in any way she sees fit, once she has determined its true purpose'.

When she read it all out to Mike, he gave a wry smile. "I don't think we need that fourth door, do we? You have most of your answers now."

"Aren't you forgetting where we are?"

"What do you mean?"

"We're not in our own time. This house is playing tricks with us again. This is the 1970s. If we go out of that door – if we even can – we'll be entering a world where the real Caroline, and Lucius for that matter, are still very much alive. We need to get back to our own time. We have no choice. We have to go through that fourth door and hope it leads us there."

Mike considered it for a second. "I wish to God you weren't right, but you are. Come on."

They returned to the kitchen and Alli gripped the door handle. They were back in the room at the summerhouse in a few moments. Mike immediately opened the fourth and final door.

As they stepped over the threshold, they found themselves once again in a dark passageway, grateful for the candles, except…. Matches. Why hadn't they remembered to bring matches?

"We can't light the candles. We have to go back to the kitchen," Alli said.

"We can't take the risk. Nothing is stable around here. Don't you get the feeling…it's like time is moving really fast."

In the increasing gloom, Alli could no longer see her hand in front of her. Although neither of them had taken a step forward, they seemed to be moving farther and farther from the entrance, and a weird sensation in her stomach reminded her of being on a fairground carousel, going faster and faster, ducking and rising on a painted wooden horse. "Mike? Mike?"

No reply.

Alli reached out with her free hand, the other still clutching the useless candles. "Mike?" Her voice echoed, bouncing off the walls. Then up ahead, a tiny flicker of light shone, growing brighter by the second. Brighter, stronger and closer. But was she moving toward it, or was it moving toward her? And where was Mike? She carried on calling out his name. No reply. Apart from her breathing and her own voice, the place was silent.

She took a few more steps and found herself back on familiar territory. The kitchen at Canonbury Manor in her own time. Alli turned back and called out again to Mike. Her voice merely echoed down the silent passageway and she knew wherever he was, it wasn't there.

Yet, despite all the craziness of the past two days, the final pieces of the jigsaw were beginning to slot into place. She was the legal owner of Canonbury Manor, however crazy that might be. She had a piece of paper proving ownership of this place. It was hers to do with as she pleased. She could burn it to the ground if she wished. She could certainly do all in her power to rid it of the evil influence of Seraphragius, Weaver, Hartmann and that cabal. Yet the warning Caroline had issued in her notebook haunted her.

Then there was Nancy. And poor Ric. He had overstepped a forbidden line when he had divulged as much as he had on his return. As she thought about it now, Alli wondered if he had even disappeared. Perhaps it was all some sort of Seraphragius-controlled ruse? Perhaps he had had second thoughts and wanted to frighten Alli into getting out of there. Whatever the truth of it, Ric had lost his life.

As for Nancy, Alli had let her down again. This time fatally. She would have to live with that for the rest of her life.

And where was Mike?

Alli went on a tour of the house, searching every room, but found no one. There was no one else there. No one living at any rate. The house was empty. Or as empty as this house could ever be.

★   ★   ★

Back in the silent kitchen, she sat on a stool and sipped a glass of water.

Alli was at first taken aback at the figure who appeared at the doorway between the kitchen and hallway.

Wispy white hair framed a smiling face.

"Caroline Rand," Alli whispered. "Grandmother."

The woman nodded, and her voice was that of an octogenarian woman, matching her appearance. "The very same. Grown older now, of course. Older than my Laurel Canyon days by many decades. This is how I looked not long before I died or, to be more accurate, before my body died. Like you, I'm destined to live on, and in my case, that will be through you. We didn't choose our destiny, dear grandchild, you and I had it thrust upon us through accident of birth. In every real sense, this is their place. The cabal. I tried everything…." She shook her head and lowered her eyes briefly. "Pieces of paper, ownership, it means nothing to them." Caroline sighed. "I can see a lot of you in me. That's why you had the visions. It's what the cabal call our 'seraphragial' link. It goes much further than a mere blood tie. You loved the music of the time I loved the most. That short and wonderful happy time in Laurel Canyon where we thought everything was possible. They took that from my memory and instilled it into yours. They let you live through parts of those wonderful days. They brought us together in that wonderful place at that blissful time of innocence, before it all turned sour."

Tears stung Alli's eyes. "I never wanted to leave. I felt safe there, with Cass and the others. John Denver was so kind to me. They all were. It was the first time in my life I felt truly...." She struggled to find the right words. "At home. Yes, that's it. I felt accepted, even though they hadn't a clue who I was or what I was doing there. I felt accepted and at home."

"As I did. At first, anyway."

"Caroline, what happened to Nancy and Ric? Why did they have to die? And Mike? The guy who was with me. He disappeared when I was on my way here."

Caroline reached for Alli's hands and clasped them in hers. This time, Alli felt no shock as their skin touched, and the spirit's hands were warm, as if blood flowed though those veins. But the contact was all too brief as Caroline gently withdrew her hand.

"Ric and Nancy never existed. At least not in the form you saw them. Their real selves were human followers of the cabal. Everything that has happened here.... Nothing was merely by chance. Ric and Nancy were there to interact with you. Nancy's appearance and personality came from the depths of your memory. A schoolgirl contemporary selected because they knew you felt guilty over the way you treated her all those years ago. And Ric? A convenient player. Together, he and Nancy placed psychological...subliminal, I believe they call them...triggers all around you. Everything was designed to put you in a certain frame of mind so you would be...I suppose 'receptive' is as good a word as any.

"The visions you had were all designed to throw you off kilter so you no longer knew what was real and what was fantasy. As for the rest of the detail.... They gave you people who each had their own issues. You wouldn't desert them, whatever happened. Especially Nancy."

Alli put her hand out to touch her, shocked when Caroline withdrew hers. "You can't touch me. Not now," she said softly. "Not anymore."

The sense of rejection hit Alli like a sledgehammer. But there was no point in arguing. She was there to listen and learn. Who knew how long remained to them? At least she had been able to hold her grandmother's hand once without the pain of an electric shock.

"Mrs. Creeley—"

"You could have done nothing. She knew what she was doing. She'd had enough, you see. Always looking over her shoulder. They would leave her alone as long as she didn't talk, but the burden of what she knew about the cabal was too great. She was killed by a manifestation of Seraphragius, but she's at peace now. Her spirit has moved on."

Alli struggled with each new piece of impossible information. Once again, those words from *Alice Through the Looking Glass* came back to her. Surely this was far more than six impossible things she was expected to believe. And it couldn't possibly end there. "But Mike…. Where does he fit in?"

Caroline sighed. "Mike is real enough. They didn't need to imprint any other personality onto him. He's an acolyte of the cabal. You probably saw the sunburst tattoo on his elbow. It marks him out to those who need to know. He's gone from here now. He left you in the corridor and is back with the cabal, but not without leaving something of himself behind."

Caroline looked straight at Alli's midriff, and she instinctively placed her hands protectively on it. "You don't mean? That night? It wasn't a dream?"

"No. The line must continue, so you must have a child of your own to pass on to. You're pregnant with Mike's child. It will be normal. Human. I'm sure you'll love it."

"But it couldn't have been. That man. He couldn't have been Mike."

"You mean because of the hair? If you look in the corridor, you'll find the wig he used. Oh, and the glasses too. He didn't want to take any chances on you recognizing him."

"I could abort it."

"They'll never let you. And, believe me, they can stop you. This house alone can stop you ever leaving should it choose to."

Caroline slid off the stool. She didn't seem as corporeal as she had a few minutes earlier. Her body had faded to an almost translucence, while her voice took on an added urgency.

"We must go. Now. You have to get away from here. You have to go somewhere the cabal can't find you."

"Where? Is there such a place?"

"I can't talk about it in here. Come with me."

Alli felt as if she were in a dream. Hell, she was following a ghost. How could any of it be real? Without a word, she followed Caroline to the front door, which opened without a murmur at the spirit's touch. Together they went down the steps and passed the bed of vivid columbine. That color. Only nature could produce hues so vivid. This blue with a hint of violet. Like....

Alli shook her head and quickened her step to catch up with Caroline.

It didn't take her long to realize the direction they were headed. The summerhouse.

"Why are we going here?" Alli asked.

"I'll tell you when we get there."

The ivy and assorted vegetation seemed to have grown back considerably since Alli's last visit, which should have been mere hours ago at most, but this looked like days or weeks of growth. She followed Caroline and scrambled up to the door. Caroline opened it and they entered.

Inside all was as it had been, except....

"There's another door." Alli pointed to the fifth door. "*That* wasn't there."

"And that's where you must go." Caroline opened the door and Alli peered in. Another gloomy, ill-lit passageway stretched ahead.

In the distance behind her, impossibly, she heard the hall clock chime nine times. For the first time, she realized the significance of the time. It came to her as some form of race memory or instinct. Nine o'clock. The hour of Seraphragius's first death and rebirth. And the hands frozen at ten twenty-five? The hour of Caroline's death.

Caroline directed her over the threshold. "Walk straight down, until you come to a door. Wait and someone will open it for you. When you get there, don't be afraid. All will be well."

"You're coming with me, aren't you? I've only just found out who you really are...our connection. I can't lose you now. You're my only family and I barely know you." Even as she spoke the words, she could tell by Caroline's downcast eyes that she would be making this trip alone.

"This is your future, Alli. I can't do any more."

On impulse and forgetting Caroline's earlier words, Alli made to hug her. Caroline backed away and once again, rebuffed the attempt at contact.

"No, we mustn't."

Alli wanted to ask why, to beg her to come with her. The look of finality on Caroline's face stopped her. "Very well. I'll do what you say, but…one last question. How did you manage to escape the clutches of the cabal?"

Caroline stared straight into Alli's eyes for a second, placed her fingers on her lips and blew her a kiss. The door swung shut with a loud click. Locked.

Alli's heart thumped, and the fetus stirred in her womb. It was far too early for any such movement, but Alli had ceased to question the passage and quirks of time in this place. She stared at the locked door for a long minute, turned and moved slowly down the passageway. After all, she had nowhere else to go, so she concentrated on putting one foot in front of the other, the ground beneath her feet seemingly constructed of compacted earth. Her footsteps made no sound. She caught sight of…it looked like a cluster of tangled rope, ahead of her. Alli bent down. On closer inspection, she recognized it. Not rope. A wig styled in dreadlocks. She touched it, then carefully picked it up between her thumb and forefinger. Something fell out. A pair of spectacles. She had last seen both items on the same person. Mike.

Alli let the wig fall to the floor and carried on walking. She soon faced a plain dark wooden door. A sense of inevitability took over. How many others had stood there before her? She waited.

They didn't keep her long.

A scratching noise as the handle was turned and then the door opened.

Gentle, classical music drifted toward her.

"Good evening, Miss Sinclair," the maître d' said. "Welcome to The Columbine. You are expected."

ACKNOWLEDGMENTS

As always, my heartfelt thanks go to Julia Kavan, friend and writer, who possesses the best instincts and uncanny knack of spotting the absurd and impossible and steering me back into the realms of the uncannily possible. As I always say, every writer needs a Julia.

Massive thanks to Don D'Auria, amazing editor, for his belief in me over quite a few years now. It is always a real pleasure to work with you, Don, and I never cease to feel a huge thrill of excitement whenever you accept a manuscript of mine. I greatly appreciate the support and help from Mike Valsted, Zoe Seabourne, Yana Koleva, and all at Flame Tree Press. Nick Wells heads up a wonderful publishing house!

My eternal thanks to Colin, my long-suffering husband, who enters into the murky world of horror and somehow emerges relatively sane if not necessarily unscathed. Maybe it's his love of all things David Lynch, and the Soska Sisters....

I must pay tribute to all the wonderful musicians and singers who helped define and reflect the tumultuous, fabulous, unique time that was the late 1960s. Some of them feature in this story and are, sadly, no longer with us, but their music and spirit live on. When I was doing background research for this story, I was able to channel my mind back to 1968/69 simply by listening to their songs. From 'White Rabbit' to 'For What It's Worth' and everything in between, my iPod became my own personal time machine. Peace and love, man, peace and love.

Huge thanks to people I meet virtually via Twitter, Instagram, Mastodon, Facebook, TikTok and elsewhere, as well as those I actually meet up with face to face at The Shippy Writers, Liverpool Horror Club, British Fantasy Society and elsewhere. A special thank you to Phil Larner at Blackwell's University Bookshop in Liverpool for being such a supportive host and all-round great person, Ramsey Campbell, from whom I learn so much about the whole genre of horror and who is so supportive – my thanks and appreciation to you and Jenny. Many thanks to James Lefebure, Dave McCluskey, Shehanne Moore and so many wonderful friends and acquaintances I could not even begin to list here for fear of omitting someone. Consider yourselves much appreciated and well and truly thanked.

And you, if you are reading this, thank you. If this is your first Catherine Cavendish, I hope you will return for many more (there have been others!) If you are returning, I hope our paths will cross again in the near future.

Catherine Cavendish
Southport, 2022

FLAME TREE PRESS
FICTION WITHOUT FRONTIERS
Award-Winning Authors & Original Voices

Flame Tree Press is the trade fiction imprint of Flame Tree Publishing, focusing on excellent writing in horror and the supernatural, crime and mystery, science fiction and fantasy. Our aim is to explore beyond the boundaries of the everyday, with tales from both award-winning authors and original voices.

•

•

Join our mailing list for free short stories, new release details, news about our authors and special promotions:

flametreepress.com